Often his hand works to
Whether it be ivory or fle
He kisses it and thinks it kisses back...

OVID, *Metamorphoses*, book X, *Pygmalion*

First published in the United Kingdom in 2020
This second edition published by
Four Elms Publishing 2021

Paperback   ISBN 978-1-8384194-0-0
.epub eBook   ISBN 978-1-8384194-1-7
.mobi eBook   ISBN 978-1-8384194-2-4

Cover Art: Egon Schiele - Sitzender Mädchenakt mit
Hemd über dem Kopf - 1910

Cover design and typeset by SpiffingCovers

YOUNG MOTHER
with
RED HAIR

M. A. DUNN

FOUR ELMS
PUBLISHING

1

So, what do you want to know? Everything, I suppose. I'm not sure I'll be able to go that far. We'll see. I don't even know yet whether I'm going to send this to you, Michael.

Where to start?

I know what you would say: "First things first", in that, "Isn't it obvious?" way you have. But then I wouldn't begin to know what the first thing might be. The day we met? That tour of the National Gallery? The day you told me he wanted me to sit for him? The first session? Or maybe I should start much further back than that, with the six-year-old girl that I once was being teased mercilessly because she had red hair and freckles.

But then, maybe "First thing" denotes the most important thing, like a supreme religious tenet, the one from which all other principles are derived: The First Commandment. Thou shalt have no other gods before me. That's much more than being first just because it's at the top of the page, isn't it?

The most important thing then: what would that be?

Perhaps why I agreed to sit for him. The truth is I'm still not sure why I did. Sometimes, I think I am, but then I decide that I'm not. Maybe this is my way of trying to find out, of working that through.

So, I think I may as well start with the first thing that comes to mind.

Can you guess what that would be?

It is the smell: yes; the smell, the scents and aromas of that house, his studio, him: first and foremost, of course, paint. It has a very particular quality, the scent of top-grade oils, quite unlike that of an emulsion one might use to paint a room. Old Holland: it is organic, earthy, almost alive and it is everywhere in that house, not confined to the two studios, certainly not to the canvases: globs of it, some still wet, some dry and crusted or drying and tacky; there were flecks of it on the walls, on the bare floorboards of the hall, enticing visitors to follow them up the stairs. I remember for a while, although it was at some point in time washed away by an unseen hand, a set of paw prints, in Burnt Sienna, that snaked its way across the tiles of the upstairs pantry where we would sometimes snack on leftovers of the previous night's supper, pheasant perhaps or grouse, washed down with a tumbler of claret.

And overlaying the paint itself, that harsher, throat-catching note of turpentine, a workshop smell, redolent of sheds and garages, the petrol-like tang that I still associate with grass-clippings and my father wiping down his old Atco after mowing the lawn in the long, regular stripes in which he took such pride.

What else? Mixed with the paint and the turps? To differing degrees, depending on the time of day, on recent events, a variable combination of wine and chocolate, cooked game, tweed and always too an acrid layer of stale cigar ash, all of it underlain with the pungent earthiness of wet dog.

And then there was him. Did you know that, except on his hands, although he bathes regularly, he never uses soap? That he doesn't use shampoo or deodorant either? Would not consider using after-shave? I hadn't guessed before he told me; so it wasn't that it left him smelling unclean or especially sweaty or any such thing, no unpleasant B.O. (if that is even a real thing and not some ad-men's concoction), but I was aware that his scent was… well, was entirely him. I think that it added to a quality he had, has, which is one of the many impressive things about him, a quality of being very much there, more there than others it often seemed to me, more definitely present, the possessor of his own, especially powerful gravity.

Oh, and I shouldn't forget the smell of that couch, the raggedy, old couch of brown cloth, torn and stained, musty and slightly soiled, on which I posed each day for weeks on end.

What next then? I think perhaps how much we used to talk, how wide ranging our conversations were. We talked about art, of course – a lot – and literature. How you must have wished you could have been there with us, just to have listened in. I wonder what you would have given for that, which is a funny question really, considering what you did give.

But we talked about so much more than art and literature; we talked about the many people he had known, friends, enemies. We talked about me, about my childhood, about us, Michael, you and me.

And then there was the silence. It can sneak up on you, silence, seem so far away, such a long time coming and then, without you noticing, it has arrived, been there unremarked for twenty minutes, more. It was not an oppressive, brooding silence for there was always the unnoticed background thrum of the traffic beyond the tightly closed shutters of his studio or perhaps the soft tread of Vivian's shoes as he paced the room.

He called it his Night Studio because he often painted in there at night and by way of a natural contrast with the other studio, his Day Studio, daylight filled, with tall, unshuttered windows looking north.

The shutters of the Night Studio were always tightly closed, an eternal blackout, so that there was no gleam of daylight, with its movement and constantly changing quality, only artificial light, constant, unchanging, and always under Vivian's control. As you know, I often posed for him during the day but inside that room it could have been any time of day or night, any season of the year. Thus, I came to think of it, not so much as his Night Studio, but as a timeless place, wholly apart from the outside, ever-changing world and its restless colours.

Does anyone come out of that room the same person who went in, I wonder. I was, throughout, an English teacher on maternity leave but how much else had changed?

I'm not sure how much I believe in talking therapies.

But then, although we talked and talked, we spent even longer in silence so that it would not really have been a talking therapy, it would have been a thinking therapy. Not that I thought that I was broken and needed fixing in any way. I still don't think I was. But I am certain that I came out of that studio on the last day I sat for him a different woman from the one who went in on that first day.

I wonder whether Vivian would consider that the process had changed him too? That's an oddly egotistical question – isn't it? – given the almost countless number of people that have sat for him over so many years, friends, family, lovers, each, given the obsessively painstaking nature of his method, of the manner in which he feels compelled to work, spending many hours with him, hours during which, I know all too well, they are the sole focus of his attention, not only the physical object that they are but also their inner self, which he tries so hard to uncover so that he can as much as possible realise it in paint.

You will certainly want to know what it was like: an ordinary, uneventful session sitting for him.

On one of those uneventful days, of which there were many, in the long periods of silence, my thoughts might drift anywhere. They might stay in the room with Vivian. I remember spending one entire morning trying to decide whether there was a physical element to his undoubted charisma, this lean and wiry man, well into his sixties, hair almost entirely grey. Was there a memory discernible in his well-worn, lived-in features of the darkly handsome man to be seen in photographs of him in his youth and into middle age? Or was that charisma, by the time I met him, a product solely of the inner person, of all the self-assurance and intensity he brought with him and the exaggerated presence of someone who knows himself to be world-renowned, believes in his own talent with genuine, immodest, unboastful certainty? Indeed, how much of my reaction was a product not of my experience of him but of my expectations, of the preconceptions that are unavoidable when meeting someone so famous, famous, not only for his fabulous paintings but also for his turbulent life and many lovers?

Or my thoughts might leave Vivian and his studio, step out of the tall, broad-fronted Georgian townhouse in West London, turn left and make their way home to you and Alice. On one occasion, perhaps my fifth or sixth sitting, when the scents and sights of Vivian's studio were less fiercely new and I had become at least partly used to the rigours of posing, of maintaining absolute stillness of posture for so long, I remember noticing in myself a delicious sense of relaxation, almost a meditative state, and thinking how lovely it was to be free of Alice's unceasing demands, her thoughtless tyranny, the heedless dictatorship of the toddler. But then, almost as soon as I had acknowledged the thought, a wave of guilt and self-loathing swept through me. How could I be so selfish and unloving of my beautiful little daughter, the most important thing in all the world to me? What was I even doing here, leaving her abandoned at home in the care of an unrelated, unqualified baby-sitter? And then, at other times, I was filled with a yearning ache to be back at home with her, to hold her tightly, press my lips to her plump, warm little cheek and breathe in the aroma of her sweet freshness.

I have been trying to think of the sort of things you would want to know. The conversations that you would have loved to have been a part of: his earliest memory of painting, perhaps.

"It is a memory of defiance," he said. "I was five – I think – at school and we were painting in class. I can't remember whether I chose the subject or whether it was dictated. Anyway, I was painting the sea. We lived on the coast and had a couple of Yellow Labradors – lovely dogs, if somewhat boisterous – and we would walk them on the beach in all weathers so I really knew my subject. I took up a pot of green paint and got to work. I was contentedly painting away when the teacher leaned over and asked me what I was doing. Painting the sea, I said, proudly. Then, to my complete astonishment, she told me that I was doing it all wrong, because the sea, she explained, is blue. I insisted that the sea is green but she wouldn't have it. We had quite a fight about it and she would not back down. I remember being puzzled. How could anyone think that the sea is blue? The sky is blue, but the sea is most definitely green. And then I was upset and angry and frustrated. I refused to change and continued with green, even though I was in tears by the time she left me, saying, as she went, that we could pretend I had painted a field. I think I have been painting that way ever since, resisting the admonishments of people who labour under the misapprehension that the sea is blue."

"I suppose I should thank that teacher," he said, studying a tube of paint in his hand, "whoever she was, and her ignorance, for being part of what makes me what I am now."

Vivian asked me once whether I had thought you handsome, when we first met. That's a very painterly question, isn't it?

I just said, "Yes, of course."

But in the silence that followed, I started to wonder whether that was true. That was the sort of thing that would happen to me in that room with him. I would say something that I thought to be obviously true but then in the ensuing silence, under his scrutinising gaze, I would start to question even the most basic assumptions.

Had I thought you handsome when I first saw you?

His first question had been what it was that I had found most attractive about you and I told him: it was how clever you are, how well you express yourself, most of all how contagiously enthusiastic you are about the things that interest you, how energising it is to be with you when you are feeling that way about something; I had noticed that right from the first time we met. But then, of course, I had to explain that it would be more accurate to say from the first time I saw you lecture, because it wasn't until weeks into term that we actually spoke.

He seemed to think it amusing that it had been at your series of lectures on Thomas Hardy. I think I understand now what he had in mind but it puzzled me at the time.

When I told him that we had met when I was an undergrad and you were one of my lecturers, he quizzed me about whether our relationship was frowned upon by the powers that be and made a joke about forbidden fruit tasting sweetest. You didn't think of me as forbidden fruit, did you, Michael? There isn't any strict rule against university teachers getting with students. And you were only a visiting lecturer; it's not as though you were marking any of my papers.

But maybe you did. What did you see in me, I wonder, when I walked up to you as you were putting your notes away and asked some stupid question about *The Mayor of Casterbridge*? That wasn't a spur of the moment thing, by the way. I had made up my mind to make a move, although it took some courage, I can tell you. I'm not naturally forward that way, as I guess you've realised. I remember being really cross with myself for blushing, when I had been planning to be extremely cool and grown-up. I suppose that was never going to happen, when I was basically a girl with a crush on her teacher.

By then, which was six weeks into term, I fancied you to bits, I promise. But had I thought you handsome when I first saw you? That was what Vivian had asked; and when I said, "Yes of course," although it was partly an automatic, unthinking answer, I'm also sure that I thought it was true.

But then I found myself wondering whether that was right.

So I lay there, as Vivian paced around the room the way he so often did, scrutinising some part of me from every angle, and tried to remember the me who went to that first lecture of yours.

I very nearly didn't go at all. I wasn't sure about Hardy in those days, found him too unremittingly pessimistic for my taste, but Sunita was a big fan and she talked me into going with her. It's so strange to contemplate all the things that hinged on that decision; without it there would be no us, no Alice and no sitting for Vivian Young.

It had been raining heavily and I hadn't noticed that my bag wasn't quite closed properly so that, when I pulled out my notepad, the pages were wet along one edge and going crinkly. I was trying to press them dry with the sleeve of my jumper when you came in and I didn't pay you any attention until you started speaking, which meant that I heard you before I saw you. I remember noticing instantly the energy and enthusiasm in your voice – not at all the bored "let's just get through this" attitude that I was growing accustomed to – and thinking that this was going to be an interesting lecture after all.

So, when I looked up at you and saw you for the first time, had I thought you handsome?

Lying there in Vivian's studio, I decided that I hadn't. I don't mean to say I thought you positively unattractive, not at all, just that you were nothing remarkable. That was quite a revelation because it made me realise how much your appeal must have grown over time. You passed from being a perfectly reasonable looking but hardly spectacular man to being someone I positively fancied, physically, not just for your personality. And I think that process had started even by the end of the lecture. You glanced at me at one point; I don't think it was a significant look on your part; you're good at making eye contact with your students when you lecture; I'm well aware of that; but, even then, I saw something appealing in and around your eyes; your expression seemed both kind and at the same time a little stern and I remember thinking that it would be nice to get to know you.

I've told you before how I started looking forward to your lectures more and more each week and found myself keeping an eye out for you around campus. That's a sure sign of an incipient crush and I could tell that I was falling for you, which was silly of me, I know, since we hadn't yet exchanged a single word. It's hardly surprising that I blushed, then, when I went over to talk to you for the first time that day; I was feeling very nervous. You might not have liked me at all or, worse, I might have found that I no longer fancied you once we talked.

But I needn't have worried on either count because of course you jumped straight into talking so enthusiastically about *The Mayor of Casterbridge*, the effect of serialisation on the narrative structure as I recall, and five minutes later we were continuing our discussion over coffee.

Vivian was very interested in how I felt about our difference in ages, your being ten years older. I thought his curiosity on that subject odd at first, when he is so famous for having had a string of younger lovers but, as I said, he looks to get under the skin of his models, each and every one of them. I made a joke once about how he had to get under someone's skin before he could paint it. From his reaction, I think perhaps he had heard that joke several times before. He looked at me like a disapproving headmaster. Actually, he looked a little the way my father looked once or twice, when he thought that I had let him – let myself – down.

It was often like that with him – Vivian I mean, not my father. We might be having a lively conversation where I felt completely his equal, sparring satisfyingly about some topic or other, then I would make a comment that he judged naïve or childish and I would suddenly feel like a schoolgirl again.

I sometimes forget that you never met my father. It often feels as though he died just months ago, not eleven years. I wonder what he would think of me now. Not very much, I fear.

Anyway, ten years isn't so much of an age difference, is it?

In a way, when we first met, I thought of you as young, being about thirty made you younger than most of the lecturers. And you've always had a sort of boyish enthusiasm.

Someone – I'll tell you about her later – told me once that part of Vivian's appeal is his youthfully enthusiastic outlook on life, so that, despite the outward trappings of age, he remains in essence young. I think you have something of that about you too, Michael.

And what about the age difference from your point of view. It's not very flattering to think that my being ten years younger than you might have been a large part of my appeal, that if we had been the same age, I might not have been quite as attractive to you. But maybe I've been kidding myself.

"It's useless to pretend that youth doesn't have its own special lustre," Vivian told me once, "the freshness and vivacity that only youth can bring, clear eyes, smoothness of complexion, elasticity of flesh. But it is much more than a solely physical thing. It's a freshness of spirit."

He should know.

At the time, I thought he was talking about me.

As for you and me, at least I have the comfort of knowing that I sought you out, selected you and made my move, clumsy and obvious though it may have been, and not the other way around, so that I can be confident that I was not the subject of some habit of picking out a first year to target every three or four years. There was a history professor at my uni who was notorious for it, always with a current undergraduate sharing his adulterous bed. I expect you heard about him.

2

It was something in your body language that first let me know that someone of significance had entered the room. When was that, your public lecture on Hardy? Only seven months ago. It's difficult to believe, isn't it?

You seemed to stiffen up. Even from the back of the lecture theatre I noticed it. Up to that point, you had shown that alert enthusiasm that I was so familiar with, like someone about to sit a difficult exam that they nevertheless feel confident of passing with flying colours. But then you almost froze for an instant and I could see that you were suddenly flustered and I noticed that you were darting furtive glances towards the corner of the room, towards the entrance. When I turned to see who or what had so obviously grabbed your attention, there he was, just a couple of yards away, and he was smiling and asking whether the place next to me was taken.

I remember, in the fraction of a second that I took to recognise him, thinking that perhaps this elderly man with an exaggeratedly plummy accent knew me. I've noticed that before with famous people; they carry with them an expectation of being recognised that is easy to mistake for an indication that it is they who have recognised you. But then, of course, I realised that it was Vivian Young.

I was struck by how slight his frame was and that he was also shorter than I would have expected. Not that he is at all short, in truth, just average – well, you know exactly what he looks like in the flesh, obviously – but, again, I think we have a notion that famous people will be bigger than they are, that they will be quite literally larger than life.

As he sat down, I asked whether he was a particular fan of Thomas Hardy and he said that he was. I remember wondering, even then, whether you might have known that, picked it up from some of your reading about him, Vivian I mean.

I watched you closely as Kevin gave his little introduction of you and the topic. I could tell how nervous you were and when you started, I was worried for you at first, because you had so evidently been knocked off your stride by the fact that someone that you admired so much and would have given almost anything to meet was there to hear your talk.

I've got to hand it to you though, before long, you were in full flow, with that excited fluency of yours that I always found so appealing. And I've always admired the freshness you manage to bring to your lectures, too. I've seen you present on that topic – what? – five or six times now and it has never been the same talk twice. That's a real talent; I hope you realise that; I really do.

But… Oh dear! I know that you will understand why I've never told you this before, Michael, but I'm afraid the truth is that halfway through your talk, Vivian leant in towards me and whispered, "What absolute nonsense this fellow is spouting. I'm afraid I'm going to have to get up and walk out."

I blushed for you.

He made to stand up but I stopped him by placing my hand on his forearm and said as quietly as I could, "Please don't do that to him. It would really upset him and he's my husband."

He looked at me for a moment and then said, "Is he really? Now that is interesting." before settling back into his seat.

"Okay, I'll stay," he said. "For your sake."

The power of suggestion: I'm afraid I spent the rest of your talk wondering whether he might not be partially right. Not that your talk might be absolute nonsense, of course not, but that perhaps some of the connections between the poems and the novels might not be so well made out or that some of your analyses of recurring themes were perhaps a little glib, a little too clever, if you know what I mean. I found myself looking at the other people attending and trying to gauge their reactions even more intently than I usually would have. But you'll be happy to hear that they seemed to me as interested and engaged as they always did and, at the end, I think their applause was genuinely enthusiastic, not merely polite.

As the applause died away and people started to file out, Vivian and I stood up.

"Right then," he said. "Please do introduce me to your

husband. But first let me introduce myself…"

"I know; you're Vivian Young."

He inclined his head and gave a slight nod, like a tiny, courtly bow from another era.

"I'm Jane, by the way."

He glanced at the notes for your talk.

"Jane Smith, presumably."

"That's right."

He offered his hand, which I shook.

"How do you do," he said and I was struck again by his exaggeratedly old-fashioned manner, which I judged to be, if not quite an affectation, then, like his accent, at the very least deliberately maintained, consciously avoiding any temptation to blend in.

We walked over to join you where you were talking with Katarina and of course you know the rest; I expect that you can remember every word of the conversation that followed.

When he told you that he had found your talk very thought provoking, you were positively glowing with pride and he caught my eye. I felt terribly guilty for being part of a sort of shared deception of you. But what could I do? I could hardly say, "Actually, he said he thought it was nonsense," could I?

Then, when he proposed joining him on a quick visit to the National Gallery – "To see the Holbeins." – it was so unexpected that I'm not sure how I felt, nearly as swept up in the excitement of the moment as you were, I suppose. And then of course there was the business of how I should really have been heading home to feed Alice and, when I said that, you looked so disappointed. Did you suggest that I could express some milk to stop myself leaking or was that me?

So, there I sat for the next twenty minutes in a cubicle of the ladies' loo with that stupid bloody pump pressed against my breast, whirring away conspicuously. When I heard another woman come in and use the neighbouring cubicle, I remember thinking, "God, I hope she doesn't think I'm in here with a vibrator." She probably did.

My mother sounded very unimpressed when I called her and asked her to feed Alice with some of the back-up formula. She even pretended not to know who Vivian Young was, although I'm sure that was just an act.

"Vivian who, dear? I'm sure he can't be more important than your daughter, however famous he might be."

I won't pretend that I wasn't thrilled, nearly as thrilled as you evidently were: A tour of the National Gallery with Vivian Young. He was so animated, so interesting and interested, so engaging. Who wouldn't leap at the opportunity to listen to such a man talking about art?

I won't bother repeating everything he said about the various pieces we stopped at, the Holbeins in particular. I'm sure you have it all committed to memory. But, Michael: the look on your face when he asked what you thought of the Stubbs painting of the prancing horse, *Whistlejacket* and you predictably said you thought it magnificent only for him to say that he didn't like it at all. If it's any comfort,

I'm sure you weren't the first to fall for that trick. I'm sure it was a trick, you know. I would have fallen for it myself if he had directed it at me. Not that I think his expressed dislike wasn't genuine – I'm sure it was – but he must have known that everyone thinks the same about that painting. It was a set-up. I felt for you; I really did.

As we continued our tour in his wake, even as I smiled and nodded, experienced the little thrills of recognition and revelation that his comments provoked, I became aware of a growing sense of frustration. I don't know whether you noticed it but, all the time, he seemed to be addressing you and only you, not exactly excluding me from the conversation but somehow not including me either, as though he were merely permitting me to listen in. It made me feel very small and insignificant. And I had a horrible feeling that was exactly how he wanted me to feel so that I began to hate myself for being unable to avoid feeling precisely that.

As we progressed and particularly each time I noted other museum-goers recognise Vivian and envy the two of us for being in his company, despite myself, I grew more and more desperate for him to say something to me, to speak to me, not only you.

And then we stopped at the Bouguereau, *The Birth of Venus*, in all its pallid, smoothed out, depilated, full-frontal, Victorian glory. Of course, you remember, that, don't you? Naturally, I immediately noticed that the goddess was a redhead like me. I remember also thinking how improbably long her hair was, all the way down to beyond her backside and that it must have been very unlikely that the model who had posed for the painting had really had hair quite like that.

"I wish I could ignore it," Vivian said. "But its absolute, transcendent awfulness seems to suck me in. To think, in his time, Bouguereau was regarded as displaying the height of technical mastery and refined good taste."

He shook his head as if in sorrow.

"Do you know how Kenneth Clark described his works?"

As he said this, I just knew that he was speaking of a personal acquaintance.

"Lubricious," he said, rolling the r with evident relish. "To be fair to the old French fraud, he knew exactly what he was doing. American millionaires paid very handsomely to have one of these things hang on their walls, the Playboy magazines of their day. I often wonder what their wives must have thought, chaste matrons in Philadelphia hosting afternoon tea in front of all that glossy soft porn."

"It's actually worth stopping to consider though, because one can see so very obviously in it, more clearly displayed than in works by ostensibly better painters, the pernicious effect of the unthinking idolatry of classical sculpture that suffused western figurative art from the Renaissance up to – well, to a lesser degree, it persists even now."

"You can see that, instead of having a model pose for him and attempting to paint an image of her, Bouguereau has painted the girl at one remove, imagined what a classical statue of her would look like and tried to represent that. It's bad statuary in two dimensions. One could study it for weeks on end and still have no clue what the girl actually looked like."

Then he added after a pause, "And of course, not a body hair in sight: another result of trying to recreate classical sculpture."

He shook his head again.

"Sadly, these days, that would be more likely to be accurate, of course. Why, I wonder, do women today so readily accept the idea that pubic hair is offensive? It's such a shame to deprive themselves of what is, after all, a potent, primary sexual signal with all that it brings in terms of sight, scent and texture."

I couldn't stop myself from checking to see whether any of the other museum goers had heard that. Apparently not.

"I suppose they think they're being hygienic," he said, as though the word 'hygienic' were itself distasteful, "when all they are really doing is mimicking porn stars. And even the porn stars only started doing it because they didn't want it to be too patently obvious that they weren't natural blondes."

Vivian had still been directing his comments to you but then he turned to look directly at me for what seemed the first time since we had entered the building and said, "Please tell me you don't shave down there. You don't, do you?"

So, there you have it; I had been hoping and hoping that

this famous artist, this unique talent, would say something to me, solicit my opinion, and then, when he did, it was to ask me about my pubic hair.

I was sure that he was challenging me, daring me to react, to take offence. I really didn't want to give him that satisfaction but then, before I could stop myself, I found myself saying stupidly, "Well, I wax my bikini line but no more than that."

He smirked and said, "I'm glad. Redheads are so distinctive It would be such a shame."

You sniggered. Do you remember that? I do.

Vivian held my gaze for a moment then turned back to study the painting again. It was obvious that he had been playing a stupid little game with me and equally obvious that he had won.

God I was angry: angry with you, angry with him, angry with myself.

"I shall have to have a bath as soon as I get home," Vivian said to the canvas, "to cleanse myself."

Later, when we stopped on Trafalgar Square to say our farewells, you were absolutely buzzing. Your feet hardly touched the pavement you were on such a high. I suppose I should be more understanding. This was someone you had admired so much for so many years, an undeniably great artist. Not only had you met him; you had spent an hour in his company, listened to some of his thoughts on painting, on art. Of course you were thrilled. But I was still angry with you and hurt that you didn't seem to have noticed that I had been feeling snubbed or to be bothered that he had made a blatantly inappropriate comment to your wife.

As I said good-bye to him, he took my hand and leaned in to exchange a kiss on the cheek. I really did not want to share a kiss with him, wanted to shrink away. But what could I do? I remember his skin felt rough and cool against mine as we brushed cheeks and I was very aware of his age and of a faint whiff of cigar smoke. Then, as we pulled apart, he kept hold of my hand just a fraction too long, staring at my bare arm; I was wearing that black, sleeveless top of mine.

"It would be a challenge to paint you," he said, "a body with so many freckles."

Our eyes met for an instant before he finally relinquished my hand and walked away with an "*Au revoir*", striding across the square in the manner of a man who owns the flagstones beneath him.

Did he say good-bye to you? I don't recall. I think he may not have. That would be very like him. I've noticed that he has a habit of shifting focus from one person to another. It can be very disconcerting, but at the same time, when his focus is on you, well...

I wanted to take the Tube but you insisted on taking a cab. All the way home, you burbled on and on like an excited schoolboy about how brilliant and insightful his ideas were. It was rather embarrassing. Daring, that was what you kept saying, how daring his mind was.

At one point, I looked at you as you were repeating what he had said about *The Ambassadors*, comparing it with other critiques that you had heard or read. You were looking out of the cab at the time and weren't aware of me studying you and I thought, You didn't even notice, did you? That he hinted at the possibility of painting me.

I went to bed early that night, confused and angry. I would say confused by myself and angry with you, but I think it would be more accurate to say that I felt confused and angry in a general, unfocussed, elemental way. Oddly, I wasn't angry with Vivian, as though he were not a person to be angry with, but something else – I don't know – like a traffic jam or a heavy downpour of rain that it would be entirely useless to fume about.

You didn't come up to bed until after I had fallen asleep. I expect you were still on too much of a high.

3

The next day, when you came back from the Faculty, you so obviously had something on your mind. You didn't do that breathless downloading of the day's events when you first got home the way you usually would and all through supper you seemed distracted. I couldn't get you to engage in any topics of conversation that I found myself dredging up, which wasn't like us at all.

When I said, "Is something wrong?", you just said, "No not at all. What makes you say that?"

But I could tell that there was something weighing you down.

You waited until we were watching television. I wonder why. Had you run out of internal reasons for delay: saying hello to me and Alice, having supper, putting Alice to bed? Or did you welcome the distraction of the sights and sounds of whatever-it-was playing in the corner?

One thing is certain: you didn't burst through the door and tell me in a rush of excitement as you might have done. Thinking about it, you could have just called me from the Faculty. I think that means that you knew it wasn't the simple thing you tried to pretend it was.

But eventually you said, "You'll never guess who called

me today."

"Obviously not. Who?"

Even then you hesitated a moment. Do you remember? Before saying, "Vivian Young."

"Wow!"

"Quite. I nearly said that, actually, when he announced himself."

"You didn't recognise his voice before then? I thought it was quite distinctive."

That stopped you in your tracks a little; I think.

"No, I didn't," you said, as though you doubted yourself somehow. "I suppose it was just so unexpected."

"So, what did he want? I assume he wanted something and wasn't just ringing up to shoot the breeze about Thomas Hardy."

You laughed. But it was a nervous laugh.

"You'll never guess."

"Yes, we've established that."

I think I was already a little irritated with you by that point; you had fallen into that slightly giddy manner I remembered from the cab ride home from the National Gallery and I was remembering how annoyed I had been with you then.

"Well... He wanted me to ask you whether you would sit for him."

I had a moment of blankness and then a whole host of thoughts and feelings and fears started jostling for pre-eminence inside me.

"Vivian Young?"

You seemed puzzled by my reaction.

"Yes."

"Vivian Young called you to ask whether I would sit for him."

"Yes."

"I don't know what to say."

"I told him it would be awkward: with Alice still nursing, I mean."

"So you're assuming I'll say, yes."

You started to look ill at ease.

"Why didn't he call me and ask me himself?"

"Err..."

"Didn't that strike you as odd?"

"I suppose he could get hold of me through the Faculty. He wouldn't know how to contact you."

"So why didn't he just get my number from you and give me a call."

"I really didn't think. That would have been weird though, wouldn't it? Hello, can I have your wife's number?"

"No weirder than: will you ask your wife to pose naked for me?"

"He didn't say anything about it being a nude."

I raised my eyebrows at that but then Alice started crying and I had to get up and see to her. It took me ages to get her back down. I tried feeding her but she wouldn't latch on, kept pushing me away with her tongue and her hard, little fists. She was probably reacting to my own bad mood, I suppose.

I won't go through it all, how we fenced and jousted

throughout the rest of the evening, how you kept saying that it was up to me (as if there were some initial doubt about that, by the way) and that you didn't care either way but then, when I said that I wouldn't, how you kept coming back to it and asking whether I was sure, or how you dealt with all my practical objections in a way that made it so obvious that you really, really wanted me to do it.

I wonder exactly what you had in mind. I can guess, I suppose, because I had similar thoughts myself later, not quite the same, I imagine, but linked. Did you picture us becoming friends with Vivian, a part of his regular milieu? The pair of us dining with him at the Ivy? Rubbing shoulders with art critics, television execs, perhaps you getting a little mini-series about Hardy? Easy fantasies that didn't involve you lying on a couch bollock naked for hours at a time and for months on end.

Did you picture yourself introducing me to people at parties? "And this is my wife. She was painted by Vivian Young, don't you know?"

You said I should be flattered at one point, which didn't seem right to me at all, given some of the people he has painted and how he made them look.

And then there was that stupid, po-faced, oh-so-innocent look on your face when I said that he would obviously want to paint a nude of me and you had the nerve to pretend that that wasn't necessarily so, as if you weren't aware that he painted practically all his female subjects that way and I lost my temper and shouted, "Are you kidding? It's fucking Vivian Young for Christ's sake."

I was so tired by the time we went to bed, Michael; I can't tell you how tired. But at least I had said a final and definitive "No," and you had agreed to call and tell him in the morning. I could laugh now, thinking about me climbing into bed, weary but glad that the whole stupid idea had been put behind us at last, that it was done and dusted, that I was very much not going to sit for the great Vivian Young.

I did wonder, by the way, whether I would regret it at some later date, passing up that chance for a little touch of fame, a sliver of immortality, but I was sure that I had made the right decision and went to sleep feeling relieved.

In the morning, I started to have a little sympathy for you, to see it from your point of view. Vivian Young was your favourite artist, someone I knew that you had admired so much since you were a teenager; here was a chance for you to become part of his story, even if at one remove, your chance to be, perhaps, a footnote in his biography someday. Not much of an ambition, granted, but it would mean a lot to you; I could see that. Maybe I had overreacted at the notion of the two of you discussing me as if I were some sort of chattel.

You do realise that was why I reacted so instantly, don't you? It was the idea of you and him disposing of me between you, like property, when he had called you, when he called you not me to make the proposal, like a nineteenth-century suitor asking a father for his daughter's hand in marriage.

In the morning, we pretended that nothing had happened between us, went through our usual routine: me changing and feeding Alice, you telling me about the classes you would be giving that day. We didn't mention Vivian once but frankly he may as well have been there at the table, sharing our breakfast.

Then as you left and we kissed goodbye, I just had to say something.

"Don't forget to give him a call. Do it early and get it over with."

Him, not Vivian: him was all I needed to say.

And you nodded and said "Yes. Of course."

I should have trusted you, I know, but I spent all that day worrying that you wouldn't go through with it, wouldn't tell him no, even though you had promised. Did you get any work done that day? You had two classes to teach, as I recall, so you would have done that at least, but did you get anything else done?

I pictured you at your desk, flicking your pen from finger to finger the way you do, chewing the thumbnail of your other hand, silently contemplating your desk-phone, trying to force yourself to pick it up and make the call that you had promised me you would.

Of course, I knew how much you had always been into him. When was it, that exhibition you saw? When you were sixteen, I think you had said, a lower-sixth school trip.

"It opened my eyes to art," you told me once, "not just

visual art, all art, music, literature, how it can transform how we see the world."

At one point that afternoon, I went to inspect the shelves where you kept your books on art and looked up at the many you had about Vivian Young, unofficial biographies, companion books to various exhibitions of his works, collections of essays, the large, high-quality, expensive volume of reproductions of all his major pieces.

We never stood a chance, did we?

But you did tell him no. At least you did that.

I wanted to ask you as soon as you came through the door that evening, whether you had, but stopped myself, not wanting to seem untrusting or rather not wanting my lack of trust to show. But eventually, after you had played with Alice for a bit and changed her nappy, I asked how Vivian had reacted.

"Oh, he was fine," you said in a gloomy voice. "A pity, I think is what he said, but not to worry, lots of people don't feel up to it, apparently."

It was quite artful of him, that – don't you think? – making modelling for him sound like a challenge that only a select few could meet. It worked too, to an extent, because I remember thinking that of course I would have been up to the task, if I had wanted to pose for him; it was just that I didn't.

Later, after supper and after I had done the washing up, when I came out of the kitchen, you were sitting at the table, slowly thumbing through a book of his works. You looked so glum. When I went to stand next to you and put my hand on your shoulder, you had stopped at a nude of a massively fat, middle-aged woman, with folds and folds of sagging flesh, mercilessly detailed by Vivian's remorseless brush.

"Is that how you want the world to see me?" I asked.

"You wouldn't look anything like that and you know it," you said.

I reached around you and turned the page. The next painting was a view of mews houses as seen from the window of a townhouse, but the one after that was of another naked woman, younger, leaner, but it remained an unflattering depiction, with fleshy creases in her flank, inevitable given the twisted pose she had struck, and there was a heaviness at her tummy that I knew she would not have wanted to see so ruthlessly reproduced.

"Who is this? Do we know?" I asked.

"One of his daughters."

What sort of man paints his adult daughter naked? I asked myself. And yet, studying it silently alongside you for a moment, it was undoubtedly affecting. She had a strength about her. Freed from a pose that might be considered in any way alluring, I felt a sense of her humanness that was touching, tender.

"Did you actually like him?" I asked. "I didn't."

"It's not a matter of liking. He's Vivian Young."

"Does it mean so much to you?"

"Yes."

I was on the cusp of giving in there and then but then you closed the book with a snap. It made me jump.

Towards our bedtime, I sat and studied you as I fed Alice. You pretended to watch television but it was obvious to me that your thoughts still dwelt on the chance we had turned down, the chance to be a small part of Vivian Young's life for a little while.

When Alice had finally unlatched herself and I was rearranging my bra and top, you turned to me and said, "Jane," but stopped yourself and we were silent for I don't know how long.

I studied Alice, sound asleep on my lap, her cheeks flushed, her little chest rising and falling in a slow peaceful rhythm. My emotions ebbed and flowed, as though they kept time with her breathing: resentment, sympathy, curiosity, self-doubt, weariness, and then a sort of all-encompassing lassitude, a feeling of being unable to care anymore, a sense of resignation.

And I said, "Okay," quietly, without feeling, told you that if you really wanted it so much, I would sit for him.

And you said, "Thank you."

And that was that.

4

How much do you remember of those days, Michael, the interregnum? Are your memories clear, precise, as mine are, or are they just the vague generalised recollections of workaday remembrance? Which moments stand out for you when you look back? I can recall one conversation with absolute clarity, word for word. Can you?

It would have been about a week after I had agreed to sit for him. You were bouncing Alice on your knee and pulling faces at her, expertly extracting giggles and shrieks of delight.

"Vivian called again today," you said across her burbling.

"Oh, yes."

It no longer seemed worthwhile to mention that he continued to communicate with you, not me.

"He was asking when you would be ready to sit for him."

"I don't understand."

That was true, by the way. It was obvious that you were sidling up to something in a manner that was becoming habitual for you, choosing a moment when we might be partly distracted by activity, playing with Alice on this occasion, but I didn't know what it could be.

"How do I need to prepare?" I said. "I just turn up and take my clothes off, don't I?"

I wanted to see whether you would react to that again, attempt to deny that I would necessarily be naked, but you didn't.

"He said something about breastfeeding."

"I still don't understand."

"I think… The thing is that it might be better if you stopped before you start sitting for him."

My mind went blank, an absolute blank. I suppose too many thoughts, too many images of Alice at my breast, too many half-formed responses were jostling for prominence that I was left with a sort of white noise where thought might have been.

"It's likely to take some months, sitting for him. You know that. And you're likely to want to stop nursing her at some point soon, even if you don't stop now. You had mentioned it, you know, before… well before."

An image of Alice just after I had given birth, emerged from the tumult of competing pictures in my mind, of when I had been propped up on the maternity bed on a post-partum high of natural opioids and the sheer absence of all-consuming pain, of when the midwife presented her to my breast for her first feed, of how I struggled to find the right position and all poor Alice wanted to do was sleep, but a reflex of hers kicked in and she latched inexpertly on and in response to her tentative mouthing, the milk started to flow, as did my tears, tears of relief, and joy, of a fresh, stinging pain and of a new, hitherto unimagined love. You bent and kissed me tenderly on my forehead, which was still clammy with sweat. I don't think I have ever felt so close to you as I did then.

"It's not such a big deal is it?" you said, dragging me back to our sitting room. "He mentioned that, well... your breasts will shrink, when you stop, naturally, and that would be a problem if it happened half-way through his painting you."

I very nearly asked you whether it had turned you on a little, discussing my breasts with another man.

But instead I said, "And you still think that I won't necessarily be posing naked?"

So the next day was the last day, my last day breastfeeding our daughter, my daughter. I looked down at her, felt the gentle, rhythmic mouthing of her jaw, edged by the sharp little row of unbiting teeth, noted for the hundredth time, more, the way her hand rested with curled fingers on the white, blue-veined flesh of my breast, felt all that for what I knew would be the very last time.

My body is not mine, I thought. It seems to be everyone's but my own: yours, Michael, who had not only the moral claims of a husband but who could manipulate me so that I had reached this point, the point where I had agreed to stop breastfeeding my child before it felt right; Vivian's, Vivian, who would have it at his disposal for weeks on end to feed his ego and bank balance and God knows what else; even poor, unknowing, sweet little Alice's, Alice, who lay there, draining me with a sleepy but remorseless relentlessness, little Alice who could make my breasts zing and tingle, make me leak milk with the faintest of cries, even from another room. And someday your body won't be yours either, Alice, I thought; all too soon some spotty boy will convince you that it is more his than yours.

She twitched and unlatched from me with painful finality as my tears fell wetly onto her plump little cheek. How appropriate, I thought, to end this as it had begun – with me in tears.

It was all too much, and I surrendered to unrestrained sobbing as Alice flopped back on the pillow and looked up at me uncomprehendingly.

One week of weaning isn't enough you know.

So once or twice a day I sat in the bathroom, milking myself with my fingers, trying to ensure that it was not so much that my body would think I was still nursing but still enough to relieve the pressure, while Alice cried in her bedroom, needing to be fed.

That went on for a few days, until the milk finally stopped coming, just in time for my first session with Vivian.

I didn't tell you at the time. It had reached the stage where anything of significance I might have told you would have sounded like a rebuke so I stopped telling you anything of significance.

I couldn't sleep that night, the night before my first session with Vivian, so much so that I imagined him calling the finished painting *Girl with Baggy Eyes*.

Do you remember what I wore? On that first day. I expect you do. It was that green and white summer dress of mine, the one I bought for your mother's sixtieth birthday party. And can you guess why I chose to wear it? Because it is so very easy to take off.

Everything seemed different that morning; no; not different, just more: colours more intense, comforting sounds more soothing, annoying sounds more grating, the scents and smells of our kitchen by turns more alluring and more pungent. I remember the smell of the coffee being layered and nuanced, arousing, stimulating, comforting and bitter at the same time, the smell of charring at the edge of your toast, offensively acrid. Your aftershave was like a miasma around you; I could taste it in the air as much as smell it. Alice's cheeks had never smelt so sweet or her soiled nappy so offensive.

I realise now that my heightened awareness, my supersensitivity to every sight and sound and touch that day, was the product of a self-fulfilling expectation, that there was no inevitability that I should be that way except that I had made it so, that, by working myself into a state of anticipation that the coming day was going to be of special significance, I had ensured that it would be.

5

Have you ever had the experience of being so wrapped up in your own thoughts that you realise with a start that you have crossed two busy roads and can't remember doing so, can't remember whether you looked to check that it was safe to cross or had crossed unthinkingly and only avoided an accident by chance? That was how I felt as I found myself standing on Vivian's doorstep for the first time with no clear recollection of the route I had taken from the nearest Tube station.

When I reached up to press the doorbell, my hand was shaking. He took an age to answer. I now think that may well have been deliberate on his part. It would have given him a nice little thrill keeping me waiting, giving me plenty of time for a last-minute change of heart. I felt so embarrassed standing on his doorstep waiting for him to answer that bloody door, thinking that every passer-by knew exactly whose house it was and would guess that I was going to sit for him and thus that I would be sitting naked in front of a stranger for the next two hours.

When at last the door swung open, there he was, Vivian Young, dressed in white cotton trousers, a baggy, cream, cable-knit sweater. Next to him stood a grey lurcher, with hair rather like an Irish wolfhound. The dog was not on a lead but clearly not tempted to wander into the street, content to stand patiently by its master, eyeing me circumspectly.

You'll never guess how Vivian greeted me.

"Ah, it's Nyssia. Come in."

My mind was in such a muddle, disarranged by so many competing emotions that I hardly registered his words, did not stop to wonder what or who Nyssia might be or why he had greeted me that way. I expect you know, don't you?

Are you hard? I bet you are.

I suppose you already know what his studio, the Night Studio, looks like, from articles and books about him. Strange to think that you have never actually been in, that the nearest you got to it was the hallway, when I have spent so many hours in there. It was all new to me that first morning, the bare, paint-flecked floorboards, with their chalk markings, little circles and lines like runes or signs of some arcane lore, the bare coffee-cream walls, the lights on stands, like a film set, the furniture all pushed to one side save for a ragged, old couch, which had been placed in the middle of the room about ten feet from the easel, the stacks of canvases leaning against the wall.

No sooner had Vivian shown me in than he stopped me by taking hold of my upper arm.

"Turn to the light a moment," he said and, as soon as I had, "You're wearing makeup."

I looked at him blankly. You know me. My daytime

makeup is, well… hardly anything at all: the faintest flick of blusher at my cheekbones, a softening brown on my eyelids, lipstick that is just a semi-tone more vivid than my natural lip-colour. I've always thought that I was very restrained and grown-up about it, been quietly proud of myself, felt a little superior to most other women on that score.

"Did you carefully note exactly what you applied?" he asked. "Exactly how?"

He seemed quite angry.

"How many strokes of the blusher did it take? Do you know whether you stroked from left to right or right to left? Because, if not and if you mean to wear make up every time you come here to sit for me, you'd better go back home, wash it all off, start again and make absolutely sure that you can repeat it exactly the same way tomorrow and the day after and every day for months to come."

I felt suddenly very small and very stupid, like a child being told off for breaking something. Despite myself, I could feel my eyes moisten.

"I didn't think."

"Is that a habit of yours, not thinking?"

I blushed.

He looked away from me as though in exasperation.

"Go and take it off."

I hesitated, not knowing what to do.

"There's a lavatory at the end of the hall."

By the time I reached the toilet I was on the verge of tears. I felt so childish, partly for not thinking about the make-up, but mostly for being so upset about what was basically nothing. At one and the same time I felt frustrated with myself for responding to his rebuke like a silly girl and also that it was all my fault for not thinking things through. As I wiped the makeup off with those stupid little wipes I have in my bag, struggling not to cry, I was angry with him for being so unkind but also felt compelled to make sure that I did a good job of removing the makeup so that he would be satisfied. Just minutes before, standing on Vivian's doorstep, I had been unsure whether I was going to go through with it but there I was, desperate to clean myself up well enough that he would agree to proceed.

When I went back into his studio, he was standing by the couch. I had the impression that he might have been pacing about the room while I had been cleaning myself up, as though he had been waiting impatiently, but I no longer had the sense that he was angry.

"Come over here."

His tone was not peremptory; it seemed to be entirely neutral.

I did as he said. He was standing near the lights that he had set up to illuminate the couch. When I reached him, he put his finger under my chin and lifted it, turning my face fully to the light. The movement was not harsh but nor was it gentle, not brusque exactly – I don't know – professional? Yes: professional, like a doctor carrying out an examination. He studied my face intently for what felt like minutes on end; his eyes can't have been more than an inch or two from my skin, moving slowly as he inspected

42

every square centimetre. As he studied me so intently, I felt incredibly exposed, as though I were already stripped and naked before him. It was also the first time that day that I was aware of the scent of him, his distinct aroma, mixed, on this occasion, with the scent of clean, fresh cotton and stale cigar smoke, the merest hint of peppermint on his breath.

I remember thinking, I'm twenty-six.

"Do you have another tissue, or whatever it is you used?"

He let go of my face and I went to fetch a wipe from my bag where I had left it by the door. As I returned to him with the wipe, he held out his hand and I passed it to him. He positioned my face just as he had before and studied me again. After a moment more inspecting me, he placed the tip of the wipe gently on my left cheek, just below my lower eyelid and wiped with the lightest of pressures, just two strokes, and then went back to studying me again.

"There," he said at last, still with that same medical air, stepping back from me.

"I'm sorry," I said, and felt immediately childish again for having apologised.

"Right," he said. "Let's get started."

He didn't ask me to take my clothes off. He just looked at me expectantly, so I reached up, undid the button of my summer dress, and stepped out of it. I remember thinking, in that instant, that I wished I had thought to take my shoes off first, but I hadn't, so I quickly stepped out of them.

Then my bra.

I had a strong instinct to turn my back to him, reveal that part of me to him first, but then I told myself not to be stupid, that there was no point in being coy, so I stayed facing him. I cringe slightly recalling it but I'm afraid I think I raised my chin and regarded him a little defiantly as I reached around, unclasped my bra, and took it off. I realise now that that defiance was every bit as childish as coyness would have been.

And then my knickers. By then I just wanted to get it over with, so off they came. He glanced down at me and I had a distinct impression that he was checking that I did indeed have hair down there, as I had promised. Promised! As I had said that I did.

I had ventured a small expression of defiance earlier, when removing my bra but now that I was fully naked, I felt exquisitely vulnerable, exposed in a way I never had before. I had never considered myself shy that way, about nudity I mean, even as a teenager, but I felt exactly like a nervously shy young girl at that moment, both shy and silly for being shy. It was all I could do to stop myself from covering my breasts with my arms. I sat for a moment on the edge of the couch, knees together, leaning forward slightly, with my hands clasped where they rested between my knees. He went to the easel, stood where I assumed he would stand when painting and considered me thoughtfully so that for a moment I wondered whether he would paint me like that. Come to think of it, there's a Munch of a girl in a pose like that, isn't there?

But I just knew that he did not intend to paint me sitting up, so, after taking a deep breath, I reclined, lifting my feet up onto the couch and resting my upper shoulders back against the armrest, so that I could rest my head on it also, conscious of the way my breasts splayed slightly to the side of my torso as I leant back.

Vivian started to move about the room, viewing me from different angles.

"How would you like me to pose?" I asked, trying my utmost to sound matter-of-fact, off-hand, as though I were asking how many sugars he took in his coffee.

He did not answer but instead kept studying me with a fierce intensity that was to become so familiar, slowly moving about the room like something feline and vaguely threatening.

Of course, I realised that, once it was fixed, I would have to maintain whatever pose we settled on for hours at a time and that knowledge made me acutely aware of my body, my flesh, the touch of my back, bottom, and legs wherever I was in contact with the couch and its slightly grubby cloth, cloth which, as a result of that heightened sensitivity, felt rough against my skin. My limbs were heavy and awkward, stiff, their position felt unnatural no matter how I arranged them. Every time I shifted a little, I felt less comfortable not more, the arrangement of my limbs more awkward and ungainly.

I tried ignoring Vivian for a while, even tried pretending that he was not there, resting my head back a little more and looking up at the high Georgian ceiling, the ornate ceiling rose, the deep cornice. There was a small patch of rough, scratched and peeling paint at one corner. But then he went to stand by the easel again, and I found that I simply had to look at him.

"That's better," he said, fixing my eyes with his. He took a step forward towards me, holding my gaze all the time, then stepped back again, still staring at me intently, repeated the process a couple of times more.

"When I'm studying any other part of you, you can look away," he said, with that level professional tone I have told you about, "with your eyes I mean; you must keep your head still. But when I'm studying your face, I need you to look straight at me."

"Can I talk?"

I felt stupid for asking, but I really wasn't sure.

"Of course."

He smiled as though to confirm the stupidity of my question.

"That's an essential part of the process."

Our eyes were still locked on each other's and we stayed like that for some time until he eventually moved and started to consider some other part of me.

I still had not settled into a pose and shifted a little. He stopped as though struck by an idea.

"Put your right arm up."

I did as he said.

"A little more to the side. Good. And bend it a touch more so that your hand is just behind your head there. Yes, resting on the couch."

He seemed at least partially satisfied.

"Will you be able to hold that do you think?"

We were clearly nearing a pose that he found acceptable.

I shifted the arm just a touch so that I was more comfortable, worrying, even though the shift was only fractional, that the change would displease him but he seemed content.

"I think so," I said.

He came forward until he was very close and stared down at my newly exposed armpit. I was acutely aware of him inspecting me there and felt suddenly very vulnerable again, almost as though he were gazing at my sex. He could have inspected my sex, of course, if he had wanted to, at least my mons, the triangle of ginger hair; I had my legs more or less clamped together, so his view would have been limited.

"You didn't ask about my armpits, did you?" I said, attempting a hint of humour. "But as you can see, I do shave there."

He smiled.

After studying my armpit for I while, he returned to his position by the canvas.

"Look at me," he said once more.

I did.

"Is that it then? The final pose?" I asked, trying to strike that matter-of fact tone once more.

He did not answer, just kept looking into my eyes. Even if I had not been under instruction to hold his gaze, I do not think that I would have been able to look away.

I have thought about what happened next endlessly, and yet I still cannot explain it, understand it, rationalise it, even to myself. As we stared so intently into each other's eyes, seemingly out of nowhere mine welled up and I knew, just knew that I would be unable to stop a tear from falling. And then, even as one did, hot and wet onto my cheek, where I left it unwiped, I slowly spread my thighs, bending my left knee as I did so, exposing myself to him.

He kept his gaze locked on mine for long seconds more, then finally relented and took a step forward, then another and studied my torso, my sex. As he gazed so intently at me, I moved my thighs just a fraction more, so that they lay a little more open and, as I did so, I felt my body settle, relax into the upholstery of the couch.

"This is it," I said, even as another tear splashed onto my cheek. "This is how I want you to paint me."

He ignored my tears.

Or perhaps it would be more accurate to say that he did not comment upon them. He simply got to work, first picking out a canvas from one of two stacks leaning against a side wall, taking a long time over his choice. This surprised me for I had expected to find a canvas on the easel ready.

Embarrassed by my tears, I was not in any mood for small talk but I feared the silence more than banality.

"You don't pick a canvas out beforehand then?" I asked.

"No," he said, carefully checking the edges of one,

"I need to have the model in position first. If I set things up before they arrive, I find I am already constructing an image unconnected with the model, imposing ideas of composition, structure that will be a block to observation."

He looked over at me, studying me and the blank canvas in turn. It was an odd feeling, the feeling of posing even though he had not yet so much as touched a brush but it was clear to me that I was to hold my pose just as much as if he were painting the finest detail.

After what seemed to me an inordinately long time, he finally settled on a canvas and set it on the easel, taking time in this process too, adjusting the height several times. At last, he picked up a piece of charcoal and made a mark. We had begun.

As he sketched me – he showed no signs of touching a paintbrush yet – I began to sense why he was notorious for taking so long over a single painting. He spent nearly all his time observing me (and on occasion, it seemed, the couch) and very little time making marks on the canvas. Not only that but he seemed to rub off nearly as much as he applied. It was clear to me that his approach was meticulous and painstaking but at the same time a process of feeling his way towards something, something that he had not yet identified.

After what I would have guessed was an hour, he stepped away from the canvas and put down his charcoal.

"I need a break," he said, stretching his arms out wide with his chin down, so that his chest bowed forwards.

"You can sit up, stretch your limbs," he said. "Stand

up and walk around if you want."

I sat up – a little too quickly, so that I was momentarily dizzy and felt that I needed to stay very still for a couple of seconds.

"Shall I get dressed?"

"Don't bother," he said, "Here!" and tossed over to me his baggy, cable-knit sweater.

I don't think I had noticed that he'd taken it off, that he was wearing just his white shirt and white cotton trousers. I think he must have taken the sweater off when I had been in the toilet wiping my face. I had been in such a state when I returned that his clothing was the last thing on my mind.

The wool felt harsh and rough in my hands. There was an animal smell to it too: his scent, I now think, but at the time, probably by the power of association, it put me in mind of the animals it had come from, of sheep, of salt air and damp grass. It was all I could do to stop myself raising it to my face and taking a deep breath of it.

I remember thinking that it would be rather uncomfortable, but I put it on anyway. It was indeed very scratchy but it was a relief to be clothed again, even if it was just my top-half. I had grown to feel less vulnerable, less exposed over the hour that he had been sketching me, but, nevertheless, to be covered up was relaxing. I felt a slight tension in my shoulders, that I had not until then been aware of, ease and lessen.

"May I look?" I asked.

"Yes, of course, but there's not much to see."

He was right. There was barely the outline of a human figure, hardly distinguishable as a woman, certainly not recognisable as me. A handful of incomplete lines, no more than that, delineated the space on the canvas where the couch would be.

"Do you plan what you're going to paint?" I asked. "I mean have a theme or an aspect of the sitter that you want to bring out."

He shook his head emphatically.

"Absolutely not; in fact, quite the opposite. I paint what I see. It would be worse than useless to try and anticipate that, to try and foreshadow it."

His answer sounded like a rebuke to me.

"That sounds like the sort of answer you would give if you were trying to impress me," I said.

He smiled.

"It's alright, you know," he said. "We don't have to fight. We can if you want but we don't have to. It's not essential to the process."

Before long, too soon for my needs at the time, he said that we should begin again and so I had to remove the comforting cover of his sweater and try to position myself back in the identical pose that I had eventually struck. Under meticulous direction from Vivian and after some minutes, I managed it to his satisfaction and he recommenced his painstaking, geologically slow work.

It's odd. Not long ago I was boasting about the clarity of my memories of certain moments, certain conversations, and yet I can recall almost nothing of that evening, the first time I returned home from posing for Vivian. I seem to remember that I stood on the pavement for a moment or two before going in and that, when I did, I went straight to Alice, picked her up and squeezed her and that it was an effort to stop myself from squeezing her too hard, hard enough to hurt her. But after that nothing.

Do you remember that evening with greater clarity? Perhaps you do. If we combined our memories of all those moments, would we be able to construct an accurate history of the whole affair?

Did you quiz me about the day, about Vivian and his methods? Or did you bite your tongue? Even if you did interrogate me, I don't suppose I would have been very forthcoming. Perhaps I cannot remember that evening because I was hardly even aware of it at the time. That would have been like me. I can obsess about a recent event with such intensity that it is as though I relive it completely and the now does not exist. I fancy I might have spent the evening in silence, reliving over and over, the moment when I had reached up to undo the top button of my summer dress.

6

The second time one does something can often seem more significant than the first. Have you noticed that? Perhaps significant is not quite right – definitive, like the second time I ever made love. The first time, I had been so wrapped up in the event, the fact of losing my virginity, the milestone on my journey to adulthood and the weight of my expectations and anxieties that it was hardly a proper instance of making love at all; it was as though it were something else entirely. But that second time, I remember thinking, This is it; I am a fully sexual woman.

I was only fifteen, but that is what I thought. I am someone who makes love.

So it was with the second time I sat for Vivian. On that first day I had been in a constant turmoil of emotions, confused feelings about you and what this might mean for us, the way he made me feel so childish at times, and then how exposed and vulnerable I had felt. But on that second day, as I stood on his doorstep once more, waiting for the blue door to swing open. I thought, Right, I'm going to do it again. This is who I am: part of who I am anyway, someone who sits for Vivian Young.

When he had led me into his studio again and I started

to take my clothes off, trying to be matter-of-fact about it as if I were at the doctors, I felt almost more awkward than I had the day before, not as vulnerable, or emotionally exposed, perhaps, but more awkward in an ordinary, social kind of way; I don't know, something like being on the edge of a conversation at a party when you haven't yet been introduced. And I found it terribly embarrassing lying back on the couch and trying to find my way into the exact pose that I had adopted the day before, wondering all the time why I had felt compelled to open my legs quite so wide.

Slightly to my surprise, he was very patient with me as he directed me into position, checking and rechecking against what he had drawn the day before.

"No, your arm a little more bent. Yes, good. Your chin a touch to the left, and a little higher. You need to shift your bottom just a fraction forward, not too much. No, back a bit."

I think I may have sighed in frustration.

"You'll get used to it," he said.

His tone was unaccustomedly gentle; it felt as if it were the first positively kind thing he had said to me over the two days thus far.

It was such a relief when he declared himself satisfied and set to work again. Looking back, I realise that the very fact of it having been such a trial, getting into absolutely the right position, made me feel happier and more relaxed lying there like that than I had the day before.

"I don't like paintings that have a structured composition," he said, as I finally settled into the correct position, "neat symmetries, that sort of thing. Or consciously studied asymmetries for that matter. They are both equally false. If you start with artifice, with what is basically a lie, you can't then impose truth; it doesn't work. If you try for asymmetry, there is discord, if you go for symmetry, then... well you end up with a Bouguereau."

"That's why it takes so long for my models to arrive at a position that will work. It has to come from them, and even after all these years, I have to work hard to avoid pushing them towards the visually pleasing."

"Wouldn't it work just to take the first pose they strike?" I asked. "A bit like photographing someone before they notice that you are going to. That leads to a lot of dud photos, I admit, but every now and then something pleasingly natural."

"I've tried it, but it doesn't really work, no. Even flopping down in a deliberately random manner has a touch of artificiality to it."

I thought of asking him whether he thought the position I had adopted was working, but I feared what his answer might be.

"There's a famous Victorian painting I rather like," I said, "of a soldier, a cavalry officer, I think, looking splendidly swanky in his mess uniform, with his legs crossed in a way that shows off the broad red stripe down his trouser leg but the result is a design that is almost abstract, so I'm guessing that it's not your kind of thing"

Vivian concentrated hard on the canvas for the next few minutes, making an adjustment, a very small change it seemed to me, although of course I could not see.

But then he said, "It's a Tissot: Frederick Burnaby; it's in the National Portrait Gallery. We could go and see it together some time. Contrary to your assumption, I rather like it, because the clothes and the patterns that they make reflect something of the man, I think. The pattern hasn't been imposed by the painter but comes from the sitter."

Then he took me by surprise by saying, "Clothes are so important."

I laughed.

"I don't know quite what to say to that, given my current condition."

He smiled.

"It's not the clothes themselves, exactly," he said, "but the way they are worn. One man will look quite different from another in the same tailored suit, and I don't mean to refer to the fit, I mean how the person and the clothes interact. Captain Burnaby certainly owns those trousers."

An hour later, for no reason that I could discern, he said, "Play up, play up and play the game," to the canvas, as he added another mark with his charcoal.

Not long after making this Delphic statement, he strode forward with sudden purpose until he was extremely close to me and bent down to inspect my left arm where it lay flat and angled slightly away from my side, the crook of my elbow. I was very aware of the physical fact of him, his being so close, and found myself studying the flecks of paint that were everywhere on his white cotton trousers.

"Why did you call me Nyssia?" I asked. "When you

56

answered the door yesterday."

I would come to learn that he would often ignore what I said, or seem to, even a direct question such as this. I think I blushed.

He continued to study me, concentrating fiercely on the inside of my left elbow, his expression giving no clue that he had even heard me. I sensed that there was no point repeating myself and lapsed into a sullen silence. Eventually, he straightened up and returned to the easel, checked his work, then began to pace about the room in a manner I was becoming familiar with. After, I don't know how long, during which he continually moved about, always intently studying me, he went back to his position by the canvas and made a few strokes with his charcoal, sweeping confident strokes.

"Look at me," he said.

It was the first thing either of us had said for a very long time.

I did.

He studied my eyes for a moment, then said, "She was Queen of Lydia, wife of King Candaules. Do you not know the story?"

"No."

I remember feeling terribly constrained by the sense that I should not shake my head, was limited to expressing myself by the negative word alone, without the naturally accompanying gesture.

Vivian added a few more strokes of charcoal to the canvas before continuing.

"The women of Lydia were famously modest, and it was considered shameful that any man other than their husbands should look upon any part of their body."

He glanced significantly at my exposed sex, a hint of a smile playing about his eyes.

"But the king, Candaules was immensely proud of his wife, Nyssia's great beauty, considered her the most gorgeous of women and it troubled him that only he could fully know just how beautiful she was. This thought gnawed at him relentlessly, obsessively for months and months until he came to long for at least one other man to know just how fortunate he was, fortunate in a way that befitted a great king."

He took a pace forward and to the side, seeming to me to be concentrating on my hair for a moment.

"Did you know, by the way, that it was not unheard of for the Ancient Greeks to have red hair. The modern Greek colouring is largely a result of prolonged subjugation to the Turk."

I didn't want passively to accept everything he told me, so I decided to challenge him.

"Is that really true, Vivian, or have you just made that up?"

He smiled.

"Now amongst the palace guard was a man called Gyges, the bravest soldier and the finest athlete in the guard."

He returned to the canvas and rubbed something away before adding a couple of fresh lines of charcoal, around about where my hair would be, if I guessed correctly.

"He and the king had been childhood companions and the king considered him a true friend. So, when the need to boast of his wife's incomparable physical beauty became too much for Candaules, he summoned Gyges and prevailed upon him to hide in the royal bedchamber so that he could spy upon the queen's nakedness when she disrobed."

I suddenly felt very conscious of the rise and fall of my chest as I breathed in and out.

"Gyges protested that such a deception was not worthy of a soldier of the palace guard, that it would do great dishonour to the queen, but the king insisted. So what could Gyges do? After all, it was an order from his king. So, he did as the king commanded and hid behind a screen, not far from the door so that he could steal away afterwards. The plan appeared to work; Gyges spied on the queen as she undressed, indeed lingered a while; for the king had not deceived him, Nyssia's body was truly luscious" – he was looking at the canvas as he said this, not at me – "and Gyges was a man, after all."

"But unknown to Gyges or the king, as Gyges slipped away, timing his exit with the moment Nyssia climbed into bed to join her husband, she spied Gyges in the corner of her eye and recognised him."

"She questioned her husband. Did he not hear something? Was there perhaps an assassin lurking? But the king said that there was surely nothing, reassured her that it could not be so."

Vivian had stopped drawing and put down his charcoal,

was entirely focussed on his storytelling.

"Now, this calm rejection of any risk betrayed Candaules; for what king is not in perpetual terror of assassination and would not hesitate to call the guard at any hint of danger? Thus, she deduced that the king had known that Gyges had been there, had made a show of her to his friend."

"In the course of a long sleepless night, Nyssia's love for Candaules, hitherto so strong, transformed into bottomless hatred: to be dealt with so shamefully, paraded for another man's titilation. So, in the morning, when the king had left her, she summoned Gyges and questioned him. When he eventually confessed the plot, confirmed her deduction, she gave him an ultimatum; she could summon the guard and have him killed on the spot or he must kill the king himself as her revenge."

"Gyges begged and pleaded but he had no choice. What could he do? She was queen. So, that same night, he hid once more behind the screen and as the queen finished undressing, which was the signal they had agreed upon between them, he leapt from his hiding place and plunged his dagger into the heart of his friend and king."

Vivian picked up a piece of charcoal, looked at me for a moment or two, then made another mark on the canvas.

"And can you guess how the story ends?"

"Yes, probably."

"Nyssia, Queen of Lydia took Gyges to her bed and he was crowned king."

"And they lived happily ever after?"

"Yes, quite happily, by all accounts."

"That's quite a story, Vivian."

"Yes, isn't it?"

I had tried to make light of it. He's teasing, I told myself. Don't rise to it. But inside I was feeling sick, physically sick to the point where I sensed the saliva pooling in my mouth and had to swallow.

"There's a very striking painting of that story," Vivian went on, "by Bouchard. You can hardly see Gyges, just glimpse his knife in the shadows. The only fully lit figure is..."

I sat up, interrupting him.

"I think I'd better call it a day."

He seemed surprised. I don't think he was used to his models deciding when a session was over. I stood up and got dressed hurriedly.

"I really need to go now."

"Of course. If you must."

As he accompanied me to the front door, I sensed for the first time that he was not completely in control of the situation, of himself, that he was even a little embarrassed, contrite, although he said nothing by way of apology. When he opened the door and made a movement forward to kiss me on the cheek by way of farewell as he had the day before, I stepped away from him out onto the doorstep.

"Don't poke fun at me, Vivian," I said. "It's not fair. I'm not sure I'll be coming back."

I sensed him stay on his doorstep watching me as I walked away, even though I did not turn to check.

7

A card was delivered by hand to our flat that evening. I'm sure you remember it; the front was a detail from a renaissance painting of the Annunciation, Mary with strawberry-blonde hair in ringlets and the angel Gabriel kneeling as if in supplication. I wasn't sure at the time but suspected that it was a da Vinci. I've checked since and it was.

You asked me what it was and when I said that it was from Vivian, you didn't know what to do with yourself, did you? I could tell that you were desperate to ask me what it said.

He had written, "Please come again. I need to paint you."

As I studied the card, trying to work out what I would do, I glanced up at you. It was obvious to me that you had been staring at me as hard as I had been staring at the card and your expression, before you hurriedly looked away… I saw in it a nervousness that was provoking. It made my mind up for me.

I'm sure you remember every word of the conversation that followed.

"I've been thinking," I said, standing up.

When you looked up at me, I could see that you were

frightened of what I might say.

"And I've decided that we should both agree that you won't ask me about what happens in the studio, that what goes on in there will remain mine and mine alone."

What thoughts did your expression betray then? Fear still, certainly, a touch of surprise, as though this was not quite what you had been expecting from me, something akin to curiosity, puzzlement perhaps.

Eventually you said simply, "Okay," quietly, meekly.

"And I mean everything. Is that clear?"

"Yes," you said, coming towards me and putting your arms around my waist.

"I love you," you said, your eyes full of a sort of questioning hope.

Then, you stepped in to kiss me, so that our fronts touched. I so very nearly backed away but that would have been too much.

As we kissed, I could feel your erection pressing against my stomach.

That night, our bedroom smelled stale to me, airless, like when we would come home from being away and it would take hours with the windows wide for the flat to feel fresh again.

My next session with Vivian was significant on several counts, perhaps most importantly because I went, when I had been nearly sure as I fled his house the previous time that I would not return. Also, it was the first time that he applied paint to the canvas. But it was also the first time, and sadly not the last, when I succumbed to feelings that my body, laid out before him on the couch, was ugly and lumpen.

You will not be surprised to hear that he took a very long time picking out paints and mixing them. There was a pile of I don't know how many tubes on a side table near the easel. Twenty-five, thirty? He seemed to have used nearly half, created several tones on the pallet, before he so much as touched a brush, all the time staring intently at me between each consideration of the mound of tubes.

When he did finally pick up a brush, instead of applying some paint to the canvas, he advanced towards me until he was extremely close and leant down to study my left breast from no more than a foot away. I was suddenly overwhelmed by self-consciousness, an irresistible notion that my breast, in particular my nipple, which he was studying with what seemed to me a profound disinterest, a purely forensic intensity, was a thing of great ugliness, a thing of great ugliness in a body that was, in its entirety, equally repellent, that my nipple was a merely functional body part with no more sexual allure than a cow's teat. I began to cry, tears rolling down my cheeks unwiped as I maintained my pose. Vivian glanced up at my face for a moment and then went back to studying my nipple, giving it once more his undivided attention.

The grey lurcher had joined us in the studio and eyed me from where he lay on a pile of rags in one corner, watching my tears snake down my cheek with indifference.

It wasn't always that way; I wouldn't want you to think that; me always sinking into a swamp of self-loathing. During one session, at least a month – no, more than that – into my sitting for Vivian, he paused in the very moment of touching his brush to the canvas and said, "It is absolutely fascinating."

"What is?"

He smiled.

"Your patterning: the way that the freckling on your face intensifies on your shoulders and arms, then how it thins out again as it reaches your upper chest and resolves itself into flawlessness, like alabaster at your breasts and stomach."

He studied me for a while more, comparing me, I think, with the paint that he had just then applied.

"It is not quite symmetrical," he said, "but, as graphic art, it is very satisfying."

I was aware that he had approached very near to paying me a compliment.

"I think it's something to do with exposure to sun over time," I said. "The bits that see the sun get more freckles."

We were silent for a moment. Then, I said, "I noticed the implication that freckles are flaws, by the way."

He laughed.

"Don't go fishing for compliments, Jane. It's not worthy of you. Let's just say that on you they are entirely congruent."

"Yes, Michael likes to say how congruent I am, too," I said. "It really turns me on."

He laughed again.

He turned back to his canvas and my thoughts drifted, as they always did whenever silence descended. But then, perhaps ten minutes later, they returned to the idea of my freckles as a discernible pattern, as though they had been placed on me by design, in a rise and fall of intensity that to this artist's eye, this man, was fascinating, coherent, and, try as my doubts might to fight the notion, by implication as something attractive rather than being, as I had come to think of them, simply irradicably there.

"Every freckly girl feels self-conscious about her freckles you know," I said. "Particularly when she's young. You wouldn't believe how mercilessly horrible children can be about such things."

I considered for a moment.

"Or perhaps you would."

He nodded thoughtfully.

And there I was, back in the playground, having approached in an exquisite torment of hope a group of girls as they played, played a game that I would, at that moment, have given anything to join, and Sonja Kerrigan, the snotty little cow, was poking her tongue at me and chanting "Freckle face. Freckle face." My ears were hot and I was trying so desperately hard not to cry but I could feel the weight of my tears becoming too much as they pooled on my lower eyelids, until one splashed onto my left cheek and I could not stop myself from handing her the victory by turning and scurrying away, wiping my tears as I went.

If only I could have been there to give the young girl that was me a hug and whisper that, in twenty years' time, one of the world's most famous artists, someone who was already famous back then, who could be seen on art programmes on T.V. if her parents would let her stay up, would tell her that her freckles were fascinating and compare the skin of her stomach, of the breasts that she did not yet have, to alabaster.

8

I did not keep a count of the sessions and so cannot identify by number the one when Vivian first led me further into the house. It may have been the fourth or fifth. I had not yet, as I recall, mastered my positioning at the start of the session as I would eventually come to do, so that seems about right. I was to learn later that not all Vivian's models were granted entry that far, that most, other than family and lovers, were not. He was, I was beginning to learn, a very private man and reticent about many things.

I had not, at that point in time, been aware of anyone else in the house. Vivian and the lurcher seemed not only the sole inhabitants but it also seemed that he did not have any visitors. This turned out to be far from the truth.

I had donned again his rough, woollen, cable-knit sweater when we took a break and I was stretching my limbs and moving my head in slow circles trying to ease my neck muscles, which always threatened to tighten up during those prolonged periods of stillness. Vivian wiped his hands with the cloth that he kept tucked into his belt while he painted.

"I'm hungry," he said, "Let's get something to eat."

I suppose it shows how far I had come in a relatively

short space of time that I did not hesitate to follow him out of the studio and up the stairs to the next floor wearing only his sweater. I think I had already formed a sense, a wordless, unexpressed notion at that point in time, of his studio as a place apart, outside of anything normal, separate from the rest of the world and, in following him then, I extended that special place to encompass all of his house. It did not occur to me to fret that a visitor might happen upon us with me wearing a sweater that only just reached low enough to cover my backside but at any sort of significant movement might rise up immodestly.

As I climbed the stairs behind Vivian, noticing as I did how narrow his hips were, how wiry his frame, a doorway, through which I could see a dining room, came into view, offering a glimpse of an expanse of mahogany table, large sash windows, and plain coffee-cream-coloured walls on which hung innumerable works of art, none of them painted by him, as far as I could determine from my vantage point. They were hung crammed together in a manner reminiscent of one of those paintings of an exhibition at the Royal Academy in the eighteenth century in which the gallery-goers strain to see paintings hung right up to the cornice. A door next to the dining room opened into a small kitchen that Vivian called his pantry, used, I supposed, to put the finishing touches to meals that had been prepared in another, larger kitchen, which there must have been somewhere in that large, well-appointed townhouse.

Vivian led me in and took a couple of plates from a

cupboard, a pair of glass tumblers from another. On a pan on a small hob sat the remains of a pheasant, much of the meat having been sliced away, but here and there were morsels of game-flesh still. Vivian took a sharp knife from a draw and expertly carved thin slices from the carcass, distributing them between the two plates.

"A couple of mouthfuls only," he said, "but restorative. Let's have some wine too."

It was not yet ten-thirty.

"Don't worry," he said, as he took a half-drunk bottle of red from a shelf and pulled out the cork that had been wedged back in. "We'll have half a glass each, just enough to enliven the senses."

I was still not sure but took the tumbler that he proffered.

"It's alright," he said, "I can't paint if I drink more than a glass, so this is definitely all we are having."

The cold pheasant had a metallic astringency that went well with the full-bodied red. Just a taste of each was all we had, but it was enough to provoke a sensation of luxury, sensuousness, that was, as Vivian had promised, quickening.

"What are you hoping to see, in the painting, when it's finished?" he asked.

"I'm not sure. What an odd question."

"In all the hours you've been posing, you've given no thought to how it will turn out?"

"That's not what you asked. I'm very curious to know what it will look like, of course I am. That's not the same thing as wanting it to look a particular way."

I took a sip of my wine.

"I suppose it would be useless to deny that I hope I won't look absolutely hideous."

I think I had meant this light-heartedly so I was slightly taken aback when he said, "That is a real risk."

I laughed a little nervously.

"Thanks."

"I'm not joking. My wife..."

He hesitated. It was the first time that he had mentioned his wife and something in the way he halted told me that he considered that a slip, an unintended lapse, a crack in the carapace of privacy that he had built around certain aspects of his life. You know all about their brief marriage so many years ago, I suppose. I was tempted to urge him to go on but thought better of it. I did not need to; after a couple of beats he continued.

"...well my wife was indisputably beautiful, everyone said so."

I noted the reference to others' opinion of her, as though he himself were not wholly convinced of her beauty.

"But of the many crimes she came to hate me for, real and imagined, I think the foremost was that she thought that I made her look ugly in my paintings of her."

He paused and looked me up and down. I had an unnerving feeling he was comparing me to her.

"She told one of our friends once that she couldn't understand how someone so beautiful could be made to look so ugly."

71

He smiled.

"She was not modest about her looks. I think she was probably trying to seduce him, successfully for all I know."

I felt, just in that instant and I think for the first time, sorry for him, that he could talk so glibly of his wife's presumed infidelity.

"Did you?"

He looked at me questioningly.

"I mean, did you think she looked ugly in your paintings?"

"No. But I understood what she saw in them that made her think that. My style then was consciously to focus on and exaggerate certain elements. That necessarily introduced a degree of distortion. That kind of exaggeration is anathema to conventional beauty, which, when all is said and done and poetry set aside, is no more than a matter of the genetic lottery and good nutrition producing satisfyingly symmetrical and regular proportions."

"It must have hurt her terribly to think you saw ugliness when you looked at her."

"Yes."

"And you painted her like that anyway?"

"Yes."

I was on the point of asking him whether he thought it had been worth it, putting what he thought his art demanded before the equilibrium of his marriage, but I stopped myself. His "art" never demanded anything, did it, of him or anyone else? His "art" doesn't exist separately from him. That term is just a kind of shorthand for him, his thoughts, his beliefs, his ego, and it's not at all difficult to believe that he thought that it was worth putting all that above the equilibrium of his marriage, above the needs and wishes of his wife. Don't you think, Michael?

When we returned to the studio and Vivian had taken up his pallet and brushes once more, my thoughts remained with his wife. She thought he made her look ugly in his paintings. I had been in tears just days before, having convinced myself how unappealing my body must look under his searching gaze. How hurtful must it have been for her to see the same in her husband's paintings of her?

Vivian's thoughts, too, seemed to have stayed with his ex-wife for he said, "Can you guess what finally ended our marriage?"

"No."

In fact, I assumed some infidelity of his.

"I had painted her on a bed with a greyhound lying next to her. In the end I called it *Woman with Dog*, but I told her that I was thinking of calling it *Beauty and the Beast*. She wasn't happy."

He had a mischievous glint in his eye.

"Can you guess why?"

I considered for a moment.

"Presumably, because you left it ambiguous which of them was Beauty and which the Beast."

He smiled.

"Exactly. Although it would be only fair to say that he was a particularly fine-looking greyhound, so it was never really in doubt. He was extremely sleek and finely muscled, what they call well-conditioned. Greyhounds are surprisingly large when they lie down. He dominated the canvas: another cause for displeasure."

After a few minutes of silent painting, he said, "What do you think of that story by the way: *Beauty and the Beast*?"

He had a habit of being silent for long periods and then simply continuing our earlier conversation, going straight to where we had left off as though there had been no pause of any length of time.

I lay in silence for a while, recalling an old book of fairy tales that I read and reread as a child. I think it had originally been my mother's. There had been one drawing that I found fascinating, a drawing of the Beast in his rose garden. I felt as though I could remember every detail, every line of it. His body was entirely that of a slim young man, clad in expensive-looking, mediaeval costume. You know the sort of thing, red hose and pointed shoes and a short, fur-lined jerkin of ribbed, blue velvet. But his head was that of a boar, all bristles and teeth and tusks, with large, hairy ears. I remember thinking, even at the age of six or seven, that his expression was not fierce at all, only sad.

"I haven't given it much thought," I said. "Not for years, anyway. I remember liking it very much. I can't remember exactly why."

"It is a particularly dangerous story," he said, emphatically. "For girls, I mean."

"I don't follow. What harm is there in it?"

"It tells them that nice, good-natured girls can tame a beast by showing courage and perseverance in the face of his beastly ways, that if they are kind and loving enough, they can transform him from a savage, dangerous animal into a loving, domesticated man. It's a completely false notion. No bad man is going to change just because a woman is stupid enough to love him. How many violent or otherwise malfunctioning marriages are maintained by the woman believing in that possibility of change?"

"Stupid, is a bit unkind isn't it?" I said. "I don't see that a woman can control who she loves."

"Love can't be turned on and off at will. That's true. But a woman can control what positions she puts herself in, with whom she gives herself the opportunity to fall in love. It's all very well falling in love with scoundrels; if that's what excites you, fine. It's the idea that you can tame that bad side that is so misguided. That's the dangerous falsehood that the story of *Beauty and the Beast* encourages."

He laughed.

"I shouldn't object really, because I can't tell you how many nice young women I've had, who put up with me for months or even years, thinking that they could transform me with their love. It used to happen all the time when I was younger" – he smiled ruefully – "not so much these days. I think it has become more and more obvious over time that I am incorrigible. My latest lovers at least know what they are letting themselves in for."

Did he glance significantly at me? I'm not sure.

"Of course, some of those nice young women who let themselves into my bedroom, years ago, were looking for something else entirely," he added, "looking to find their own, inner Beast and let her out. That was much more achievable."

It was later in that same session that he said, as though out of nowhere, "You might not believe it, Jane, but some of the people who sit for me are really very dull. I try to coax something intelligent out of them, but it's a huge effort. And dull people lead to dull paintings. It's always a relief when my sitter has something about them, a spark."

But my thoughts kept returning to his brief marriage.

"There were real crimes then?"

"I'm sorry?"

"In your marriage; you said that she accused you of many crimes, real and imagined."

He did not answer. His face was set and I began to think that I had displeased him, probed too much.

"Did you even attempt to be faithful to her?"

"I intended to be, was, right up to near the end of my marriage I would say, spiritually faithful to my wife."

"Just not actually."

He paused, in a way that was unusual for him, not being silent because he was absorbed in the process of observing me or mixing paint or applying it to the canvas but in a manner that seemed to me to suggest his leaving the room for a moment, remembering.

"No," he said.

"She must have hated that."

"Do you think so? You seem to be assuming that she was faithful to me."

He was right. I had been, whatever he had said earlier about her attempting to seduce a friend.

"I came home once to find her in bed with another man," he said, as though he were recounting something of limited importance, nothing more than an anecdote. "Not someone I knew."

"Jesus! Poor you. What did that feel like?"

"It was very strange. I was upset, much more upset than I had ever expected I would be. But not in the way you would think."

Something on the canvas demanded his complete attention, interrupting his narrative.

"No, that's not quite right," he muttered to himself, before taking up his pallet knife and scraping paint away.

"The thing was," he said, as he picked out another tube of paint from the side table, "they were literally sleeping together. They must have dozed off after making love in what might have been termed "the marital bed". I think it was the insouciance of it all that disturbed me."

"What did you do?"

"Nothing. I just left them there, went out and stayed away for a couple of hours. When I got back, he had gone, whoever he was, and she was having a bath, washing the scent of him away, I suppose. I never saw him again, never spoke to her about it. I had been unfaithful too many times by then to be judgmental."

"So you had an open marriage?"

"Not so much open as ajar. We had a tacit understanding, I think you might say, without ever having put anything into words. We really did live amongst bohemians. It was more or less the done thing at the time, amongst that set."

"I couldn't live in your world," I said.

"It's not my world, Jane; it's the world."

I let it rest at that and silence took up residence in the room as it so often did. My thoughts were drifting away from the studio to some distant memory or other or perhaps to an image of a young Vivian standing at a half-open bedroom door, looking on blankly at a sleeping couple, when, without warning, the door opened and a man walked in. I reacted instantly, sitting up, covering my breasts with one arm, clamping my legs together and placing the other hand so that it covered what remained visible of my sex.

"Christ Vivian!" I said. "What's going on?"

The man, who was about forty, slightly tubby with thinning, sandy hair, went instantly red about the face.

"I'm so sorry. I didn't think."

Vivian smiled.

"Jane this is Colin. He's been away."

I was confused.

"He lives here," said Vivian. "He's my... actually what are you Colin?"

"General manager?" Colin replied. "Chief of staff? A.D.C.?"

"Too military. I know this place is a shambles but it's not that bad. General dogsbody? My Boswell? Yes, let's

78

stick with Boswell."

They might be in the mood for banter, but I was very unhappy that we had been barged in on and very conscious of being naked in the company of two clothed men, one of whom I did not know at all.

"I'm not a slab of meat, you know, Vivian?" I said angrily. "Just because I've agreed to sit for you doesn't make my body public property."

"I'll leave," said Colin and made to go, but then stopped. "But before I do, I meant to say that Alan Beckwith asked if he could meet for an interview, ahead of the Berlin retrospective."

Vivian shook his head.

"Tell him no. And also tell him that he knows better than to ask, the wheedling, little shit."

"Right," Colin said; then, turning back to me with a contrite smile, "Sorry again."

This time he did leave, closing the door behind him, with what seemed to me deliberately ostentatious care.

"I'm not happy, Vivian," I said.

"I can tell. Look, I am sorry, really. He shouldn't have barged in like that. Normally, he would have been here when we started and introduced himself, so that you would have known that he would be about."

I sighed.

"Shall we take another break?" he asked.

"No, No. It's alright, it was the shock, mostly."

"Would it help if I told you that he's gay?"

"A bit. Is he?"

"Yes. Very."

I considered for a moment. I had moved my arms from their defensive positions, but I was still sitting up. I didn't feel quite up to getting back into position, a process that I had become more proficient at over time, but that still required a series of micro-adjustments before Vivian would be satisfied.

"Actually, can we take a break?" I said. "I could do with a coffee."

He smiled.

"I'll get Colin to make us one."

As we drank our coffee, freshly brewed, with a distinct woodiness and a hint of dark fruit, Vivian said, "What you said earlier, about your body not being public property. You know, that's quite interesting because when this is finished..."

He had wandered over to the painting and was studying it.

"...in a way, it will be."

That night, I found it difficult to get to sleep, ruminating on Vivian's words: that my body would become public property when the painting was finished. It might seem strange, but until then I had been so wrapped up in the process of sitting for Vivian, of being painted by him, that I had hardly thought about what it would be like to have a painting of me by him out there in the world, hanging on a wall somewhere for hundreds of pairs of eyes to see, maybe thousands if it were exhibited. I had, in a vague, unformed way, imagined a finished painting there in the studio but I had not given much thought to where it might end up: in a museum? On some millionaire's living room wall, above the fireplace next to his fifty-six-inch screen that his mates gather round from time to time when the football's on.

I found myself wondering what it would be like for me to stand in front of it in a public space, watch others' reaction to it. If I were standing there, would someone who didn't already know guess that I was the woman sprawled naked in front of him in the picture?

9

After he had returned from being away, Colin would usually be the one to answer the door and, in those first weeks, take me directly into the studio. Vivian might be there already or not. If he wasn't there, I would sit on the couch and wait; he wouldn't keep me waiting long. When he arrived, or if he was already there, we would greet each other casually, like work colleagues, and I would strip while he arranged his paints and prepared his pallet. He used to tuck a rag into his belt, a fresh one each day, for wiping brushes, his pallet knife, his hands. I would get myself into position aided by a prompt or two from him and away we would go.

One afternoon, though, when I rang the doorbell, the door was opened, not by Colin, but by a young woman, younger than me I would have said. She was blonde, naturally so I think, with lovely blue eyes and a general air of vivacity.

"Hi," she said, with just a hint of a questioning tone to her voice.

"Hi, I'm Jane," I said. "I'm sitting for Vivian."

"Oh, right, come in. Night or Day?"

"Night."

She smiled.

"Figures," she said with a mischievous twinkle in her eye as she led me into the studio. "I'm Clare."

She said this in a way that left me with the impression that she expected me to know who she was. I didn't and wondered what her relation to Vivian might be and how she had licence to answer his door. That and her relaxed air of being thoroughly at home made me wonder whether she might be one of Vivian's children.

"Ah! You've met Clare," said Vivian, entering the room shortly after us. "Hopefully, the pair of you will get on."

Although I did all I could to hide it, I bristled a little at that. It was another example of him referring to me, to Clare and me on this occasion as if I, we, were schoolgirls.

"Oh, I'm sure we will," said Clare, smiling broadly, "I expect we have a lot in common."

"She means she thinks I'm sleeping with you," he said. "Shall we tell her the truth or keep her happily ignorant?"

I didn't give an answer. None was expected.

"I'll let you get on," said Clare, as breezily and as cheerfully as she had first greeted me.

She went to Vivian and they exchanged a peck on the lips, him putting his hands lightly on her hips as they did so. Evidently, she was not his daughter.

"Is it the Ivy, again tonight?" she asked.

"No. We're going to Femi's."

"Oh, lovely. Right. I'm going to pop out to do some shopping and I'll see you later."

He turned to me.

"Clare is my Pompadour."

I don't think she liked being called that. I could tell that it was not the first time Vivian had described her as such, as, in effect, his official mistress. She hid it well, sustaining her broad smile, but I detected a slight hardening at the inner corners of her eyes that betrayed her irritation.

She said goodbye and left.

It was becoming obvious to me that Vivian had a habit of labelling people: I was Nyssia, making you Candaules, Michael; Colin was Boswell and now Clare was Madame Pompadour, making him Louis XV. I think in labelling us all, and others, like this, not only did he exert a kind of control over us all, more or less intentionally, expressly assigning roles to us and by doing so making it more likely that we would conform to those roles, but he also made himself the one who was free of any particular tag, for he was at one and the same time Gyges, Dr Johnson and the king of France – a multiplicity of identities and therefore not constrained by any single one.

There is something of this, I now think, in the way he deals with fatherhood. He is not a father in the way most men are, the way you are with Alice; he is many fathers, fulfilling that function, to the extent that he does at all, in different ways to the different clusters of children he has by so many women. I have seen him acting with one child like the cuddliest, most generous grandfather, unable to resist spoiling him with toys and sweets, and yet with others, his grown-up daughters, he is like the most austere patrician, a father from a bygone age.

We think we look the world in the eye when we talk, but we don't, do we? I learnt that in the studio with Vivian. Only the most loaded words would be exchanged with our eyes locked on each other's. I would often study him while he spoke, but he would as often as not be speaking to the canvas or to his pallet, or he might be studying some part of my body, perhaps glance in the general direction of my face without making real eye-contact. And most of my talking would be addressed to the ceiling or the walls. When we talked about art or literature, we sometimes had entire conversations without our eyes meeting. As you can imagine, sometimes, sitting for him was like attending an art lecture.

"It is a revelation," he told me once, "when one is first told that when viewed from directly in front, the eyes are at the middle of the head, measured from top to bottom. Of course, the usual first reaction is denial, because they just don't seem to be there. But then one checks and finds that it is true. And one also discovers that in terms of producing an image that is reasonably lifelike, it is a huge help, knowing this, and instead of drawing faces that are weirdly alien, one can suddenly produce images that look almost human."

"But the real lesson to be taken from this, at least for anyone with a spark of intelligence, is the revelation of how erroneous our notions of what people look like are. Because the features around the eyes and down to the mouth are those we concentrate on most, almost to the exclusion of all others, we sense that they also dominate the space of the head in a way that is not in fact true. Thus, the naïve artist places the eyes much further up the head than they are. In effect, one draws a face, rather than a head."

"Amusingly, people make much the same mistake with women's breasts."

"But there is a danger, lurking within this discovery; the application of that rule has such a pleasingly transformative effect on the quality of one's work, that one starts to apply it rigidly, and quite probably will go in search of other such rules to assist the felicity of one's drawings. That results in work that is every bit as false as those earlier, alien faces. One is not then drawing what one sees but drawing according to a rigid cannon of rules of proportion. Rigid being the *mot juste*."

To my ears his French pronunciation was faultless.

"It's funny what you said about people drawing breasts in the wrong place." I said. "It's exactly like that with breastfeeding. You would think you'd know where your own nipples are but you don't. The whole thing is supposed to be natural and easy but it isn't; it's awkward and feels completely unnatural at first. Neither you nor the baby knows what they're doing and it hurts. It does get easier, of course, when you've both learnt what to do, but at the start... I suppose I was hoping it would be all mystical and quasi-sexual but it isn't. Not for me anyway. Perhaps it is for others."

"So what does it feel like?"

"It's hard to say. Efficient."

Vivian raised his eyebrows.

"That's not quite right; that makes it sound too clinical; but I guess I mean that I like the feeling of being useful. It's like a low-grade contentment, a bit like the feeling you might have when you realise you've been humming to yourself when doing the dishes or something."

"It's funny for such a passive thing, but I thought I would get a lot of reading done while I was feeding, catch up on some contemporary novelists – it's ironic for an English teacher, but when I was teaching full time, I just didn't have the time – but reading doesn't feel right somehow. I don't even really like to watch the television; I find my mind drifting from the screen too readily. The one thing that does feel completely natural while feeding, is chatting. Gossiping with my girlfriends, that sort of thing."

"Chewing the cud while sitting around the campfire," said Vivian.

"I suppose."

"Do you miss it."

"I did at first, very much. That's fading now though."

I wondered for a moment whether he would say something that hinted at an apology for his bringing that about prematurely, but he didn't.

10

We had finished for the day and were standing by the door to the studio, as we did after each session, he with his appointment book in his left hand, a pencil in his right, me standing expectantly. He turned a page, another, affording me a glimpse of the indecipherable hieroglyphs written there.

"I have a lot on this week," he said, studying the pages with an air of resignation, as though the appointments in it had come about without his involvement, like a stretch of bad weather in summer. "Friday afternoon? At three again?"

I studied him for a couple of seconds. In the resulting moment of stillness, he looked up at me expectantly.

"You can be very unperceptive at times, Vivian."

He shook his head slightly as though confused.

"I always say yes to whatever next appointment you propose. Hadn't you noticed?"

He raised his eyebrows.

"You're right. I hadn't noticed."

He looked down at his book, turned back to, I think, the page where he had started, then closed it with decision.

"In that case, let's go and get something to eat."

"Now?"

"Yes, now. Since you always say yes, let's go. I'll get my jacket. Bentley's, I think. I'm in the mood for fish."

Less than three minutes later, we stood together on the pavement outside his house; it was the first time we had done so. A passing woman noticed him with a look of recognition that he studiously ignored.

"Tube?" I said, teasing.

He raised his eyebrows sardonically.

"Cab."

It was the wrong hour to hail a cab instantly and although I was aware of an irrational expectation that taxis would simply appear for Vivian, it was not so; we spent at least five minutes watching a seemingly endless procession of unlit "For Hire" lamps pass before I finally managed to hail one at the cross-roads where Vivian's street met the next.

As we watched and waited, even after all the time that we had spent together, I was aware of a feeling of freshness, of renewed excitement. I am going to dinner with Vivian Young, I thought. When another passer-by, a Catholic priest by the look of him, evidently recognised him, I thought, Yes, you're right. That is Vivian Young and he and I are indeed looking to hail a cab together.

The priest glanced at me too. I wonder what he was thinking.

If we had done this weeks earlier, I know I would have thought of you, of how envious you would have been of me, but I'm afraid that I had ceased to have those kinds of thoughts by then.

When we had finally clambered into the taxi and were bracing ourselves as it carried out a tight U-turn with the uniquely challenging turning-circle of a black cab, Vivian sighed and said, "It's only a thirty-minute walk. I used to walk nearly everywhere. But it's next to impossible these days."

Out of habit, I fastened my seatbelt, struggling a little to fit the metal end into the correct red plastic-fringed slot. Vivian didn't bother. It was such a small thing, but it really struck me. Isn't that odd? I remember wondering whether it was a matter of different generations, of his having grown up before seatbelt wearing was compulsory, or whether he was being deliberately rebellious. It made me feel terribly conformist, even though at an intellectual level I knew that I was simply being sensible, and he was the one being stupid, if he had even thought of it at all. He must have, I suppose, as I took so long scrabbling around to find the right bit to fasten into.

During the journey, a thought struck me.

"You like game, and fish, don't you?" I said. "Wild things."

"They're more real," said Vivian. "More real than sheep or cattle. Wouldn't you say?"

I turned to face him in the cab.

"I'm not even remotely wild," I said, "just so we're clear."

He studied me for a moment.

"Perhaps not" he said. "We'll see."

At the restaurant, he was welcomed with what I can only describe as studied restraint, a deliberate effort not to make a fuss, even though there was not the slightest doubt that each and every member of staff knew him; I noticed that the manager instantly went to study his book of reservations with an air of barely concealed concern as Vivian made his way, without, I think, actually being led there, to a table near the back, tucked away, the perfect place to see and almost not be seen.

I don't think I've ever felt so nearly famous as I did then, following Vivian across the room, picking our way between the tables, neat and elegant with their white tablecloths and sparkling cutlery. It was as though a barely perceptible but distinct tremor, low on the Richter Scale but observable by appropriately sensitive apparatus, emanated from him as each diner at each table first noticed him and then inspected me. Forearms were touched, elbows jogged as those who saw us first alerted their fellows and heads discretely but unmissably turned to see the great man and his young companion.

I could have been anyone, a journalist, an art critic, someone from Christie's or Sotheby's. For all they knew, I could have been one of his daughters, but I could not stop myself from feeling that each and every one of them would assume that I was one of his mistresses. I was a little embarrassed, although I think I just about avoided blushing, and... well, I'm afraid the truth is, a little bit proud that that was what they thought of me, even though it wasn't true.

Vivian's chosen table was a table set for six and he placed himself in the farthest corner, indicating that I should sit next to him, which meant that we would both be looking into the restaurant. I remember thinking that he could have sat on the other side and offered his back to the room and noting that he chose not to. I'm sure he enjoyed surveying the room, our fellow diners – who doesn't? – but I think he also preferred to face the world, not have a score of pairs of eyes boring into his back throughout the meal. Glances were thrown at us from time to time, but I felt sure that we would have been scrutinised more intently had he been facing the wall.

A young and very fresh-faced waiter approached with a couple of menus. Vivian waved him away with a curt but not unkind instruction to bring a bottle of Meursault and a dozen oysters followed by two Dover Soles.

"I've just realised something about you," I said.

"Oh yes?"

He glanced sideways at me with a questioning, slightly amused expression.

"And what is that?"

"You're very much a creature of habit, aren't you?"

The young waiter had returned with the bottle of wine, distracting us for a moment with scents of wood-smoke and peach and oak, a hint of apricot.

"Here, for instance," I said after taking my first sip, "how many times would you say you've dined here?"

He laughed.

"Too many to count," he said. "I've been coming here

for decades."

"Exactly. And always this table, I'd bet."

"Were you expecting uninhibited bohemian debauchery? Endless innovation? I've done all that. It's very tiring. I stopped trying to live up to other people's expectations of me long ago."

The manager, whom Vivian addressed as Stefan, brought the oysters and he and Vivian shared small talk for a minute or so. What do you think of me? I wondered as Stefan smiled at me from time to time, including me in the conversation with his looks whilst not actually speaking to me. You must be used to Vivian bringing guests of all types here, I thought. What assumptions might you have made about me?

When Stefan had left us, Vivian started on the oysters.

"Oysters and a glass of wine or three, little matches it for uncomplicated pleasure," he said. "I'm sorry to disappoint you, Jane but I'm much more of an epicurean than a hedonist, despite what you obviously think of me."

"You didn't introduce me to the manager."

He smiled.

"I took sympathy on him," he said. "He has enough on his mind already."

The oysters were nearly as delicious as the wine. They reminded me of Vivian's jumper, the cable-knit sweater I habitually wore when we took a break in his studio; like it, they were redolent of sea air and salt.

"I'll introduce you next time he comes over, if you'd like."

"How would you introduce me?"

"What an interesting question. You have a habit of surprising me."

"Well?"

"As a teacher, of course: a teacher on maternity leave."

It was my turn to be surprised and when Stefan returned to clear away the plate of empty oyster shells, Vivian did indeed introduce us. Stefan smiled suavely but I could see in his eyes, though he did his best to hide it, that he was trying to judge whether I was someone whom he should remember for the future. How could he possibly know when I did not know myself?

I'm afraid it was only then that I remembered that you had something on at the Faculty that evening and wouldn't be back at the usual time to relieve Helen. I called her. She took an age to answer, my motherly instincts filling that time with grim disaster, famine, fire, and flood, but when she answered all was well and she accepted the necessity of extending her hours with good humour, almost as though she had been expecting it.

Later, when I had been to the toilet and was making my way back to our table, I saw that Vivian studied me, as I approached, every bit as intensely as he observed me in the studio.

"I'm guessing you stared at me just as intently when I went," I said, as I sat down.

"Naturally. The opportunity to observe a sitter in motion is not to be missed and those moments when they don't realise that they are being studied are often the most fruitful: not solely those, mind you; it's the contrast between the relaxed person, unaware that they are being observed, and the consciously observed, projected persona that is so telling. The gap in between those two is often where I try to place my paintings."

He took a sip of his wine, eyeing, over the rim of his glass, a portly middle-aged man in a three-piece suit who was himself making his way back from the toilets.

"Mind you," said Vivian, "no one is ever completely relaxed when they walk through a restaurant, are they?"

"Not even you, Vivian?"

He smiled but did not answer.

When we had finished and Vivian summoned the bill, he paid in cash, from a thick bundle of notes held together by an elastic band that he pulled from his jacket pocket.

He winked and said, "We were never here."

11

What did you think of Helen, by the way? I hardly saw the two of you together. Either she would have gone by the time you returned from the Faculty or, as I began to spend evenings with Vivian, she would be gone by the time I returned.

You were in such a hurry, the day when she first came to babysit. Do you remember? You had mislaid some notes and had started to panic a little at the thought that you would arrive at your seminar late and noteless and, although I found them for you in Alice's room, you were still in a panicky rush as you hurried out, calling goodbye and shouting, "Vivian's babysitter's here."

I remember thinking that made it sound as if she were going to babysit Vivian rather than Alice, but I knew what you meant. Inauspiciously, Alice had just done a posset so that I greeted Helen, who was there standing at our open front-door, joggling a grizzling child while a gobbet of milky vomit dripped down my back.

I think you had sensed that I had been growing increasingly uneasy at the notion of leaving Alice in the care of an unknown babysitter sent over by Vivian, one chosen by him applying God knows what criteria, but you seemed markedly sanguine. I must admit that I, like you, did feel that we had been imposing on my mother more than was fair. Despite that anxiety, when Helen offered her hand and introduced herself with her warm unaffected smile, I started to relax, even more so when we chatted a little and she told me that she would be going to Bristol in the autumn to study modern languages.

God, I can be so middle-class sometimes – all the time I suppose – relaxing and thinking that everything would be fine just because she was well-spoken and was going to a nice, Russell Group university. But, although I had attained a moderate level of equanimity by the time I left, my motherly anxieties revived themselves as I made my way to Vivian's. I could barely quell the urge to turn around and go back, just to check on them.

Vivian's intense concentration on me in the studio made him extraordinarily perceptive of my moods. That highly developed perception of emotions must be a large part of his charisma, I suppose, even though, logically, he must be the same way with all his models, at least I assume so.

Anyway, not long into the session that day, he remarked that I didn't seem to be in the room.

"It's the new babysitter you sent round," I said. "I can't help but be a little anxious about her, since I don't know her properly yet. She seemed nice and sensible, but…"

He smiled and said, "Don't worry. Helen's a good girl, I promise."

I was not reassured. I had heard men, arrogant sportsmen or the like, describe young women as "good girls" in a very different context; the juxtaposition was disconcerting.

Of course, everything was fine, as you know; but I remember regretting that you had arrived home before me so that Helen had left and I hadn't had the comfort of seeing Alice and her together – how settled or otherwise they had been without us.

At the end of that session, I apologised to Vivian, for not quite being able to control my anxiety.

"There's no need to apologise," he said. "I'm painting you, not a platonic ideal of woman. That mother's anxiety is an additional layer of your personality that I might be able to incorporate."

I asked him whether he consciously adapted whatever image he was painting to take account of such characteristics, ones freshly observed. He said not, that he would observe them, note them, note perhaps the expressions that attested to them and then hope that they would work their way onto the canvas in due course, by a process that he could not and perhaps would not want to understand.

"All painting, even the most immediate, impressionistic *en plein air* sketch is a work from memory," he said. "There is always a gap between the observation and the application of paint to canvas, so perhaps the memories of a sitter's movement, of an expression noted at another time and in another context, intrude themselves during the process."

It wasn't until at least a week later that I found out who she was; Helen I mean. I realise now that I don't know when it was that you found out. How odd.

The journey home had been a nightmare; I was stuck on the Tube for half an hour outside our station. It was very hot and I was anxious and flustered by the time I reached the flat and, in that state, I was not thinking straight so, as Helen was about to leave, I delved into my purse and took out all the notes that happened to be in there. I can't remember how much it would have been.

"Is this going to be enough?"

She seemed puzzled.

"No, no," she said, pushing the money away, "Dad's subbing me for this already."

"Dad?"

"Yes, my Dad."

We regarded each other with mutual incomprehension for a moment.

"I don't understand," I said.

"My father is paying me for this: Vivian Young."

I was dumbstruck. This pretty eighteen-year-old that Vivian had sent round to baby-sit was his daughter.

In those early days, the first weeks, my thoughts would often drift to you, during the silences.

"What did you say to Michael, when you first called to ask that I sit for you?" I asked Vivian once.

He looked up at the corner of the room.

"I honestly can't remember. Nothing particular, I would

have thought."

"You mean it didn't mean anything whether I agreed or not."

"I wouldn't say that. I definitely wanted to paint you. But some people say no; some people say yes. I'm used to both."

His pallet took his complete attention for the next five minutes.

"I don't make a pitch," he said eventually, "give reasons for wanting to paint someone. I'm not even sure I could if I wanted to. I just have a sense that the process of painting whoever might be rewarding, might result in something worth creating."

"So, it wasn't my freckles that made you want to paint me?"

"I'm not sure that I can remember what the main characteristic was."

I think that answer disappointed me and I sulked a little through some minutes of silence, but then he said, "I don't mean that it was so unimportant to me that I haven't bothered to remember; I mean that the layers of what interests me about you have built up since then, so it would be difficult, and pointless, to try and remember which strata were present then and which have been laid down since."

"Outside the National Gallery, you said that painting me would be a challenge, because of my freckles."

He stepped back from the canvas and regarded it as though my comment had reminded him how unsatisfactory his work so far had been.

"I wasn't wrong about that, I can assure you," he said.

"He has a thick volume of reproductions of your work, you know."

"Who does?"

"Michael."

"Does he? It's not a good way of seeing my pieces, he must know that."

"I'm sure he realises that, but what else can he do? There are only so many on public display and you can't spend your whole life touring galleries."

"I don't think of my paintings in that way."

"What way?"

"As something other people will look at."

"Really?"

"I know they do of course. But it's not how I think of them when I'm painting."

"You mean you paint them only for yourself?"

"I suppose so, yes. I'd never quite expressed it that way before but I think that is true yes. I try not to be introspective, particularly about my method. I'm a bit superstitious about it; as though, if I open up the workings and peer inside, the whole machine will grind to a halt."

"You don't care what anyone thinks of them?"

"It would be easy to say yes but that wouldn't really be true. I'm vain enough to want the people I admire to like them. I think I mean that the only person I am setting out to please as I take up my brush, is me."

He sighed.

"It's sad in a way as I'm never really pleased with any of my works. I have a target audience of one and routinely disappoint him."

I wanted to ask him what he really thought of the painting but was frightened to, somehow, as though asking that question would cause him to be dissatisfied with it, even more so than he sometimes appeared to be.

"Will this end up in the next volume of your works?" I asked. "You can't begin to understand how odd that feels: that anyone might have a reproduction of a painting of me on their shelf."

"There are self-portraits of me out there too."

"That's not the same."

"No, you're right. I find self-portraits extremely challenging. More challenging than an armful of freckles."

I think he meant that as a joke.

"The temptation to interfere, interpose whatever it is you want to say about yourself is so great. Obviously, there's the temptation to make oneself look more visually pleasing but I'm way beyond that now. But I might still be tempted to make myself look, I don't know, wiser, more intelligent or maybe more inscrutable than I am. There is even a definite temptation to make oneself uglier than one really is, both physically and morally: a different type of egoism; look at me; look how physically hideous and spiritually empty I am."

"I don't think you're spiritually empty."

"And neither do I. I wasn't fishing for compliments."

"Or physically hideous."

He had been mixing paints on his pallet. Hearing this, he looked up at me and met my gaze.

I blushed and looked away.

"Would you ever consider painting Michael?" I asked. "It would give him such a thrill."

"A compelling reason not to paint him."

Vivian advanced towards me to study some part of me, my knee perhaps. "I look for something new, interesting in every painting. Keenness bores me."

"Really, how strange. It was exactly that quality that I loved so much in him. I love my daughter; of course I do; but, sometimes I miss the way we were, Michael and I, before we had her. I used to love to watch him work but somehow that doesn't happen anymore."

That was true. I did use to love to watch you work, in the first year of our marriage before I got pregnant. You would be so obviously, completely absorbed in your work, such a contrast to my own methods. My mind drifts continually and I don't even notice myself doing it, but you... Sometimes you would look across at me, when we were both working at the kitchen table, and look right through me. One might possibly be offended at being seemingly treated as a none-person like that but I never was. I knew that you weren't really there in the room with me at all but gazing on unfamiliar constellations in the twilight above the veldt or breathing in the scents of a Wessex orchard.

I remember my father doing much the same, reviewing his notes late into the night, letting the room around him go dark with just his papers glowing white under his desk lamp. I could sit there, unseen in the armchair, unnoticed until long past my bedtime until my mother, having realised that I hadn't said goodnight, would come and fetch me.

My knee kept Vivian's attention for a couple of minutes.

"You used the past tense," he said, returning to the canvas.

"Sorry?"

"You used the past tense, regarding your husband's enthusiasm; you said loved not love."

"Did I? I just meant that was one of the things I loved about him when I was falling in love."

"So, you still love him?"

"Yes, of course."

What else could I say?

"Anyway, the enthusiasm you are talking about is, I think, your husband's enthusiasm for his subject. That, I grant you, can be appealing. But it's quite distinct from the enthusiasm of the fan, what the French call an *amateur*. The last sort of person I would want to paint would be someone looking at me with puppy eyes."

"And yet you paint your lovers."

He smiled a wry smile. We both knew, I think, that Vivian's lovers were unlikely to look at him "with puppy eyes" as he had put it.

"You don't seem to think very much of my husband."

"I've hardly met him."

"It's very disconcerting."

Vivian, as was not uncommon, seemed only half

engaged, focused on some detail of light or shade or tone of paint, and our conversation petered out. In the silence, I thought of you when you had returned with a copy of your latest published article, of how you glowed with a restrained but all suffusing pride and then how you mentioned over supper a couple of days later, some compliments offered by your colleagues.

"I admire him very much," I said, "and so do his colleagues at UCL, so there is an odd sort of dissonance when you so evidently think him… I don't know; what do you think of him?"

"You admire him?"

"Yes."

"Do you think that's a sound basis for a marriage?"

"I assume your wife admired you."

"My ex-wife admired me very much, yes."

Silence again. It must have been nearly an hour later when Vivian next spoke.

"It's a huge burden being fêted, hailed as the next great British artist," he said. "There were times in my twenties when I could hardly bring myself to pick up a brush. The first few months of my marriage were the worst. I think, now, that more than anything was what doomed my marriage, not the infidelities or the resentment, but the expectation. My wife would look at me with her huge trusting eyes, radiating a fierce belief in my genius. That's even worse than being fêted or lionised, being trusted."

"You didn't have any children with her, did you?"

"No."

It was later still, when he said, "I'm not sure I've told anyone that before, about the burden of my wife's trust in me. You seem to make me want to confide in you Jane."

12

It ate away at me, his low opinion of you. That makes me sound terribly shallow, doesn't it? Maybe I am. I realise now that his charisma was such that I fell all too easily into seeing things the way he saw them, seeing the world his way.

Right from his very first comment during the talk about Hardy when I first met him, I began to have doubts. I would find myself considering the things you said with the ears of a critic, rather than an unthinking admirer, and found myself often disappointed by your pronouncements, leaving me with a sense of you as a man who is not as clever as he thinks he is or, in fairness to you, as he has been told he is.

I did fight back for you though. I did, honestly.

During one session, when he had said something disparaging about your ideas – I forget what – I remember thinking that he might have been right and then immediately feeling guilty at that thought, guilty at being disloyal. It must have been in the early weeks, then, I suppose.

"It's easy to be dismissive, Vivian," I said.

That stopped him, I think. He paused for a moment – not for any reason to do with painting, I would say – before resuming his work.

"And it's an easy way to make yourself feel superior, isn't it, being dismissive? You just say – I don't know – Dickens' plotting is inherently unbelievable and you instantly make yourself seem a little bit smarter than those who are simple enough folk to enjoy his novels."

"I like Dickens," he said.

I smiled.

"You can do it with anything more or less," I said. "A television programme, a restaurant. If someone says how much they enjoyed a meal there, you just say 'Really? I found the food there terribly insipid and uninspiring,' and they are left feeling foolish and lacking in taste."

"I remember when I was at school telling a friend, well a half-friend, how spooky a ghost story on the television had been. She laughed and said she couldn't understand how anyone would think it was even the littlest bit scary, that she had been completely bored throughout. At first, I thought she must be right, that I was too susceptible and should have been less scared, which I'm sure is exactly what she intended, but later I thought, Hold on. I let myself go, became immersed in the story, and had a delightful hour of being thrilled, whilst she, if she was telling the truth, just sat there being bored. Why does that make her superior to me? It doesn't make any sense."

Vivian could always fall back on silence, concentrate on his pallet, his paints, and did.

I think it was later in that same session that I asked him how he reacted to criticism of his own works. He is routinely fêted as a genius these days, of course, but he must have received more than his share of criticism in the first half of his career.

"Oh, I have not the slightest difficulty coping with unjustified criticism," he said, and then smiled. "It's justified criticism that really stings."

But my heart wasn't in it, my defence of you, Michael. I could see what he was up to; of course I could; I'm not stupid. He was deliberately undermining you in my eyes. But somehow that realisation didn't diminish the efficacy of the trick.

It was the same with the story of Nyssia. I knew that he had deliberately planted the notion of me as Nyssia and you as Candaules in my mind but stories have such power when you have been introduced to them on the basis that you are living them, don't they?

That story worked away inside me, just as I was sure Vivian had intended. I was going to be his lover; I was Nyssia. I may think I have some control over events, of whom I do and don't sleep with, but that is an illusion. I was Nyssia and was going to take Gyges to my bed and make him king, not out of love for him or even lust, but out of hatred of my husband, a husband for whom my body was not a treasure for himself alone but a symbol, a signifier of his great worth: look how beautiful my wife is; gorge on her nakedness and see displayed to you in her body, proven by her curves, how great a king I am.

"This is my wife, Jane. She posed for Vivian Young, don't you know? Yes, a nude. You can see it online if you Google him."

I noticed more and more that people I met who knew I was sitting for Vivian simply assumed that I was sleeping with him: Helen, for example.

The afternoon when I found out that she was his daughter, I had just said, "Oh, I see," told her when we would next be needing her and said goodbye. But the next day, when she arrived, I apologised for my stupidity.

"He didn't mention that you were his daughter," I said. "He just told us he would send someone round."

There was an awkward pause as we both considered what his reticence might connote. I struggled to think of something to say to move things on and grasped at the first question that came to mind.

"How many children does he have, then?"

I realised even as I asked that this implied that I assumed that there were many and revealed also that I anticipated that they would not be her full brothers and sisters, but only half-siblings, hence my choice of the neutral term: children.

"I don't know."

I think from her expression that my shock at her ignorance must have shown on my face.

"Did you expect me to keep count?" she said. "Why bother? There's at least twenty. And that's just the ones we know about. Anyway, there'll be another one along soon."

She eyed me as though she half expected me to announce that I was indeed pregnant by him and it was then that I realised that she assumed he and I were having an affair. What a strange position for a young woman to be in – her, I mean, not me – thinking that the woman you are babysitting for is sleeping with your father.

"My eldest sister, half-sister, is thirty-eight," she said. "Her name is June."

She smiled. It was a warm smile, warmer than I felt I had the right to expect from her at that moment, as though she were already halfway to forgiving me for prying so thoughtlessly.

I blinked.

"How old are you?" she asked.

"Twenty-six."

She whistled.

"Twenty-six and married with a child. That's not so common these days. I can't believe I'll be married by that age."

She paused and considered for a moment, folding one of Alice's tops neatly as she did so.

"I can't see myself marrying at all really. Although I would like to have kids someday. Alice is adorable, by the way."

She looked up at me.

"But you knew that."

It was my turn to smile.

"Thank you. Yes, she is adorable. At least most of the time."

We shared a smile and I felt the awkwardness between us dissipate.

13

Parties, exhibitions, drinks receptions, book launches, private showings, I suppose these were the kinds of thing you were hoping to be involved in. I did go to some on Vivian's arm, a fair few over the months. What to tell you about them? That they pall after a while, that some, most, were not memorable at all; I couldn't list them even if I wanted to; they have merged so much in my memory, involving, as I soon learned, the same faces, the same drinks and canapes, the same conversations. Only the venues seemed to change.

Of those that were memorable, one was at the RAC Clubhouse on Pall Mall, Corinthian splendour in Portland Stone and marble. It may even have been the very first I went to with Vivian. I remember feeling a mixture of excitement and anxiety as we arrived, which suggests that it was at least one of the earlier ones. I'm afraid I can't remember what it was marking.

"Do you enjoy these things?" I asked Vivian as we climbed the broad, sweeping stairs towards the salon where drinks and nibbles were being served.

"Like all parties, that depends who's here. Speaking of which…"

A man, short and moderately overweight, a glass of champagne in hand, approached as soon as we crossed the threshold of the room. I would have said he was in his forties.

"Vivian! I didn't think you'd come. I'm so glad that you did."

"This is Guy Johnstone," Vivian said. "He writes about art."

Vivian's tone suggested that writing about art was a very lowly profession, very lowly indeed, and Guy had the air of a man preparing to be insulted while at the same time knowing that he would not be able to retaliate.

"About two thirds of what he writes is absolute nonsense," said Vivian.

I had a sense that Guy had been on the receiving end of this jibe before. He smiled a thin smile. I tried to feel sorry for him but something about the way he accepted that dig without any hint of protest, not even in his expression, quelled that emotion.

"In fairness, that puts him at the very top of his profession," said Vivian.

I don't think that coda was enough to make up for the initial put-down. Guy looked the kind who would store such jibes away, jealously guard them.

Vivian tilted his glass of champagne towards me.

"This is Jane."

That was all I got from Vivian by way of introduction on this occasion. Guy seemed to accept that my first name was all he needed to know of me and they launched into a lively conversation about a recent exhibition at Tate Britain. Notwithstanding his initial teasing and occasional further dismissal of Guy's comments, it seemed that Vivian enjoyed discussing art with Guy and valued some of his insights. From time to time as they spoke, Guy would throw a glance at me as though to say, "You see. I am someone of consequence after all. You thought I wasn't, didn't you? But I am."

On occasion I noticed other guests looking our way. They were not the furtive glimpses at a famous person that I had observed when dining out with Vivian; presumably most of the guests had seen him before, perhaps many knew him. I suppose that I might even have been the new element that they were looking to assess.

We had been chatting – well, Vivian and Guy had been chatting – for about ten minutes when I felt instinctively that someone was studying me. Looking about the room, I saw a new arrival standing at the doorway who was indeed watching us. The newcomer was tall and thin, with snow-white hair. It was clear that he could tell that I had spotted him looking at us. Unconcerned by that, he looked about the room with an air of benevolence, as if he were our host, then sauntered from group to group saying a few words to each. Before long, he made his way over to us.

Guy greeted him enthusiastically.

"Oliver! How are you?"

"I grow more and more decrepit each day, I'm afraid Guy," Oliver said, then turned to me with a suave smile saying, "which is a very great pity."

He offered his hand.

"Oliver Brown. How do you do."

"Jane, Jane Smith."

"And what brings you here? Did Guy drag you along?"

"No, I..."

I hesitated, not knowing quite how I wanted to introduce myself.

"I'm painting her," said Vivian, taking that burden from me.

"Ahh! Very time consuming, posing for Vivian."

I nodded.

"Very."

He looked thoughtful for a moment as though he had been about to say something but had thought better of it, then he turned to Vivian and asked whether he had seen a recent film. I forget its title but you know the one; it had caused something of a stir with its treatment of necrophilia: not my type of film at all. Just as Vivian had earlier with Guy, he launched into a lively conversation with Oliver, this time on the topic of art-house cinema.

I do not think that was the first time I had witnessed how Vivian could shift his focus so completely from one person to another but I think it was the first time that I consciously noted it. Although Guy notionally remained part of the conversation, neither Vivian nor Oliver made any effort to address him or solicit his input. I noticed that he began to tap a finger against the stem of his champagne glass. I was similarly ignored but I was sufficiently interested in observing this newcomer and in listening to their conversation not to feel snubbed.

Oliver was the first person of a similar age to Vivian that I had seen spend any time with him. They had an air of relaxed intimacy as they chatted; there was no fencing, no jousting for superiority. But I also sensed a slight reticence, a little as though one of them had a relative who had passed away not so long ago and they had tacitly agreed not to mention it. After a while, with apologies to me, Oliver led Vivian away saying that there was someone who needed to speak to him, something about an upcoming auction, I think.

I was left alone with Guy.

"You don't know who Oliver is, do you?" he said.

"The name rings a bell but I'm afraid I can't place it, no."

He shook his head.

"Oliver Brown is a world-famous film director. He was the enfant terrible of British cinema in the seventies."

"Ahh!" I said, feeling a little foolish, because of course I had heard of him. "Yes, of course."

"Admittedly, he concentrates on production these days, but you really should have recognised him."

"Should I?"

Guy eyed me with a distinct air of malice.

"I don't understand how they do it," he said.

"Who? Do what?"

"Vivian and Oliver. Remain so civil. Actually, it's more than that. I think they really are friends. Not that they see much of each other these days, I think, not as much as they once did."

I was confused and looked blankly at him.

"You're not telling me you don't know," he said, accepting a refill of his glass from one of the catering staff.

"Evidently not."

"Vivian has been having an affair with Oliver's wife, Susan, for as long as anyone can remember."

He did not bother to pause until the waiter was out of earshot before imparting this startling piece of information. The waiter, however, showed no sign of reacting. Perhaps he did not hear, had developed a habit of blanking out the meaningless snippets of conversation he might overhear at such events. Perhaps he did not care. Perhaps he already knew.

"It may even have started before they married. Oliver and Susan, I mean. Yes, I'm sure that's right – shortly before if the rumours are to be believed. It's quite notorious. I thought everyone knew."

Was this revelation, delivered with such evident relish, his act of revenge for having the spotlight of Vivian's attention move away? Guy had the air of someone who knew that I had taken a dislike to him but did not care. I've met several people like that. Do you remember Derek Carter? He was one. They seem to embrace the distaste that they provoke in others, as though it gives them a licence that the rest of us do not have, caring, as we do, what others think of us.

"In some ways Oliver is responsible for Vivian's success," he said, "although, I like to think someone with such visceral talent would have succeeded whatever happened."

I was not warming to Guy but I did note the generosity of that comment.

"Oliver was the brightest, most brilliant director of his time. His championing of Vivian back in the seventies made a huge difference."

I watched Vivian and Oliver chatting to another couple of guests, each so seemingly at ease, and wondered whether the affair Guy had mentioned was ongoing; he had certainly implied that it was. Who here knew of it? Everyone? I don't understand this world, I thought. The world of Vivian and fame and celebrity, where a friend repays professional advancement by sleeping with the other's wife and yet they remain friends, where they chat amicably at parties when everyone around them knows their circumstance.

I couldn't think of anything to say to Guy and smiled a little awkwardly.

"Excuse me," he said. "There's someone I promised to say hello to."

It's not the done thing is it, leaving a newcomer on their own at a party without introducing them to someone else first? But frankly I was glad to be left alone. Thoughts engendered by the revelation of Vivian's long-term affair took up too much space in my head to leave room for the work of making small talk with new acquaintances. I looked over to where Vivian stood. The group he was chatting to had swelled to four or five, each of the others noticeably deferring to him, like students at a supervision. Oliver had moved away and was talking to another clutch of guests. Vivian showed no sign of any concern for my well-being, or even that he remembered that I was there and I decided to slip away without saying goodbye.

Thinking about it, you might remember that evening, because you were in a foul mood when I got home and explained where I had been. Anyone would have thought that I had stayed out beyond midnight, when it wasn't even gone nine. In your defence, Alice was playing up that night, which is always unbalancing. I expect you were also conscious of missing out on exactly the type of things you had hoped to be included in.

That night in bed, I couldn't stop myself from wondering what Susan Brown might be like, she who had had such a lengthy, persistent affair with Vivian.

14

In the morning I caught myself wondering about Susan Brown again. I thought about asking you about her. I knew you had read so much about Vivian that you might have heard of their affair if it was as notorious as Guy Johnstone had said. But I didn't.

In the studio that day, ruminating on Guy's revelation, I found myself asking Vivian whether he had ever painted anyone, he disliked.

"Oh, yes," he said, "Many times."

He shook his head.

"More often than I should have, in hindsight. I've never set out to paint someone I already didn't like, but I have grown to dislike some sitters. That can go one of two ways. Mostly it means I find the process so inherently disagreeable that I close the project down but, a handful of times, my dislike has come through on the canvas in a way that produced something interesting. It's tiring keeping on top of my emotions in those circumstances though, so I haven't done that for a while."

As he did so often, he returned to the same topic minutes later as though he had not even paused.

"There was one; he was a financier and he had agreed

to pay a very substantial sum to be painted by me, not because he knew anything about art; I'm not even sure he liked my paintings; he was just paying the price of my high reputation, making an investment. I didn't know him before he started sitting but some people whose opinions I respected spoke highly of him. He certainly had a name for being brilliant with money. I didn't fall out with him in any obvious way. I didn't even take a dislike to him. But before long, after only one or two sittings, I started to feel that there was something not quite right. I began to develop a strong sense that he wouldn't sit still, that somehow he was moving whenever I looked away, even though, objectively it was clear that he wasn't."

"I persevered for a few sessions, but that feeling that he was constantly moving wouldn't leave me. It became an absolute block on making any progress and I eventually had to call it a day. He was quite offended when I told him I would have to stop. Of course, I couldn't explain what the problem was to him and had to say simply that sometimes it doesn't work. It's not you it's me; that sort of thing. He obviously thought I was playing a game to try and up my price. It took me some weeks to convince him that that was not the case and that I really wasn't going to paint him."

"I never saw him again and had almost forgotten the whole thing when, some years later, he was exposed as a one-hundred percent, copper-bottomed fraud. His supposed magic touch was a carefully crafted illusion; his fund was basically nothing more than a glorified Ponzi scheme. His investors lost everything."

Was that story completely true, I wonder. At the time, I believed him unthinkingly. I'm sure there must be a basis in truth but how can one really know? A painting didn't work out. That has happened often to Vivian over the years, I know. Later the sitter is revealed as a fraud, and then it would be so easy for Vivian to tell himself that he had always felt that there was something wrong, wouldn't it? It would be a short step to an interesting little anecdote to bring out and show people at parties, not so much made up as built up, an enhanced truth, with the added benefit of tending to polish his reputation as an exceptionally perceptive artist.

None of these thoughts occurred to me as I listened that day. Quite the opposite, really, for I found myself worrying what his special artist's intuition might be sensing in me. It didn't help when he stopped in mid-brushstroke and said, "Something's not right."

"Is it the pose?" I asked, hoping that it would be something mundane like that, "I'm sure this is it,"

"No. The pose is correct. It's not that."

He was comparing me with the half-formed image on the canvas with an air of frustration. He looked a little like someone who was searching for the right word, one on the tip of the tongue that just won't come.

I'm embarrassed to admit that, as he was searching for whatever it was that was disturbing him, I began to fear that I had perhaps put on a little weight since we had started.

"It's your hair."

"My hair?"

"It's grown. It's perceptibly longer."

"Oh... Hair does that."

I didn't know what more to say. I thought that he might add something, but he didn't. He sighed audibly, picked up his pallet and brushes and started to work.

After twenty minutes or so of silence, I said. "I'll get it cut."

Our eyes met for a moment before his returned to the canvas.

"How much needs to come off?" I asked. Trying to make it seem like a trivial matter, although to me it was far from being so.

"An inch," he said, without looking up from the painting where he was working at something with his trowel.

I don't think you even noticed – did you? – that I had my hair trimmed regularly from that day on, to keep it at the same length. Perhaps I'm being unfair, asking you to notice a lack of change, rather than a transformation. After all, it was not as though I had my hair restyled, quite the opposite. And I didn't mention it at the time.

Do actresses do that when they're filming? I suppose they must, for continuity purposes. And actors of course. I'd never thought.

That moment of doubt about my weight stuck with me, I'm afraid, and it was from then that I began being more careful than I ever had before about what I ate.

Do you remember that evening when you had cooked lamb chops and ratatouille? Perhaps you don't. It may have seemed a trivial incident to you.

You had made some mashed potato, too. It was all very tasty and I did enjoy it; but I trimmed away the fat from the lamb and left about half the mash. Then, when you were clearing up, as you were scraping the leftovers into the bin, you remarked on how much I'd left.

I remember you literally peered into the bin after you had scraped the leftovers into it as though you were seriously considering hauling them back out and weighing them.

"Well," I said, "I'm no longer breast feeding. And anyway, I need to keep trim for…"

And stopped myself.

"You mean you need to keep yourself trim for Vivian."

I felt suddenly very embarrassed.

"I was going to say for the painting," I said.

That wasn't true.

I said I would check on Alice and went upstairs. I'd got into the habit of doing that quite often when things got awkward. Did you not notice?

There is another thing, I'm afraid, more than just starting to worry about my weight. The truth is that I used to lie there wondering why he hadn't made a move, this man who was so famous for his unrestrained libido, his almost countless conquests. Was I so truly off-putting? Was it my body? Was it as lumpen and ugly as I sometimes let myself imagine it? Was it something in my character, something forbidding, sexless? And of course, hard on the heels of such thoughts, came thoughts of how I would respond if he ever did make the attempt. And the truth is, I didn't know.

I've been trying to remember when I started lying to you, Michael. Before long, it became an easy habit, something of no consequence, just the way I was. How could that happen so quickly? A year ago, I wouldn't have believed that I could ever have been that way with you; I'm not talking about trivial matters or white lies; I mean deliberate, conscious deception.

I'm fairly sure that the first occasion was a morning, at breakfast. I don't suppose you remember that morning. Why should you? You couldn't know until now what happened. But it was very significant for me because, when I lied, I found that it came so very easily. Alice was playing up, pushing her beaker away with her hands and sometimes her feet; you know what she can be like. Her little shrieks of frustrated rebellion seemed to slice right through the centre of my forehead and the room was stuffy and close, oppressive, so much so that it seemed smaller than it really was. I felt that, if I had reached out with my arms spread wide, I could have touched both sides of it at the same time.

I had an overwhelming, irresistible urge to leave, to get away from the both of you. So, I turned to you and said that Vivian and I had shifted the time of my sitting forward.

But that wasn't true.

As I closed the door of our flat behind me, I felt no trace of remorse at the lie, only a sense of release at being free of the two of you for a while, you and Alice. Poor Alice. I hate that I felt that way about her.

I had had in mind that I might wile away the extra half an hour in a coffee shop but then I unthinkingly made my way straight to Vivian's. It wasn't until Colin answered the door that I wondered how Vivian might react, given how angry he had been when I had been late.

Have I mentioned that? I haven't yet, have I?

It wasn't my fault. The Tube was almost completely clogged so that Helen was late arriving at ours and it took me much longer than usual to get to Vivian's. He didn't care about any of that, of course.

"You're late," he said, by way of greeting as soon as he opened the door.

I should have known better than to try and make light of it.

"What does it matter? You take hours anyway."

His left eyelid pulsed with a tiny tremor.

"You have no idea what it's like to be me, have you?" he said, quietly but with real menace.

I remember thinking, for the first time, that he might well be capable of hitting me. I'm not sure I can explain exactly how that felt. I would say that it was arousing. I don't mean in a sexual way. (Or do I? God, I hope not.) I mean in the way that watching a horror film is arousing, or an intense burst of physical exercise, stimulating, something that heightens awareness, reminds one that one is alive, related I imagine, though only remotely, to how a soldier might feel when he first comes under fire.

"I spent all night," he said, "all this morning, obsessing about a particular freckle you have just above your right elbow, one that is very nearly but not quite a perfect crescent shape and you've kept me waiting an extra twenty minutes to check it."

He took hold of my arm, quite roughly, there in the hallway and stared down at it for a minute before letting go.

We hardly spoke during that session, although at one point I said, "You said that I have no idea what it's like to be you. Of course I haven't. Any more than you have the faintest idea of what it's like to be me."

"Did I hurt you when I grabbed your arm?" he asked.

I told him that he hadn't.

Where was I? The first morning I was early, the first time I lied to you. Colin showed no signs of knowing that I was significantly early but he said that Vivian might be a while and led me up to the dining room to wait there, pointing out a handful of newspapers on the sideboard that I could look at, if I wished.

When Vivian appeared some twenty-minutes later, I apologised for being early.

"It's being late that's intolerable," he said. "I don't mind you turning up early, not in the least."

After that day, I would usually arrive at Vivian's earlier

than we had arranged. It became a matter of routine. Colin would show me up to the dining room and I would read the papers or a book I might have brought with me for half an hour, more, or simply gaze out at London life as it passed by below in all its endless variety, unified solely by its ignorance of my vigil.

The dining room, I soon realised, had become a sort of unofficial waiting room and over the weeks I met there an assortment of those involved in Vivian's life. I bumped into Guy Johnstone several times.

One morning, I entered to find a woman I didn't know sitting there. She was smartly dressed, fine featured, elegant, in her fifties I would have said, sitting at the expansive, mahogany dining table, reading a newspaper. She looked up at me as I entered.

"Hello," she said, "you must be Jane."

"Yes," I said, wondering how she could have known who I was.

She seemed to read my thoughts because she added, "It's the red hair that gives you away: so striking."

She glanced at her newspaper for a moment before looking back up.

"I'm Susan Brown."

I tried not to react visibly, to not show that I had heard of her and her longstanding affair with Vivian, had been wondering whether I would ever meet her, what she would be like.

"Pleased to meet you," I said as neutrally as I possibly could, wondering whether she had called on Vivian that morning or had stayed the previous night.

She smiled.

"Vivian is having a bath. I expect he won't be long. Did you know that he bathes several times a day, and that he never uses soap?"

I had a feeling she was not really expecting me to answer.

"I suppose he's told you all that. I wonder what he hasn't told you. That would be the really interesting thing to know, wouldn't it?"

"Yes."

She turned a page of the newspaper.

"My husband mentioned you, the other day," she said, "after he met you at that reception. You left an impression on him."

"Did I? I hardly said a word I'm afraid."

She looked at me as though she thought I was being deliberately stupid.

"Yes, well, Oliver is easily impressed."

I heard the noise of a door opening from the floor above, where Vivian's bedroom was, and footsteps on the stairs. A few seconds later, Vivian appeared at the door and greeted me with a nod and a good-morning.

"You've introduced yourselves?" he said. I thought I detected just the merest hint of unease in his manner, an uncertainty.

"Yes, we're practically best friends already," Susan said, rising from her chair.

"Well, I'd better go," she continued. "Oliver is giving

a television interview. I said I'd go to lend moral support. Why he still feels he needs help with that sort of thing after all these years, I wouldn't know. But it's the least I can do, I suppose, as the dutiful wife."

Vivian went to her. With a glance at me, she offered her cheek, which he kissed.

"See you around," she said to me as she left.

I noticed that Vivian didn't see her to the door, that she let herself out.

I met her for the second time about a week later. I don't remember quite how we got there, but she ended up rattling off the different parties and events that Vivian had attended during that week. I think perhaps she wanted to emphasise how much she knew of all the comings and goings of his life.

"His energy is inspiring, isn't it?" I said.

Susan raised her eyebrows.

"At heart he's still a young man," she said. "I've known him longer than I would care to admit and outwardly he has aged; of course he has; but, inwardly... While the rest of us have been battered and bruised by life, gradually worn down until we are cynical and downbeat, he is just as playful and optimistic, as full of vigour, zest for life as the day I met him. I don't mean to imply that he hasn't been buffeted by the same vicissitudes that affect us all. It's just that they don't seem to have altered the essence of the man. He may as well still be twenty-one, judged by his outlook on life."

She smiled at me.

"Oh, to be twenty-one again," she said. Those were her words but it was clear that she wouldn't really embrace the opportunity to start again at twenty-one, to relive her life: quite the opposite.

"Does that make him healthier, mentally, than the rest of us?" I asked. "It might be an indication that there's something wrong with him, mightn't it, that there's something missing, even if it doesn't lessen his charisma."

She looked at me quizzically. For the first time in our brief dealings, she looked at me as though I had surprised her a little.

"I couldn't say," she said. "Perhaps."

15

"I've felt for a while now, that there is something not quite right, that there is something missing."

"Clothes?"

Vivian gave me a straight look.

We had finished for the day and I was pulling my dress on. Vivian had put down his pallet, his brushes, wiped his hands but he was still standing by the canvas studying it.

"No, I've just realised what it is. I can't believe it didn't come to me sooner."

I went to look at the painting, knowing that I would have no clue what he meant.

"One of the reasons I like to take my time painting, is so that I can get to know the sitter as intimately as possible, in the hope that will work its way onto the canvas. It's one of the reasons I like to paint my friends and family. That provides a kind of short-cut."

"So?"

"So, what is the most important thing about you at the moment? What is the most significant aspect of your life?"

I smiled and said "Alice."

"Exactly. Alice."

He turned to face me.

"Will you bring her round?"

The house did not seem a child-friendly place, not for one newly toddling. Our own flat had not long before undergone the transformation that all households must go through when the first child reaches a certain age, when breakable or dangerous objects, hitherto freely distributed, are put away or moved to higher ground.

"I don't know, Vivian," I said doubtfully.

"I don't mean to pose; I'm not going to paint her; that's not my point at all. I mean that I need to see you with her, see how you interact."

"Much the same as any mother and child, I would have thought."

He raised his eyebrows.

"You're right," I said. "That was stupid."

"Yes," he said. "It really was."

I looked at the half-formed image of me on the canvas. How could he possibly hope to convey something of the presence of an absent child? Would he add an extra layer of wistfulness? Looking back, I think that he wanted to see the physical me interacting with my daughter, see whether and how my eyes might light up, witness the special smiles I reserve only for her, hoping, perhaps, when next I posed for him, to note the difference, which surely there would be, between the me with Alice and the me without her, looking for that gap I had heard him speak of.

"Okay then. I'll bring her. But you realise there's no way I could possibly pose while she's here: the idea of her letting me be still; well…"

He smiled.

"Oh, I know. Believe me."

We arranged our next appointment.

"With child," he said with a wry smile as he made the notation in his appointment book.

I turned to leave but then a thought occurred to me.

"How old is your youngest child, Vivian?"

"He's four."

"Wow!"

"Yes, wow!"

All the way home, I thought about that unknown child of an unknown mother. What sort of life could he look forward to? Financially comfortable, presumably, although, in truth, I did not know how involved Vivian tended to be with his children in terms of either money or time. I had not yet seen him with any of them. The only one of his children I had met at that point in time was Helen. How very old Vivian would seem to his youngest son as he grew up. By the time the boy was twenty, at university, say, Vivian would be in his eighties, if he were still with us. I had been so very conscious of the age of my own father, how old he had seemed in comparison to others' parents, yet he had been only in his forties when I was born. Vivian was well into his sixties.

As I neared home, my thoughts turned to Helen, herself only eighteen.

I had not, before then, quizzed Helen about her relationship with her father but I could no longer resist.

"He was hardly there at all, when I was growing up," she said.

I smiled inside at the implication that that process was over.

"Mum was living with him when we were born, Sophie and me. But, by the time I was three, she had had enough."

She sighed.

"I don't remember any of that time of course. He had just bought the house, back then, I'm told, so it was my first home. He seems to like having a main squeeze at any one time and Mum was it for six years or so."

How much hurt was encapsulated in that simple sentence. I thought of Clare fulfilling that role for him, now: main squeeze.

"But he was never faithful to her," said Helen. "It's just not in him. It got to her in the end."

Alice demanded, silently but eloquently with upstretched arms, that I pick her up. I stooped down and swept her up, prompting a burst of delighted, delightful giggles.

"He's not really a bad father," said Helen, smiling at Alice, "but he's certainly not a good one. He would pop in and see us sometimes, a few times a year, maybe on or around our birthdays. He had a knack of buying presents that were not quite right, for the wrong age perhaps, too tomboyish for Sophie, too girlie for me."

You would never be like that with Alice – would you Michael? – I just know you wouldn't.

"The only decent length of time I've spent with him was

when I posed for a painting. For me, sitting for him was the price I had to pay for spending time with him, for a chance to… well, to get to know him a bit. I wouldn't know what he got out of it: just another painting, I suppose."

My eyes teared up. It happens to me a lot these days. But, of course, I thought of my own father and the idea of not having an opportunity to spend any time with him throughout my childhood, only having a chance to get to know him, just a little, when I was seventeen.

Alice twirled her little fist in my hair and I kissed her cheek.

"She's going to have your colouring, isn't she?" said Helen. "She's lucky."

I paused for a moment, wondering whether that was true. That Alice was lucky, I mean. It's always been obvious that she has my hair and skin tones, hasn't it?

"Michael has a big book of reproductions of your father's works," I said. "There isn't one of you in it."

She seemed amused.

"You checked?"

"I'm afraid I did, yes."

I was suddenly very embarrassed.

"I suppose I wanted to see how he had painted someone I knew."

"Worried, how yours is going to turn out?"

I smiled.

"It was only last year," she said, "so I guess you'll have to wait for the next edition. Perhaps we'll be on consecutive pages, you and me."

She gathered up her things, made a note of when she would next be needed, and said goodbye to Alice.

At the door she stopped.

"The answer's yes, by the way."

"I'm sorry?"

"The answer to the question you wanted to ask is, yes, the painting of me is a nude. So are the ones of Sophie. He's done two of her."

"Would you pose for him again, if he asked?"

She did not hesitate.

"Yes, of course. He's my father."

I found myself wondering, that evening, what she had meant by that. Did she mean simply that she felt she had to do what he asked of her or did she mean that she would do anything to spend some more time with her father? Just as I would, to spend some more time with mine.

It was one of the few times when you straightforwardly asked to be included, when I took Alice to see Vivian. At least you had an excuse: as you said yourself, it would have been handy, in practical terms, to have your help for the journey across town, but I knew that wasn't the dynamic Vivian was looking to observe, the family; he was expressly looking to see Mother and Child.

He took us up, not to the dining room, with which I was familiar, but to another room across the landing. The room which he termed the sitting-room was more library than reception room, had something of the air of a rundown gentlemen's club. Book-crammed shelves lined every wall, volume after volume of art, art-history, and art-criticism, nearly as many biographies and histories, an entire bookcase of nineteenth-century novels, some twentieth-century ones too, but not as many of those I noticed, very few contemporary ones.

As I watched Alice carefully making her way from one piece of furniture to another, like an intrepid mountaineer picking her way slowly across a cliff-face, my thoughts returned to Helen and the conversation we had had about her father.

"When you painted Helen, did you see yourself in her or see her mother?" I asked.

Vivian turned a little in his seat to look directly at me.

"Now that is an interesting question," he said. "The actual question is fairly interesting but what's really intriguing is what you really meant. Do I see my children as reflections of me, my progeny, fortunate bearers of my genes, or are they a haunting reminder of betrayed women?"

He said this with a mischievous twinkle in his eye and a wry smile but I could tell that he was only half-joking. Perhaps there had been a sense of that in my reasons for asking that question, not articulated to myself but there for all that.

"Well, which is it?"

"The honest answer is also the dullest, I'm afraid, and that is – both. Not at the same time, mind you, but changing from session to session. I wouldn't know whether that was caused by changes in my mood or theirs."

"You couldn't flip it, in your head. Like one of those two-pictures-in-one images. You know: elegant woman or old crone."

"No, not at all."

Alice had almost managed to reach a book that I had thought would be out of reach and I hurried to move it to a safe spot.

"Are you careful when you paint your children?" I asked.

"I always take great care when I paint; you know enough of my method by now."

Was he being deliberately obtuse?

"I mean are you careful not to paint them in a way that might upset them?"

He studied me intently. For a moment it was like being in the studio.

"My very first art teacher told me something that I've never forgotten," he said. "He drew a bottle on the blackboard, a simple outline in chalk and asked us what it was. We all duly said that it was a bottle, but he said, No. It's not a bottle. It's a picture of a bottle and its crucial to any effective representational art to keep that always in mind."

It seemed to me that he had evaded my question, not just ignored it.

"What has that got to do with how you paint your children?"

"I mean that a painting of you isn't the same thing as you. You do realise that, don't you, Jane? It's no more, and of course, no less than an image of you mediated by the artist. It's very important for you to remember that; I would say for you in particular."

I noticed the phrase "for you in particular."

"I'm not thinking that it's going to be like *The Portrait of Dorian Gray*," I said, "if that's what you're worried about."

"Picture."

"I'm sorry?"

"Picture; it's *The Picture of Dorian Gray*, not portrait."

"Oh."

"I think Wilde wanted to emphasise that he was referring to the physical object, the canvas in its frame: hence, picture. Portrait carries connotations of the concept of the man, the idea of him, a portrait in words as much as an image. So, you have James' *The Portrait of a Lady*, where the book itself is the portrait. You can paint a picture in words too, of course, but portrait nudges us that way more definitely, I think."

"So which are you doing of me: portrait or picture?"

"I prefer the word painting, because the paint itself… well I've grown rather obsessive about paint over the years."

"You know that makes me sound no more significant than a jar of daffodils."

I meant that to be light-hearted but Vivian just said, "Indeed," in a very serious manner.

Vivian had said hello to Alice and pulled a few silly faces when we had first arrived but, after that, he showed no sign of any desire to interact with her, preferring, it seemed, to observe the two of us together. I had brought some toys of hers, which I took out and tried to distract her with. I was anxious that she might break something. As I played with her, I felt self-conscious under Vivian's gaze and as a result started to worry that there was an artificiality to the situation that would defeat the object.

That feeling returned when it was time to leave. As I strapped her into her pushchair, I said to Vivian, "There, satisfied now?"

He took so long to say anything in response that I turned to look at him, expectantly.

"No, not really," he said. "I feel I know you less now, not more."

"What could you possibly mean by that?"

He remained thoughtful.

"Less isn't quite right," he said. "I suppose I mean that there is even more to you than I had thought."

"Should I be flattered? We're all more than we seem on the surface, aren't we?"

"Yes, of course, but I thought I'd got beyond that, way beyond."

I made light of it at the time; but in the taxi going home, I fretted about what he might have meant by that comment. Did he mean that I had not shown a normal mother's affection for her child? I had thought I loved Alice with every bit of me.

I doubt that Vivian meant that he had detected some lack in me as a mother, but what it was that had disturbed him, I do not know.

I think it was several sessions later when I asked about something that I had been obsessing over since the visit with Alice.

"What did you mean the other day," I asked, "when you said that it was important to remember that the painting wouldn't be me? I mean when you said that it was important for me in particular."

He looked up from the pile of tubes of paint that he had been considering.

"You know, Jane," he said, "I've had countless models sit for me: men and women, clothed and naked, lovers, family, but of them all I feel sure that you are the one who has been most invested in it, given of yourself the most."

I do not think it would be an exaggeration to say that I was stunned.

"Right from the very first day, even in the way you undressed, you have brought an intensity to the studio that I only hope I can give some hint of in this painting."

16

Colin had brought a coffee up to the dining room for me while I waited. I asked him how he had come to share his life with Vivian.

"I was in – Oh God," he shook his head ruefully, "such an abusive relationship. I kept leaving my partner, then finding myself going back. I don't know how many times I'd left but I always went back to him, partly because I'm weak, but also because I didn't have anywhere else to go. When he heard about my troubles, Vivian said I could stay here, if I wanted."

He touched the back of one of the dining chairs as though he needed to confirm the reality of his being there.

"The thing is, I hardly knew Vivian at the time. We'd met for the very first time just a few weeks before."

He smiled a little bashfully.

"He's the most generous man I know."

I was beginning to become more and more aware that I had seen only some parts of Vivian: the obsessive painter who was a tyrant in his studio, the relentlessly inquisitive intellect, the insightful art-historian; but these were aspects only of the whole.

"I suppose he can afford to be."

"Now, yes," Colin said. "But you'll find most rich people aren't. And from what others tell me, Vivian was being generous long before he became rich. I asked him about it, once. What he said was interesting."

"How?"

"He said that, if he was generous, it was because he was impulsive. He might have been being modest, but he isn't a fan of modesty."

"No."

Colin was, I think, the person who most admired Vivian: Vivian the man, as distinct from the painter.

"Psychologists say that impulsiveness is a marker for criminality," I said. "Did you know that?"

Colin laughed.

"Yes," he said. "I can see that side to him."

When I next sat for Vivian, I mentioned Colin's description of him as the most generous person Colin had known. He made light of it.

"What a fine judge of character Colin is," he said.

I waited to see whether he would repeat the notion that his generosity was an aspect of his impulsiveness but he didn't so I mentioned it myself.

"Did I say that? I don't recall. I suppose it might be true. I try to avoid introspection, just do what I do."

He was applying paint using a trowel, around the spot where I judged my midriff would be. I found the notion that he needed a trowel to paint my stomach disconcerting.

"Because I paint so obsessively," he said, without

looking away from the canvas, "I have sometimes been praised for my work ethic. Completely misplaced praise I can assure you. I feel compelled to paint. It is neither a pleasure nor an unpleasant toil, it is feeding an addiction."

"So that's your philosophy of life, is it, always do what you feel you want to do?"

"When I'm hungry, I eat. Nothing more, nothing less."

I assessed his lean, wiry frame. He did not look like a man incapable of restraining his appetites. But then, he spent so much of his time on his feet, pacing back and forth around that room, that there was no especial secret to his remaining slim. Of course, he wasn't really talking about food.

"You should try it," he said.

"You make it sound so simple, but it isn't, is it?" I said. "Unrestrained hedonism: it has consequences. Eat what you like, sleep with whom you like, ignore any obligations that may arise as lover or father."

"I do not ignore my responsibilities as father."

"Yes, you do."

He stopped in the act of applying some paint to the canvas and looked at me.

"You sometimes act as a father, but not because you feel obligated to; it's because you sometimes want to and it's only when you want to. It's nice being a father sometimes. I don't know – going to the pub with Helen and Sophie. They're charming and pretty and they love you. Look at my pretty daughters. Aren't they charming? And listen to us discussing art. They're clever too. See how proud they are of me."

His silence was inscrutable. But he did not appear to be studying me or the canvas, his brushes were ignored for once.

"It's just as you said: when you're hungry, you eat."

He seemed to have remembered his brushes and, after a moment's consideration, made a mark on the canvas with one, one of the very finest.

After some silence, a half-formed notion, something that had been coalescing from different elements of thought over recent days, became clear to me.

"Actually, you're not a pure hedonist, are you? You're like Faust, all that hedonistic behaviour is part of the deal. In a way, you've sold your soul and you've done so with a purpose, a Faustian pact. You think it's the way you have to live in order to create great art. You have to have had all those experiences, have people around you that have been touched by you, broken by you, so that you can paint them, knowing that that is what they are like, knowing that with absolute certainty because you're the one who's made them that way."

"It's an idea, I suppose," he said, trying to make light of my words.

I let it rest for a moment and permitted my thoughts to drift. I was aware of having got the better of him in our exchange for the first time and I wondered how that made me feel. I don't think I particularly enjoyed it, yet at the same time had a notion that our relationship, whatever it might be, had moved on, transmuted ever so slightly, as it seemed to do from time to time.

After some minutes, I said, "He offers to burn his books, at the end of the play you know, Doctor Faustus, the one by Marlowe, in a last attempt to save his soul."

"And what would I offer to burn, do you think? My finished works? Like Botticelli offering up his paintings to the Bonfire of the Vanities. My brushes and paints perhaps?"

I smiled, and as I did so I realised that I had managed to put a label on him that was not of his own choosing. A small triumph, but a triumph all the same.

"In the play, it is far too late for that," I said.

My thoughts stayed with the idea of labels and the expectations that they impose.

"It's not quite as apposite as you like to think, is it?" I said. "The whole Candaules, Nyssia, Gyges triangle."

"How do you mean?"

"The whole point of that story is that it was Candaules' idea in the first place. But this wasn't Michael's idea, was it?"

He eyed me thoughtfully.

"It was yours."

17

I never told you much about my father's death, did I? Perhaps, when we first met, it was all too raw still, even though it had already been nearly four years. And if you don't talk of these things in those first few months of getting to know each other, perhaps you never will.

But I told Vivian. It was the sort of thing that felt natural to speak of during the many hours we spent alone together.

I was sixteen and I had been fretting over a French vocab test. My French teacher, who was, as it happened, Italian, had a knack of making me feel stupid. I don't know quite how she did it. It was something in the way she looked at me with an air of mild exasperation. It had gone well enough in the end, even if she had managed to make my reasonable mark seem little short of astonishing, so I was feeling pleasantly relieved as I made my way home.

I called a greeting to my mother as I dropped my bag in the hall, having seen her shadow on the floor through the half-open kitchen door so that I knew that she was there. It was to be my last moment of normality for a very long time, I might almost say ever.

My mother didn't reply, which was not like her, so that

it was with mild curiosity that I entered the kitchen. The first thing I noticed was that my mother's face was deathly pale; she was sitting at the kitchen table clutching a cup of tea, her knuckles white too, her fingers pressed hard against the black china of the mug; and then I saw that my father was there, which was unexpected; he would normally not return from work until much later.

"Oh! Hi Dad."

He smiled. His face was not white like my mother's but there was a noticeable firmness to his expression, which was tensely controlled.

He started with, "I've just been telling your mother," as though he were going to say that he was planning to take Friday off work to play golf.

But it wasn't that.

He'd come from the hospital, where he'd had an appointment with a consultant, an appointment that he hadn't told us about. He didn't want a fuss.

The combination of hospital and consultant was enough for me. The rest was detail. It was cancer, lung cancer, one of those rare ones that some contract even though they have never smoked. Unlucky was the word he used. No word has ever seemed so inadequate.

As presented by him, death was not a factor worth mentioning, nor even sickness. He spoke of neither. There would be hospital admissions, chemotherapy, more tests, monitoring, shifting to working part-time, all practical matters to be ticked off, as though illness is no more than a matter of procedure. But it wasn't like that. Oh, there were tests and drugs and so much more, forms and charts, boxes crossed or ticked, waivers signed. But what there really was, was sudden transformation, from husband, father, man, to man with cancer, and above all failure, failure to prevent the cancer from metastasising, failure even to limit the acceleration of its spread.

I know it upset my mother that he hadn't told her that he was undergoing some tests.

"He didn't want you worrying unnecessarily," I told her later, when we were alone together.

"But it's my job to worry," she said, "and it wouldn't have been unnecessary, would it?"

I was too young to understand why she should have been upset by that. But it was a deception, wasn't it? Something more significant than a white lie. It betrayed a lack of trust and I think that hurt her. I expect that it was the last time he deceived her though, except perhaps for his trying to hide how much pain he was in, in the last days.

Later that same day, I disturbed them when they were hugging wordlessly, standing in the dark in our unlit living room.

I realise now that I don't really know what sort of marriage they had. Once, I would have said unthinkingly that they were obviously very happily married; but, with the habit of relentless questioning formed in Vivian's studio, such pat answers are rendered transparently inadequate. I can say that outwardly they seemed happy together. They argued about the sorts of stupid things that couples argue about, but how many marriages are free of such moments? They seemed to enjoy each other's company, which is a sign of real happiness, I think. But what really passed between them by way of love, I couldn't say.

She cried for hours and hours when he died, so I suppose she really did love him. But tears can flow for so many reasons. If you died tomorrow, Michael, I know that I would cry, but the tears wouldn't testify that I still loved you. They would flow from regret and remorse, and sorrow, guilt that I had hurt you so much and that you hadn't had time to recover from that hurt before your end. So I wonder whether the source of my mother's tears might have been in part remorse, regret at harsh or unkind words spoken, loving ones not uttered often enough. I can never know. If she submitted to interrogation, would she even know herself?

"Anyway," my father said, after he had broken the news, "how did your vocab test go?"

I missed his death. I had promised myself I wouldn't, that I would be there for him alongside my mother at the end, but I missed him go because I was in the loo. I knew he had gone because, when I returned, my mother was no longer by his bedside but sitting on a chair in the corner of the room. Her face was wet with silent tears. She didn't say anything to me or shake her head by way of gesture, just looked at me with wide, tear filled eyes that said all there was to say.

They say a natural part of grieving is denial, don't they?

That we all go through a phase when we refuse to accept that the loved one really is dead. It was like that for me in the crematorium. It wasn't an active denial, a refusal to accept reality; it was an overwhelming feeling that my father was still alive, that he simply couldn't be gone. I couldn't shake the notion that at any minute he would walk down the aisle and come and sit next to me. I pictured him doing so, dressed soberly for the funeral just like everyone else, and saying something banal like "Not a bad turn-out," or, as it was murky and drizzling, "Appropriate weather for a funeral."

I will tell you something that I didn't tell Vivian, something about my father. It is a memory of him that is nothing out of the ordinary really but has somehow taken on an extra significance for me lately.

He had taken me to a concert at Wembley Stadium, when I had just turned fourteen. When we came out onto the concourse after the show, the crowds were immense, moving in waves that seemed a force of nature rather than a collection of rational individuals. There was a clear risk that we might be parted by a rip tide as we were buffeted along, so he reached for me and took my hand. It must have been years since we had last walked anywhere hand in hand. I clung on to him all the way down Wembley Way, only letting go when we reached the station. I wish I had kept hold of him for longer.

18

On a day of unusual heat and humidity, such that I wondered whether Vivian might not wish to paint (he did), I was sitting at the dining table, reading, and drinking a welcome glass of iced water that Colin had brought for me, when I heard first the doorbell, then Colin opening the front door, and unfamiliar voices entering.

Footsteps ascended the stairs and, looking up from my book, I saw a young woman standing at the doorway. She was nineteen or so, I would have guessed, slim, with long chestnut hair in full-bodied waves. She smiled a slightly sheepish, artlessly friendly smile.

"Hello," she said.

"Hello."

Oliver Brown, in a linen suit, clutching a panama hat, appeared behind her, hot and visibly perspiring about his flushed face.

"It's Jane, isn't it?"

"Yes, that's right. How are you, Oliver?"

"Bloody hot."

The pair of them entered the room, Oliver patting his face with a handkerchief.

"This is Maggie, my daughter."

"Hi," I said.

So, this was Susan's daughter. Could I see anything of Susan's features in her? I thought I could, yes: something in both the colour and shape of her eyes.

"And this is Jane. One of Vivian's models."

"Pleased to meet you," said Maggie, offering her hand, which I shook.

"I'm not solely one of Vivian's models, you know," I said. "I'm also a secondary school teacher: English."

"Are you?" said Oliver as though this information were extremely surprising. "How interesting."

I studied his face for a moment, trying to assess whether he was teasing me in a manner that I didn't quite understand.

"Oh God, a teacher" said Maggie. "I'm just done with all that, thank God. Are you very strict? I bet you are."

I laughed.

"Yes," Oliver said, "she's finally left school and is twiddling her thumbs and generally getting up to no good before going up to university."

He eyed his daughter with what was clearly feigned disapproval.

"I told her she'd be better off getting a job, get straight out there doing things. A degree's no use to anyone these days."

Maggie rolled her eyes, but her expression was more affectionate than exasperated.

"Why miss out on three years of fun?" she said.

"Three years of fun at my expense."

He mopped his brow once more.

"Mind you, at least it's a lot less than the school fees. I'm glad that's finally over."

"Everyone knows you're indecently rich, Dad; don't pretend," she said. "Anyway, I'm not twiddling my thumbs. I help out at the gallery on Pont Street."

Oliver turned to me.

"It's unpaid, of course. Young people have no conception how much money it takes to live a reasonably comfortable life."

"You're talking to a teacher on maternity leave," I said, "who's married to a junior English lecturer."

He smiled. Comparing the two of them, father and daughter, I thought I could see a resemblance there too, particularly in the line of the jaw, despite the difference in elasticity of flesh between an aging parent and a young woman fast approaching her physical peak.

"Vivian!" said Maggie.

He was at the door. With a childish enthusiasm that made her appear momentarily even younger than she was, she went to him to exchange kisses on the cheek as though he were her favourite uncle.

"Maggie, Oliver," said Vivian.

He looked at me and smiled, greeting me wordlessly. Somehow, it made me feel a more established part of his household than the others, who were thus more clearly categorised as visitors. I thrilled a little inside.

It transpired that Oliver, who was on his way to see a dress rehearsal of a play that he was backing (taking

Maggie so that he could "keep her out of mischief"), had dropped by to talk to Vivian about something to do with a vintage car, a Mercedes, I think. I was left with the vague impression that they were joint owners but I made no attempt to follow their conversation, exchanging instead some small talk with Maggie about her forthcoming studies.

When the two men had finished their discussion and Oliver and Maggie were about to leave, Maggie took hold of Vivian's forearm with both her hands and said, "When are you going to come and visit us again, Vivian? I love seeing you at Court Lodge."

The two men exchanged glances. For the first time, I noted a hint of tension between them, just for an instant as their eyes met.

"I'm busy painting," said Vivian.

"You're always busy painting."

"Precisely."

I think now that there was something significant in how forceful the scents of that place seemed to me, right from the very first day, from the moment that broad, blue door swung open and he was standing there with his dog, the lurcher, the two of them inspecting me sardonically.

How does one describe the intensity of a smell, its depth, something more than the banality of saying that it is strong? I could say intoxicating, but that is not quite right. Heady, perhaps? I want to say compelling, but does that make any sense? Can there be compulsion in a scent, a combination of aromas? And anyway, I don't mean to imply that I was compelled to do anything, not really, not to the extent of a will overborne. Perhaps powerful is the nearest I can come, the closest to a word that might convey what I mean, the sense that those scents, those smells were meaningful, took up a significant portion of my attention, were an ever-present, always noted quality of each of my many visits throughout those long months.

There is another scent that I will always associate with that room, one I forgot to mention earlier – no; forgot is not quite right; let's just say didn't mention – the scent of me.

I had been wondering whether I was going to tell you everything.

Well: here goes.

At the start of another session, one not long after the visit with Alice, I had lain back and positioned myself, as always – I was very proficient at it by then – but instead of picking up his pallet, his brushes or a tube of paint, Vivian stood considering me for a brief moment and then did something that he had not done before; he went and fetched a high stool, one that stood in the corner of the room farthest from me, an object that I had barely registered before, and placed it next to the easel, precisely where he would stand when he was painting; then he sat on it, studying the canvas and me in turn for about half an hour.

I had not seen him behave in quite that way before.

Yes, there were always periods of intense scrutiny when he might be still for many minutes but always he would move eventually, approach, retreat, shift his angle, apply some paint, remove some. On this occasion, however, his mood was different, passive. I also noted that he was spending more time studying the painting than studying me, which was completely the other way around from his usual method. I began to wonder whether he was considering that it might be finished, even though, when I had glanced at it on the way in, (I tended to avoid giving it any close scrutiny.) it had seemed far from complete.

And then I started to think that maybe he was going to stop, that it was not working for him, that he would tell me to go home, throw the canvas away and move on to another sitter. You had told me that he sometimes does that. That thought made me feel suddenly queasy, dizzy even. It was a moment of revelation for me, and I realised that my life over the past weeks had been in this room, that everything else, the ordinary things outside those walls, spending time with you, caring for Alice, all the humdrum daily matters, were unimportant, incidental detail. All that was important was happening here; the thing of first importance to me at that point in time was the painting and that it should be good, more than good, significant. The idea that Vivian might put down his brush and stop threatened to overwhelm me.

I found myself saying, "Is something wrong?" like a woman with a terror of heights who is unable to stop herself from approaching a cliff-edge.

He remained silent for a while, not in the manner he often had of not having heard my question, but as though he were carefully considering his answer.

And then he said, "Yes, something is wrong."

My stomach lurched, and I swallowed.

"What?"

He eyed the painting with something approaching a frown for about a minute more and then said, "Come over here."

I don't think I can fully convey how significant it felt to break my pose, get up from the couch and take those few steps across the room to him, completely naked as I was. It doesn't make any sense, I know. I had spent many hours naked in front of him by then, and his characteristic method of studying his sitters so intently meant that he had so very often stood extremely close to me, bent down at times to study my most intimate parts with merciless thoroughness, but, at all times when I was fully naked, I had been there on the couch, sitting for him. It had always been as though there were a barrier of purpose around me, an exculpatory reason for my being there, for my nudity, a charm of protection, all of which dissipated as I walked across the room to him.

If he sensed the significance of that act for me, he did not show it; he just kept studying his work. When I reached him, I turned to stand close next to him and joined him in contemplation of the painting, very aware, as I did so, of the physical fact of him, the space he took up sitting on the stool, the faint, barely perceptible rise and fall of his shoulders as he breathed in and out, the scent of him. For no reason that I can explain, other than that it felt the natural thing to do, I put my hand on his shoulder. We remained like that for minutes, a naked woman and a fully clothed man, studying the half-painted figure on the canvas.

I knew that I could not see what he could see, could not discern whatever incongruity or lack of something it was that was troubling him. It was far from finished, but the draughtsmanship, the mastery of form, the weight of the image of my body, torso and limbs, head, each resting with discernible gravity on the couch, forming together a coherent whole, seemed to me of an equal with the very best of his works. Surely he could not be contemplating throwing it away, when it seemed to me at least half-way to greatness.

At last he turned to me and looked up into my eyes.

"I need to see what you look like after you've made love," he said.

The moment had come. The moment that I had been anticipating for so long, fixating on, if I am to be completely honest with you. The moment of proposition. I hesitated, of course I did, before being unfaithful to you, before letting another man make love to me, enter me, thrust himself inside me, even though it had been there all the time, hadn't it? – when he had suggested painting me, before then even, a hint of a suggestion that infused everything that passed between us when the three of us were together, a possibility. It had been there in the moment when I had lifted my hand to undo the button of my summer dress on the first day that I had sat for him, and the next day, when he had teased me with the story of Candaules and Nyssia. It had been there all the time: the question of whether we would become lovers.

I remember that, as I hesitated, I was very aware of the warmth of his body through his cotton shirt where I had placed my hand on his shoulder and thinking, even then, how old he was. He is so old, I thought, but his flesh is firm and warm.

"Okay," I said, in the faintest of whispers.

I did think of you, Michael, I promise I did, as I took his hand and led him back to the couch, watched his penis stiffen as I pulled his trousers down, felt sorry for you, sympathy for you, even though we had both known - hadn't we? - that it might come to this and that you were willing to risk it. But then he was suckling at one of my breasts and jolts of sensation were zinging though me, radiating outwards from my nipple.

I didn't come, by the way, in case you were wondering, which I'm sure you were. Not that first time. But I did enjoy it, the newness of it all, the different ways he had, the different ways I found myself responding to him.

He did not take long to finish, which was what I had anticipated. That first time was essentially a matter of his covering me, of my giving myself to him, so that, although I had been enjoying it, I was not so disappointed when he came so soon, not left feeling frustrated as I would have been in other circumstances. The fact of having done it was what mattered to us both. Nevertheless, I still wanted to share soft kisses with him as we regained our breath entwined, feel his hardness soften inside me, caress his tongue with mine gently in the afterglow of sex. But he was heedless of any such wish, pulled out almost as soon as the last pulse of his cock had subsided and stood up brusquely, handing me some tissues saying, "Clean yourself up and get back into position," in a horribly peremptory tone, devoid of any tenderness or affection. Instantaneously, I could feel a deep unhappiness, a hollowness opening up in me in the face of such a blatant, careless lack of regard and as I sat there, feeling worthless and duped, scooping his mess out of me, my nostrils flaring involuntarily at the soapy, salty scent of his ejaculate, I could sense an abyss of self-loathing into which I was about to fall.

But then I glanced up at him where he stood watching me, having pulled his trousers back up and refastened his belt, and I saw a new expression on his face, one that I had not seen there before, a sort of avidity, an eager anticipation, a hunger, and then, after I had dropped the sticky, soggy clump of soiled tissues onto the floor and stretched back into that by then familiar pose, right arm up and bent with my hand resting behind my head, armpit exposed, my left arm lying limply flat away from my side, my thighs spread, exposing myself to him, my chest still noticeably rising and falling as I struggled to get my breath back, conscious of a sheen of sweat on my torso, knowing how blotchy and mottled my flesh would look, his eyes were everywhere, all over me, darting from place to place, scrutinising every part of me as he paced back and forth and I was filled with a fierce exultation that I could be so fascinating to this man, this great artist, this unique talent.

When he had finally returned to the canvas and picked up a brush, started to apply paint for the first time that day, he radiated an intensity, a sureness of purpose that he had not shown before. I revelled in it, his need for me, a need of which I had not the faintest doubt, the absolute necessity for him, at that moment, that I should be there, looking just as I looked, so that he could paint, paint an image of me that every fibre of his being insisted he must paint.

The journey home, home to you, was a seemingly unending series of surreal moments. In the studio, I had been composed, unrepentant, I might almost say exultant, but with my clothes back on and out on the streets of London, away from the world apart that was his studio, his house, I bumped up hard against reality. I am an adulteress, I thought. I have cheated on my husband. I should hate myself. Perhaps I do.

I thought about taking a cab, but I just knew that I would feel as though the cabbie could tell what I had been up to, that, if I caught him inspecting me in his rear-view mirror, I would read in his eyes an expression that said, I know what you've been doing. You've just had sex, haven't you? And not with your husband. I can tell.

And then when I descended into the Tube and sat next to a young family on the train, I thought that I must reek of sex, dreaded the little boy turning to his mother and saying, "What's that funny smell, Mummy?"

"It's the smell of whore, Baby Boy: cheap, adulterous whore."

And, of course, every turn of the train's wheels, every step I took along the platform after I had alighted at our stop, was taking me towards you, towards you and a life of deception.

You don't know which day that was, do you? The very first time. But then, why should you? It was a Tuesday, there was a stiff northerly and some showers, nothing special, an ordinary day, just the day I fucked another man.

Or perhaps you do know. Because I went and had a shower, very soon after I came back. That's right, I remember so clearly now. I had not forgotten so much as put it out of my mind, not renewed my memory by actively remembering. So much has happened since then.

But now I remember thinking that you might guess because of that. I had not been in the habit of showering when I got home. Why change now? And then I thought, I don't care. Let him guess. He put all this in place, has known all along that it might come to this and done nothing about it, gone along with it. I hope he does guess. I won't give him the satisfaction of telling him, but I hope he does.

But then, when I consider the way you acted throughout the whole of that time, I sometimes think you assumed that I had been sleeping with Vivian from the very first day. In fact, I'm almost sure of it. You were incredibly aroused that night. Do you remember? I mean after my first session sitting. I think, now, that you assumed that I had already done it, on that very first day, and that it turned you on.

What sort of man are you Michael? What sort of woman do you think I am? Did you really think I would just walk in and shag him? When you wanted to make love that first night and I rebuffed you, did you think that it was because I didn't want to sleep with you at the same time that I was sleeping with Vivian? It wasn't that, not then. I was just tired, tired and confused.

How could it possibly turn you on, thinking that I was being unfaithful? I really want to know. Was it because he's famous? Was it some perverse proof of your own attractiveness? Of all the women that this famous man could sleep with he has chosen my wife; was that it?

When you imagined introducing me at parties: "She was painted by Vivian Young, don't you know?" Were you looking forward to adding, "She slept with him too."?

I've often tried to picture you on the other side of our front door in the moments after I had left to go to him that first time. Did you go upstairs and wank as soon as I left?

19

I have mentioned before the significance of the second time. God, how true that was that morning as I made my way back to Vivian's studio, knowing that we were going to make love for a second time. There was not the slightest doubt in my mind. We would make love as soon as I had removed my clothes ready to pose. We had to because that was how he needed to paint me.

And because I wanted to.

The thought was like a physical presence in my head, had been all morning, making my skull feel heavy. I don't mean in the manner of a headache, I mean literally heavy, to the extent that my neck muscles began to tire with the effort of keeping it upright.

Did you not notice how quiet I was? Of course, you don't know which morning that was do you? At least I don't think you do.

I had expected to feel guilty or self-conscious, but I was too wrapped up in the simple fact of what I was going to do to feel either.

I'm going to make love to Vivian again.

That thought went around and around in my head.

I'm going to make love to Vivian again.

As I fed and changed Alice, as we sat and had breakfast together, when you left for work and we said goodbye.

I'm going to make love to Vivian again.

It was like a clamour in my head when Helen arrived to babysit.

I'm going to make love to your father for the second time today, I thought, as I watched her playing with Alice. Can you not tell?

I wonder whether she could tell. I don't suppose so. Perhaps, just as I now think you had, she had assumed that we were lovers already.

As I lay trying to get my breath back, after that second time, to control the rise and fall of my chest and settle fully into my pose, I thought of you, where you would be, what you would be doing. I think you had a seminar to take that morning: *Drummer Hodge*. I pictured you calling on one of the students to read out her prepared notes and had such a clear image of you, with your head cocked thoughtfully to one side, nodding now and then in encouragement, asking the room how much they thought *The Drums of the Fore and Aft* had a different tone or mood, and whether that difference in tone was significant or whether the two pieces were perhaps closely linked in sentiment, whatever we like to think we know about Kipling: the everyday routine of your life as a lecturer. And all the time, your wife was lying on a couch, with her legs spread, having just made love to another man.

The image of you, of the seminar room was so clear in

my mind that it was almost an out of body experience – the irony. And then I realised that I had fallen out of the habit of thinking of you while posing for Vivian. I had used to think of you so often at the start, not happy thoughts, mostly, but still thoughts of you, yet that this was the first time I could remember doing so in years.

I just wrote, "years." What made me do that? It had been only a few weeks, if that.

"Come back please," Vivian said.

I had indeed been so far way – well a couple of miles away to be precise – that I started.

"I'm working on your face," he said, "so I need you present."

"I'm sorry."

He smiled, then, some minutes later, he asked, "Where were you anyway? I don't think I've seen you so far removed from here before."

"I was thinking what Michael would be doing now. He will be taking a seminar until noon: one for the Masters students."

"Guilty thoughts? I wouldn't bother with those if I were you," he said. "Guilt is an entirely useless emotion."

I wasn't at all sure that I had been feeling guilty exactly, just contemplative.

"Isn't guilt a necessary part of being a moral being?" I asked. "That emotion is what prompts us to be better in future, isn't it?"

"Is it? It never has with me."

I didn't believe him.

"I know we have this notion of guilt being something foisted on us by priests and parents," I said, "but I'm not sure that's right. It's such a universal emotion that I think it must be something innate in us. Sure, what makes us feel guilty can be moulded by the times – an indigenous Amazonian isn't going to feel guilty about missing Mass, obviously – but the feeling itself is there, ready to be provoked. Guilt, remorse, contrition, apology, making amends, they're part of our nature as social creatures, wouldn't you say?"

He didn't answer, did not engage in the conversation any more, seeming lost in the intricacies of mixing paint, but I could tell that he was listening.

My thoughts returned to you. By then you would be finished; perhaps you would be saying goodbye to the students as they filed out, putting your papers back in your bag. Perhaps a student would linger, wanting to ask a question, as I had done, all those years ago.

I tried to remember when we had last made love, what we had done, how I had felt, but I couldn't. And then I thought of when we had first made love. That I could remember. It was in the flat that you had rented for the year while you were on placement at my uni, all in a rush one Friday afternoon as though it were a race. Thank God for us that I won, I suppose.

And then I thought of my very first time. I haven't told you about that before, have I?

It was a family friend, James. He was married. I feel

guilty about that now, but I'm afraid I didn't at the time, even though I liked his wife very much. Anyway, they're still happily married so no harm done. Well, they're still married. I wouldn't know whether they were happy or not, whether they are now.

I'd had a crush on him since I was about ten, I think – not long after I'd started noticing boys, I suppose. He was a journalist, a travel writer, which seemed very exotic and adventurous to me when I was growing up. He would turn up from time to time throughout my childhood, tousled and tanned, and shake the sand out of his hair over my parents' dining table with a mischievous twinkle in his eye. I always thought him very handsome, in a crumpled, lived-in sort of way. He had that knack some people have with children, so that he would talk to me as if I were not a child at all but a grown-up. It was very flattering. I remember always feeling at ease when I was with him in a way that I didn't tend to feel with other grown-ups. You know how it is, the way they always ask stupid questions that lead nowhere like "How's school?" He wasn't like that at all, although it must give you a huge advantage having a job like his rather than being an accountant or whatever. I used to feel comfortable and at the same time a little bit awe struck, whenever I was with him.

I've been trying to remember how he came to be so close to my parents, because he was some years younger than they were. I think he was a cousin or nephew of one of my fathers' old friends from Sheffield and somehow my parents ended up putting him up for some weeks when he was on his uppers, struggling to get a foothold in journalism and without a place to stay. I don't remember that time, when he was staying with us; I would have been three or four then, I think.

It started when he dropped by for supper one evening. His wife was with him. As you would expect, she was very pretty. She'd been a secretary at one of the papers he wrote for, if I remember correctly.

"Come and sit next to me, Jane," he said as we took our places, patting the chair next to him.

I've told you that I was fifteen, haven't I? I had already made up my mind to sit next to him, but it always gave me a little thrill when he singled me out like that.

He'd just come back from a tour of Central America, parts of which were very out of the way and risky places to travel at that time. I suppose they still are. He made them sound so dangerously exotic. I couldn't have been more impressed. At one point, he was telling a very animated tale about how he, his driver, and a local Mr Fixit he had hired were held up at gunpoint when my knee accidentally brushed against his under the table. I moved my leg away, feeling a little embarrassed but he didn't seem to have noticed.

And then I thought, "Why not?" and moved my leg back so that my knee brushed once more against his. My heart was pounding and I felt sure that somehow one of the others would guess what I was doing. I remember thinking that I ought to join in the conversation so that no one would think that I was doing anything out of the ordinary but I couldn't think of anything to say and ended up staring at my plate.

James showed absolutely no sign of having even noticed, so, after a while, I shifted a little in my seat so that a length of my thigh was touching his and he couldn't possibly not realise what I was doing. It was summer and I was wearing shorts so my bare thigh was pressed against the cloth of his chinos and I could sense the warmth of him, of his lean leg, through that single layer of cloth, just a thin piece of cotton between his flesh and mine. I felt as though my entire being was in that stretch of thigh where it touched his. I was elated and, at the same time, terrified that he might shift away, dismiss me as a silly young girl not worthy of his attention.

But he didn't.

They were exquisitely delicious, long minutes as the meal, the animated grown-up conversation continued, with all the time our thighs pressed hotly together under the table; then, when someone else was talking, James turned to me just for a moment and smiled. I don't think I had ever been more thrilled.

The rest of the meal was a blur. I could hardly follow the conversation. At one point my mother even asked whether I was feeling well, because I was so quiet and at another, I caught his wife, Kim looking at me too, just for a moment, and in that moment, I was convinced that she could tell that something was going on between the two of us but then she looked away and seemed quite at ease and unsuspecting, not perturbed in any way.

Towards the end of supper, when my father was holding forth on some topic or other, something about third-world debt, James turned towards my father slightly as he listened and thus away from me, but then he oh-so-casually slipped his hand under the table, placed it on my bare thigh just below my shorts and gave it a little squeeze. His hand was hot and heavy against my skin. I sensed its strength. It was all I could do not to gasp.

When the meal was finally over and the grown-ups had had their night-cap in the sitting room (Not me; I was only permitted one small glass of wine with the meal.) and we all said good-night, James and I exchanged kisses, one on each cheek as we always did, and he placed his hand lightly but very deliberately on my waist.

"*A bientôt*," he said in a flawless French accent.

It was without doubt the sexiest thing anybody had ever said to me and his touch at my waist was like molten metal against my flesh through the cloth of my T-shirt. That night, when I took my top off to go to bed, I actually inspected myself, half expecting to find a burn mark there. And when I climbed into bed, well... Let's just say it was some time before I finally rolled over and tried to get some sleep.

School the next day was a torment, a delicious, heart fluttering torment, but a torment none the less. I think you know that I was mostly a good girl at school, keen to study. However, that day I found concentrating on my schoolwork unthinkable. My teachers were quite cross with me, crosser than they would have been faced with the same behaviour from others because it was so out of character. But I didn't care about that; the torment was all inside, my thoughts a dizzying mix of my memories of the night before, fervid analysis of every glance he had thrown my way, every touch, combined with lurid fantasies for the future and hazy, unfocussed plans for what might come next.

The chief difficulty was that I couldn't see how I was going to find a way to be alone with him and in reach of a bed. I was quite determined; I wasn't going to settle for a kiss and a cuddle. I was going to go all the way, if he would let me, and I was going to use all my charms, such as they were, to ensure that he would. But I didn't even know when I would see him again; it was often weeks between his visits, sometimes months. The thought of having to wait two or three months before seeing him again was almost too painful to contemplate.

I needn't have worried. Only a few days later he dropped by at our house unexpectedly, so that when I came home from school, it was to find him standing in the kitchen, chatting to my mother, exuding his customary raffish charm.

I wonder now whether my mother might have fancied James too, just a little. That thought didn't occur to me at the time but I have an image in my mind's eye of her chatting to him in our garden on another occasion and sweeping a stray wisp of hair back over her ear in a way that makes me think perhaps she did. I wonder whether she still does.

That afternoon, I hadn't been expecting him to be there and was embarrassed and unhappy that I was still in my school uniform when he first saw me. I wanted him to think of me as a sexy and sophisticated young woman, not a schoolgirl, so I rushed upstairs and hurriedly got changed, fearing that perhaps he would be gone by the time I went back down but he was still there and, as I joined them, he turned his broad confident smile on me with a mischievous twinkle in his eye. I couldn't not blush.

I had put on the same shorts that I had worn at the supper. My mother's look, as it had that evening, told me that she did not approve but James' eyes told me that he did.

"I was just telling your mother how absolutely overcome with boredom I am at the moment," he said. "I'm between assignments and Kim's gone back to work. We need the money; I'm afraid; travel journalism doesn't provide the relentless torrent of riches that you might imagine. She doesn't get back until past seven most nights, so I'm left twiddling my thumbs at home all day. It's purgatory."

"You're welcome to pop in here, anytime, James," my mother said with a smile.

I longed to be alone with him, share improper whispers, invite him to touch me, touch me anywhere, everywhere. Another caress of his hand at my waist, like molten metal through the cloth of my T-shirt, would have been ecstasy and I prayed that my mother would need the loo or have some other reason to leave us alone, even if just for a couple of minutes; but she didn't; she stayed and chatted relentlessly, unmoving, happily ignorant of my designs.

Every now and then, as the conversation meandered on, James and I would share a smile, nothing more than would be normal in a lively, good natured discussion between friends, but each time our eyes met my heart would leap.

He loves me too. I thought.

You will think me – or at least my fifteen-year-old self – naive, but I had barely noticed his words describing his dull days spent twiddling his thumbs alone at home. I had been too flustered by his unexpected presence in our kitchen to pay adequate attention to what he might have been saying in those first few minutes after I came back downstairs after changing, concentrated too much on his body language, the twinkle in his eye, the mischievous smile, to note what his tongue was telling me. But later that evening, with a set text propped open and unread upon my bed, his words came back to me, rather in the way a searched for name or fact will pop into your head long after it is needed.

He spends all his time alone at home. His wife doesn't return from work until past seven. That day was a Tuesday. I had orchestra practice after school on Thursdays.

It wasn't the lie itself of which I was ashamed, it was the ease with which I told it, and the trusting, unsuspicious way that I was believed. The credit I had built up with my teachers over years of being dependable and honest, of being a good girl, was easily sufficient for me to draw down upon that day. My father had arranged for me to meet a colleague who might be able to offer me some work experience in the summer; he was a very busy man and that Thursday afternoon was the only time that he could make for me.

"That's no problem, Jane. I hope it goes well."

I changed out of my uniform in the toilet of a McDonald's, having decided, after much feverish deliberation, not to wear the short shorts again, but a seemingly more modest skirt, one that reached almost to my knees, but the real purpose of which was to permit him easy access. I had brought some thigh high socks to wear as well – you know the type of thing: the ones that have a look of stockings about them – but decided at the last moment that they would have been too much.

You can imagine how my heart was pounding as I stood on James' doorstep and rang the bell. I had rehearsed what I was going to say, word for word, and practised the off-hand way in which I was going to deliver my lines.

"I've been thinking about you, all alone and twiddling your thumbs all day; it makes me sad, so I thought I would drop by to see whether there is anything I might do to alleviate your boredom."

But then I panicked when he opened the door so that I just said, "Hi, it's me."

"Hello, Me," he said, as though I were exactly the person he had been expecting to find there on his doorstep at four o'clock in the afternoon.

And once inside, all my plans of seduction, of how I would make my move, proved unnecessary, for we kissed fiercely as soon as he had ushered me in and closed the door behind me, his hands cupping my backside under my skirt, pulling my body hard against his.

I lay there afterwards, on his bed, and let myself fantasise about him leaving his wife and marrying me in her place; although, that would have to have been in a few years' time; I knew that we couldn't do anything of that sort until I was some years older. Lying there, snuggled up against his firm, warm body, savouring the scent of our mingled sweat, I felt so safe and loved that I could have stayed there for days; but, of course, I had to leave, had to leave so much sooner than I would have wished, before my mother started worrying that I was late, even for a day when I had orchestra, and wondering where I was. What would she have thought if she had known? I don't think she would have believed it possible.

Since I couldn't return to my house in my change of clothes and knowing that I wouldn't have time to change in a loo somewhere as I had on my way, I had no choice but to get dressed back into my school uniform in front of James, much though I would have wanted to avoid doing so. He lay on the bed and watched me. When I was done, he got up, came to me, and kissed me long and hard, naked as he was.

After our third time together, two more conscienceless

deceptions, two more snatched hours of increasingly vigorous lovemaking, he let me down, gently but firmly. Despite my schoolgirl fantasies of sharing my life with him, I think I had known all along that it couldn't last, and it only took a few kind words from him to bring that realisation to the surface. I felt special and heartbroken and treasured all at the same time.

When we met every now and then afterwards, ostensibly as no more than the family acquaintances that we had always been – it seemed less often than it had been before somehow – he would wink and smile his roguish smile and I would feel happy and grateful, grateful for the pleasure he had given me and the gentleness of the parting, but sad too, that it couldn't have been more than it had been.

I wrote those pages about James yesterday. I had always thought I knew exactly what happened: Young woman seduces handsome family friend and is introduced to sex by an experienced, caring yet vigorous lover; but I've read it back just now and somehow it looks different set down in black and white.

It's not right; is it? Sleeping with the fifteen-year-old daughter of close family friends, no matter how much she bats her teenage eyes at you and gives you the come-on, or how grown-up and womanly she thinks she is, feels herself to be. Even if you are gentle and kind when it comes to the deed itself, that doesn't change the fundamentals. When I think of my pupils at St. Bede's that are the same age that I was then...

I wish I hadn't written it, now.

We don't understand our own lives, do we? Even though we live them.

20

This is the first time in days that I have written anything. I had to take a break.

I haven't been able to stop what happened between James and me – what it might really have been, as opposed to what I thought it was – from going around and around in my head. And on the back of that, I have fresh doubts about so many things.

You invited me for a coffee, didn't you?

I had forgotten that detail, but perhaps it's important. I've always remembered that moment as "and then we went for coffee." But the truth is, you suggested it. I had asked my question about *The Mayor of Casterbridge* and, as you were expanding on your initial answer, we had walked out of the lecture theatre together – God! When I think of me nodding along, trying so hard to look coolly intelligent. How embarrassing! – but then we were out of the building and you had said something like, "I'll see you at the next lecture." I think we had even taken a step or two on our separate ways when you stopped and said that you had some time before your next appointment and did I want a coffee.

I'd never really considered it that way before now but

we were a bit furtive, weren't we, at first? At least until you went back to UCL and I used to travel into London to see you at weekends. We hardly went out together before then, I now realise, not out in public; we would just stay in, in the flat you had rented for the year, and make love. Were you worried it might look bad after all? Don't get me wrong; staying in suited me just fine; as well as really enjoying the sex, I used to love the way we would chat and chat in bed afterwards, about anything and everything. I could feel myself falling in love with you more and more each time. I used to enjoy how we would have our supper in bed, too. I would feel satisfyingly sexy, sitting up and sensing you gazing at my body, perhaps noticing you start to get semi-hard again under the sheets as we chatted and ate.

But even the straightforward pleasures of our earliest times together now seem somehow less pure, tainted. Did you pat yourself on the back for being a stud? For having nailed a cute young redhead, a fresher? Was I even your first? Student I mean; or was I part of a pattern? We never really talked about our previous lovers, did we? You said you didn't like to think of me in another's arms, which seems laughable now.

I remember when you first introduced me to you oldest friends, Paul and Ian and Geoff, at a pub in Chiswick. Of course, they were charming and friendly; they're decent people; but, looking back, I can't help but think that you were showing me off to them. When I went to the loo and you were alone together, did Paul slap you on the back and congratulate you for being such a player?

I know we were in love when we married, when we had Alice. Perhaps I should be content with that, not try to overanalyse those early days. It's hard to stop though, once you've started. I used to feel so safe in your arms, Michael, whenever we hugged, when I rested my head on your shoulder, breathed in the scent of you, or in the morning, before we moved in together, when I stayed over at yours and would wake to find you there and I would place my hand on your back or thigh and feel completely at ease in a way I don't think I had since I was a young girl and used to clamber into my parents bed on Sunday mornings.

I'm not sure I will ever feel that safe again. I've never felt that way with Vivian. There you are; you have one on him in that at least.

I saw a programme on television yesterday, a stupid, lightweight puffball of a programme in which people bring family heirlooms to be repaired in a ridiculously perfect, chocolate-box-cover of a converted barn. There is seldom any artistic or cultural merit in the items that they bring, their only real purpose being to serve as vehicles for memory. The whole thing is a cynical exercise in mawkish sentimentality, every moment of it calibrated to that end, archly leading from conversations about patina and clock mechanisms through final repair to the moment when the piece is re-revealed to its owner, who then obligingly dissolves in tears, usually saying how much they wished their deceased relative could be there to see it.

I fall for it every time.

Yesterday, an elderly woman had brought two ancient teddy-bears: one her own, the other her husband's, both treasured since they were children and hence, dirty tattered and torn. Her husband had died the year before, after more than fifty years of marriage. As she duly cried and cried when the lovingly repaired bears were returned to her, mumbling, "I'm so sorry. I'm being stupid." I thought of me, the me I was less than a year ago, who would have dreamed that she too might one day suffer the sweet loss of a long-loved husband after decades of marriage.

I cried for more than an hour.

21

Vivian and I had taken a break and were sharing a pot of tea in the pantry. I was wearing just his cable-knit sweater as had become a habit. The telephone rang and Colin shouted to Vivian announcing someone important on the line. Vivian does have a smartphone, but incoming calls always go to the landline to be vetted by Colin.

"I wouldn't, if we were still in the studio, but..." Vivian said with an apologetic shrug.

"That's fine," I said. "I'll have another cup."

As I poured the last dregs of the tea into my cup, I heard the doorbell and then the sounds of Colin admitting someone below: a woman. I thought I recognised her voice; and I was right; it was Susan.

"Ah, Jane," she said, as she came into view near the top of the stairs. "Were you getting chilly, or are you wearing that in the painting?"

"I just threw it on, as we were taking a break," I said, but then felt foolish for having given an explanation, when clearly one was neither needed nor expected.

Susan seemed amused and joined me in the pantry. It was the first time we had seen each other since Vivian and I had become lovers – we had made love not two hours earlier. I felt sure that she could tell and I was newly conscious of my semi-clad state. It was all I could do to stop myself from pulling the hem of Vivian's sweater down a touch.

"How long is it now that you've been posing for Vivian?" she asked.

She does know, I thought, as I told her that it had been nearly two months.

"Still many, many sessions to go then," she said.

"I suppose so."

She smiled, not at all a friendly smile.

"Do you think you'll stay the course?"

"Of course."

"Many don't you know."

"I have a feeling I'll manage it."

That smile again. It made me grab for something to defend myself with, anything.

"Do you know what Vivian told me the other day?" I said.

Her only response was a relaxed, mildly inquisitive look.

"He said I bring a special intensity to the studio."

It was a mistake, a foolish, juvenile attempt at a boast; I realised that, even as I finished speaking.

"Oh, I'm sure he did, Dear," she said, with false motherliness. "And I'm quite sure he will have meant it at the time. But, well..."

Her eyes drifted down for a moment to the point where the hem of Vivian's sweater met my upper thighs.

"...he'll probably say the same to some other pretty

young thing in a few months' time."

I blushed, but I wasn't going to back down.

"How many times has he painted you, Susan?"

It was enough to move her focus off me, just for a moment.

"Five times, over the years," she said, her tone betraying a hint of introspection.

"When was the first time?"

She laughed.

"Long, long ago. Too long to put a figure to."

"Where you married to Oliver, by then?"

"You know Vivian told me once," she said, turning to face me square on and looking me in the eye, "that when he paints, the painting he is working on is the only painting that matters to him, is his obsession, to the extent that he blanks out all ideas, thoughts or even memories of any other painting. He says he even sometimes manages to reach a point where it feels as though it is the only painting he ever has or ever will paint."

Her unrelenting gaze dared me to look away.

"Of course, you know that he usually has as many as four or five paintings on the go at any one time."

I tried not to show my surprise but I think I must have failed. I had not consciously considered whether Vivian would have other ongoing projects but, as soon as she said this, I realised that I had wordlessly assumed that mine was the only painting that he would be working on.

"You didn't think he would only be painting you for all this time, did you?" she said, still searching my eyes for a reaction. "How sweet!"

I felt undeniably foolish, but also irritated with her, more than irritated; I felt a well of antagonism towards her opening up within me. Why did she feel the need to belittle me in this way? Was it simple jealousy? Surely, she had learned to live with that over all those long years of her affair with Vivian. Was there something about me or Vivian's relationship with me that she found particularly provoking?

Just then, Vivian returned. I think he must have sensed a tension in the room but he gave no indication of having done so. I left them together and went to wait for him in the studio.

With Susan's taunting words fresh in my mind, I looked over at the familiar stacks of canvases leaning front-side against the wall. What had I made of them before? It seemed odd that I had not considered that they might include other ongoing works. What had I thought of them? That they were all blank canvases stored there for when they would be used? Perhaps. I honestly think I had not considered them at all. They had been simply there. Now, they were a distinct presence, like a shadow at a window of someone that you know to be eavesdropping. What faces, what bodies might they have on them? Whose?

I noted again, as I had on the very first day that I had posed for him, the tiny chalk circles and lines that dotted the bare, paint-flecked floorboards. They marked the positions of the different items of furniture that those other sitters were posing on, I realised: the armchair, the stool, the camp-bed; just as my couch had its own four circles, fixing it in space. My couch? It wasn't my couch. It was Vivian's.

During the remaining half of that session, it seemed to me that these other sitters had somehow joined us, joined us in the room like unseen ghosts, ghosts that were neither malevolent nor friendly but very definitely there.

When the session was over, after I had re-covered myself with the patina of civilisation that my clothes provided and we stood in the hall to fix a time for our next appointment just as we always did, his pocket diary, like those canvases leaning against the wall in his studio, now had a definite presence. I could not stop my eyes from studying it as we spoke, not exactly trying to read anything that was written there but attempting to assess how full it might be. It was impossible to tell from such a brief sight of its well-thumbed pages; I glimpsed only a few pencil marks; they could have been hieroglyphics for all I could make of them. After checking it briefly, he closed it with a definitive snap that nearly made me jump, such had my focus been on its pages.

As I walked towards the Tube, I found myself imagining Vivian returning to the studio and lifting the canvas of me from the easel, perhaps turning it to the light and studying if for a moment but then turning its face away and setting it with the other canvases against the wall, out of sight, putting it, putting me, out of mind. Would he be taking one of the others and placing it on the easel, ready for another session?

I imagined him moving the couch. I thought it must have been quite heavy; perhaps he would ask Colin to help. Together they would place it against the wall and move – what? – the armchair? Yes, the armchair to the exact place required, as marked by four little chalk marks on the floor, ready for whichever man or woman was going to sit for him and take up, for that time, all of his attention.

When I reached our flat and relieved Helen, I went and took down the big book of reproductions of Vivian's pieces. I hadn't looked at it since my fruitless search for any painting of Helen. Thumbing through it, I didn't take long to find what I was looking for, a portrait of Susan; *Woman Smoking* is its laconic title, so that I could not have known who it was before having met her. She must have been about thirty when Vivian painted it. Only four years older than I am now. To think!

Do you know it? She is fully clothed, sitting cross-legged in an armchair, gazing knowingly out at us, a lit cigarette in her hand, which she holds with a cocked wrist to her side. She looks the embodiment of enticing sophistication; her expression seems to say that she knows all the viewer's darkest secrets, darkest thoughts, darkest desires and that hers match them. Vivian must have been partially in awe of her when he painted it. It was an aspect of his character that was new to me. I found it hard to believe that he could ever have felt that way about anyone.

Muse. Does it mean anything more than a woman that an artist has managed to convince to sleep with him on the basis, real or imagined, that doing so is essential to his production of great art?

I suppose at least the artist in question usually convinces himself that it is true. Men have a habit of rationalising their desires, I think, like all those moderately successful, middle-aged men, convincing themselves that it is the irresistible forces of evolution that compel them to ditch their wife of thirty years for a younger, more nubile version.

You will have understood what it meant, that statement made by Vivian that he needed to know what I looked like after I had made love, my agreement to it. How typical of him to say that he needed to see me like that: needed not wanted. It meant that I had agreed that we would make love at the start of every session so that my body would look exactly right, exactly the way he needed it to be for the painting to have that extra layer of meaning, that crucial extra depth: me freshly fucked.

Sometimes, he would remain naked when he painted me. We would make love; then, as I arranged myself into the correct pose, he would pull his boots back on – you know how he has to prowl about the room as he paints – and get straight to work. He was quite a sight, with his wrinkled, slightly saggy flesh, his grizzled body hair, bollock naked, his cock slowly returning from semi-turgid to fully flaccid, staring at me with all his usual intensity, the laces of his boots undone and the tongues of leather sticking up.

That conversation that I mentioned near the beginning of this, the one about me thinking you handsome when we first met. I'm afraid that was one Vivian and I had directly after we had made love. I didn't say that earlier because I couldn't just jump straight in and hit you with that right from the start.

Colin walked in on us once, when we were doing it.

I sensed, without being aware of anything to prompt the feeling, without hearing any noise other than the rhythm of the couch springs under our thrusting and my own little animal grunts keeping time, that the door was open. With an effort, I opened my eyes and saw that Colin stood at the doorway, only half in the room, his hand on the doorknob, as if frozen in the act of entering. His eyes did not meet mine but were fixed on the backside of his companion; he would have been able to see Vivian's balls as they swung back and forth between his slightly splayed thighs, slapping against the lower cheeks of my backside. He appeared to be transfixed. In the couple of seconds that I was able to look at him, his expression showed neither surprise nor lust; it seemed to me only a kind of sorrow. I had no time to be angry or shocked because I was far too close and simply had to shut my eyes, and then there was nothing else for me other than the place where my body was locked to Vivian's and I was coming, coming very hard, unable to stop myself from crying out as I did so.

As the last tremors of my orgasm dissipated and Vivian momentarily slackened the pace of his thrusting, I reopened my eyes. The door was shut. Colin had gone. I think I clung even more tightly than usual to Vivian when he ejaculated inside me some minutes later.

"Colin was at the door. He saw us making love."

Vivian seemed unsurprised and unperturbed, not in the slightest bit upset or embarrassed and said nothing, just kept concentrating on the precise point on the canvas where his trowel touched it and made a tiny mark or adjustment.

"From your reaction, I guess it's not the first time he's walked in on you with someone," I said.

"Did it upset you?" he asked.

I had been trying to work that out and was still unsure of the answer.

"No. I don't think it did, and I find it rather disconcerting that it didn't."

22

I would love to know what your memories are of that time we dined with Vivian at Simpson's, how different from my own they might be. The entire evening was close to surreal for me because of course by then, he and I were lovers. But what was it like for you? What did you think when that journalist came over and Vivian introduced us to her, for example? Were you thrilled to be seen in his company and in that company to meet a well-known writer or were you wondering what she thought of us, whether she was asking herself if I might be sleeping with him and whether you knew? By then, I had grown used to people looking at me in a peculiarly circumspect way when I was with him, with a look that was akin to reticence, but I noticed it anew with you there to see it too and it was a fresh experience to see how people reacted to you being with us. Just for a moment, I thought you looked a little shamefaced when she turned her gaze from me and inspected you but perhaps I imagined it.

When Vivian had told me to invite you to dine with him – yes, it was as blunt as that, an instruction – I knew exactly what he had in mind; there was no need for explanation this time, as there had been when he had asked to see me with

Alice; if he were going to paint a picture of an adulterous wife, he would naturally want to observe her interacting with the cuckold husband. (Does that word sting?) Just as my love for Alice was such a key part of who I was, so was my betrayal of you. I don't mean to imply that he was dispassionately interested solely as an observer, that he didn't take a mischievous delight in the situation; I'm sure he did. But I realise now that for him that is all wrapped up together, the manipulation and his art; the delight in toying with his lovers, his friends and family is all of a piece with his acute observation of the results; it is his way of life, one might say, laying waste those around him so that they will be more interesting to paint.

That evening, as I lay on the couch and the clock ticked round towards the time when you were due to join us, I remember thinking that I didn't want you to witness Vivian painting me, didn't want you to observe me in my pose, not out of any embarrassment but out of a desire to keep that part of my life private for the time being, something to be shared only with Vivian. That doesn't make any sense – does it? – since the whole world would eventually see the painting. It makes even less sense bearing in mind that, by that point in time, Colin was in the habit of wandering in and out of the studio as he saw fit; and, I had grown used to him doing so, so much so that I no longer even twitched whenever he entered the room.

No, it didn't make any sense, but it is how I felt.

With that thought foremost in my mind, as time crept

on, I was beginning to fear that Vivian would indeed still be painting me when you arrived, that Colin might usher you in with me still lying there; but then, at last, Vivian put down his brushes, his pallet and wiped his hands in the resigned, slightly rueful manner he always did when we were done for the day.

"We'd better stop," he said. "Your husband will be here soon."

Then, as I broke my pose, stretched a little and sat up, he said, "Don't get dressed just yet though," and came towards me.

"We can't Vivian," I said. "We just can't."

But we did.

I'm afraid the truth is that it turned me on, knowing that you would be there any minute. In fact, we were not long done when you did arrive, and I was just finishing getting dressed when you rang the doorbell.

Vivian smiled and said, "Perfect timing. Why don't you go and let him in?"

Which is why it was I who answered the door.

"Come in. Vivian and I have just been making love," I didn't say. But I was tempted.

Instead, of course, I told you that Vivian was arranging things in his studio and would be ready to join us soon.

"He's just putting my canvas to bed," is what I think I said.

Did you notice how closely I watched you as we waited for him? I was checking to see whether you had an idea of what we had just been doing. Frankly, I found it difficult to believe that it wasn't obvious; I'd only just managed to get my breath back and I felt flushed and sweaty. And the smell... I thought I reeked of sex. At least we didn't go into the studio. You surely would have noticed the mixed scents of Vivian and me if we had.

I honestly couldn't tell whether you did suspect us. Sometimes I feel I can read you like a book; at other times I find you quite inscrutable. I could, however, read the way you looked longingly along the hall and up the stairs. It was obvious that you so wanted to be taken up there, to be permitted entry further into his house; and, when we heard Colin moving about upstairs, you practically got a crick in your neck as you craned to try and see who it was. You didn't hide your disappointment well, by the way, when Vivian emerged from the studio and we went straight out.

Did the walk to our table across the restaurant partly compensate for your regret at not having been shown into Vivian's house? It was a mark of how often I had dined with Vivian that by then I was almost, but I admit not quite, used to the attention we always drew when we arrived anywhere. Even those who didn't recognise Vivian seemed to sense that he was someone of importance. What is that, I wonder. Does it emanate from within him, an innate significance, or is it prompted by the reaction of those who greet him, the exaggerated care and attention shown by managers and waiters, whose every twitch of body language cries out that this is someone of special status? I had grown accustomed too, to the diners assessing me also, particularly the women, each making their own rapid evaluation of me with that forensic exactitude that we bring to the judgement of our fellow sex, in marked distinction to the more simplistic contemplations of the men.

I remember now that it was you who first pointed that out to me, that when a good-looking woman enters a room, everyone in it looks at her, all the men, naturally, but all the women also; and, that a man, even a good-looking, well-groomed one, needs a status or a notoriety before he will provoke any similar reaction.

It may surprise you to learn that I was, for want of a better phrase, rooting for you that evening; I really was. I didn't want to see you humiliated or belittled, certainly not in any straightforward bullying sort of way – Vivian is quite capable of that; I can assure you – but also not by means of any secret joke shared between Vivian and me, which I feared was his intent. In the end, you held your own; you really did; well, mostly. It was clear that you knew much more about the Romantic Poets, for example. Of course, you should, being an English lecturer but I know they're hardly your specialist subject and the depth of your knowledge was evident. Some of Vivian's views on them are insightful; I think you will agree; he has that sort of mind; but I think they are almost something in the way of hunches rather than being drawn from a deep well of understanding. That was in noticeable contrast with your own more firmly grounded opinions that night.

I could tell that you were a little put-out when I pleaded at the start for us not to talk about Thomas Hardy all evening but what you couldn't know was that I did that for your sake. He is too close to your heart and I knew that Vivian didn't rate your ideas, so I had to steer the conversation away from Hardy and I'm glad I did.

At the next table, in the central section across the walkway from our booth, sat a young couple. Do you remember? She was quite pretty with lovely dark hair in a bob, whilst he was a little gauche and self-conscious, but pleasant looking. I could tell that they were excited to be dining in such a famous old restaurant, that they were not used to those surroundings. I imagine that they couldn't really afford it, not regularly anyway, but had decided to treat themselves. I expect they had booked months in advance. They might have been us a year ago. Every now and then throughout the evening, I would study them for a moment or two, trying to work out whether they were in love. I couldn't decide; perhaps not quite yet, but very much enjoying each other's company. It was sweet. That sort of innocent enjoyment of life seems a distant memory for me now. And for you too, I assume. Poor you.

Naturally, Vivian dominated the conversation when it came to art; but then you were happy, eager, for him to do so; of course you were. He might have closed that topic down, you know. He does sometimes, if he doesn't value the other person's opinions so, in an odd way, you were favoured.

But then he turned the conversation to your future plans and my insides tightened, because I didn't know, yet, whether we had a future together anymore. Did you notice me withdraw into myself, stop participating in the conversation? I had the impression that you did. I tried nodding along and smiling at what might have been appropriate junctures – God knows why: habit, common politeness, wanting to avoid a scene that sullenness might provoke – but all the time, while you were outlining the various career paths open to you, the opportunities that might come up at other universities, how that would have to dovetail with my teaching, I was wondering why I was still with you, why I was still pretending to be your wife, when I wasn't anymore, not in the most fundamental way. I had only been having sex with Vivian for... what? Two weeks. But the distance between you and me was already so great in my mind as to seem unbridgeable. I was the mother of your child, that much remained true, but nothing more, not for me.

And then he asked whether we were planning to have any more children. It was the one moment during the meal when I think he was intentionally cruel.

"That's the plan," you said. And it had been, I know it had, but by then...

You went on to say that it was early days and we were in no rush, that we would see how we got on with Alice before thinking about it seriously, that money was a factor. Stock, meaningless phrases.

I think I laughed. Yes, I did, didn't I? For a moment you looked distraught. It was just a flash across your face and then you composed yourself. I wonder whether Vivian noticed it. I had been wondering whether you might have been provoked into losing your temper. If you were going to, that was the moment. I know how even tempered you usually are; but, well-hidden though it is, I also know that you do have a temper, a fierce one.

I made excuses for my laughter by saying something about how expensive children are and that we certainly couldn't afford another one at that point in time but what I had actually been thinking was that another child would require what would practically be a second Virgin Birth because I could hardly bear you to touch me.

And then I thought, Or it could be Vivian's.

We were so silent during the cab-ride home, weren't we?

It was that thought, that I might get pregnant by Vivian and let you think the child was yours, that carouseled through my thoughts endlessly and stopped me from talking. Could I really be that cruel?

What were you thinking, hunched silently in your seat the way you were? Were you still trying to assess whether Vivian and I were lovers? Or did your thoughts too, dwell on what the future might hold for us, whether there was still an us?

I had shocked myself with that thought of bringing up Vivian's child as yours, didn't recognise my thoughts as my own, which is why I let you make love to me that night. I almost stopped you, when I felt your hand first touch my hip and I had a reflex, only just suppressed, to shrink away from you. But I had to give you a chance, a chance to provoke the feelings that had once come to me so naturally in your arms.

But it didn't work at all for me that night; I'm sure

you realised that. Your fingers between my legs were annoyingly tentative, clumsy and uncertain, and the artless probing of your tongue in my mouth felt demanding and needy at the same time.

When you came so quickly, which in fairness to you was always likely, as it had been so long, I'm afraid it was a relief. And then, when you clambered off me and said that you loved me, I just couldn't bring myself to lie. I'm sorry.

There's one more thing about that evening. Perhaps I shouldn't say.

When Vivian told me to invite you to dine with us, it had been one of those occasions when he had stayed naked while he painted. I think he relished the incongruity of the scene. He can be like that.

He did not hesitate to quiz me about our sex-life, even before we became lovers. I know it will sound strange, but I felt no compunction discussing us with him. I should have, I know, but I've already explained how outside normality our sessions so rapidly became for me, how other his house and particularly his studio felt.

It's a terrible betrayal, discussing the secrets of the marital bed with another man, isn't it? But when he asked me whether I sometimes faked my orgasm I simply had to tell him the truth, which was that I did.

Not every time, Michael, I swear. But sometimes, when I just knew that it wasn't going to happen for me – I usually know early on; it's much more dependent on my own mood than anything my lover might do – and I would see that you were trying so hard, delaying your own pleasure in a way I knew to be futile. Then I would feel my arousal draining away and I just had to do it, let you let yourself go. Honestly, it sometimes felt less like a deceit than a little secret gift from me to you, a gift that you received unknowingly, a present, given in a spirit of love, freeing you of that burden of performance and letting you just enjoy yourself.

And then he asked me how often we did it, and I had to tell him that lately it had been less than once a week, at least since Alice was born.

How did we come to that point so soon, Michael? The point where it felt as though you had to wheedle sex out of me. I did feel like it sometimes; I promise I did. And I never stopped loving you, not then, not before. But sometimes, too many times, you would come back down from putting Alice to bed and you would say that you were going up too with a significant look on your face that I would pretend not to have noticed and I would say that I would just watch the news before coming up. Your disappointment would hang about you like a heavy cloak as you poured yourself a glass of water or did some other last-minute, delaying task in the kitchen, obviously hoping that I would notice that you were still around and that I would take the hint so that we could then go up together. I'm afraid I found you terribly off-putting at those times, clinging and irritating and needy. I'm sorry, Michael; I really am.

I wonder if it was my body, not prepared by the forces

of evolution to assimilate fully the notion that the pill could possibly be effective and in that ignorance telling me by means of something approaching revulsion that it was too soon to risk having another child, to the point where, sometimes, when you would turn to me under the sheets and place your hand tentatively on my hip, it was all I could do not to physically recoil.

One morning, Colin greeted me when he answered the door with the news that Vivian had been nursing a heavy cold the day before and had not yet emerged from his room. He led me up to the dining room, made a pot of coffee for me and went to check with Vivian whether he would be fit to paint. I could not stop myself from straining to hear their conversation as it drifted down from the floor above, where I had not yet ventured, but their words were tantalisingly indistinct.

Colin returned with the news that we would have to postpone my next session, probably for a day or two; he would give me a call to arrange a time; also, Colin had somewhere to be himself. As I had just poured myself a second cup of coffee, he invited me to stay as long as I wished, rather than turning straight back; it would be fine to let myself out.

It has only just occurred to me now, writing this, that it might not have been true, that Vivian had a cold I mean, that he might have been up there entertaining another woman, not Clare presumably, as he would not have taken any precautions to keep her presence secret from me. Thinking back, he had shown no signs of an incipient cold during our previous session, nor did he show any signs of lingering sickness the next time, so perhaps my new suspicions are well founded.

Not thinking any such thoughts at the time, I nursed my coffee for as long as I could, inspecting some of the paintings and etchings on Vivian's dining room walls. I stayed so long, not out of any marked desire to linger there but from not wishing to return straight home. Eventually, there was no use pretending that there was any coffee left or that I had any excuse not to go. I was halfway down the stairs on my way out, when the thought occurred that I could look into Vivian's studio. There was a risk, I supposed, that he might have ventured out of his room, but he had showed no signs of stirring yet. I could not resist. Those stacks of canvases, facing the side wall of his studio were calling me, Siren-like. When, if ever, would I have another opportunity to inspect them?

With guilty steps, as silent as I could make them, I went in. The lights were on. I did not take any note of that at the time but later it struck me as odd. Had Vivian left them on all night?

I hurried to turn the first of the painted canvases.

It was of a man, in his fifties I would have said, wearing an old-fashioned, tweed, three-piece suit, predominantly green, and a red knitted tie. He was depicted sitting in the armchair, legs crossed in a very relaxed pose, looking completely at ease with himself and the world in general. Without quite being able to name him, I had a feeling that I knew his face. Was he a politician? I rather thought he was. The painting seemed to me to be finished and it occurred to me to wonder how long after the painting of me might appear to be done Vivian would keep me there, obsessively checking, repainting and retouching, which I was sure would be his way.

I carefully placed this first painting so that it leant against the wall next to the remaining pile and picked up the second, a larger canvas in a landscape orientation. I remember quite distinctly holding my breath as I turned this second canvas to inspect it. It seemed barely begun, just discrete, solid blocks of colours between and around a sketched outline, but it was clearly another nude, a naked woman lying on what appeared to be the camp bed, the camp bed that stood not two feet from me where it had been pushed out of the way against the wall. It was too soon to tell but something of the proportions of her limbs suggested the litheness of a young woman. There was something oddly challenging, almost sinister about the featureless blocks of paint. I felt as though they might resolve themselves by an innate magic into a clear image even as I studied them and I was unable to stop my mind from filling in the spaces with a body and face of improbable beauty.

Who was that long-limbed girl? When had she last lain in that position on the camp-bed? Exactly where?

I glanced over my shoulder. Checking against the angle of the walls and the line of the floorboards, the camp-bed would appear to have been set up rather more to the right and at a different angle from the orientation of the couch when I was posing on it. When would she lie there again, taking up, for that couple of hours or so, all of Vivian's undivided attention, being for him at that point in time the only subject matter worthy of being painted by him, seeming to him for that time at least, the only thing he ever would paint?

The amount of talking Vivian and I did, the length of the silences changed over time. To begin with we would talk in intense little bursts in between periods of prolonged silence but gradually, as we grew to know each other better, became familiar with our modes of thought, the conversations would be easier, gentler and take up more time, flow. Then as the weeks turned to months, the silence reasserted itself, longer again, but different in quality, relaxed, easy.

"I almost miss her," Vivian said one day.

"Who?"

"The anxious, uptight, self-conscious young woman who started posing for me."

"Do I look different, then, from that other me?"

"Of course."

I felt my eyes moisten.

"Which are you painting, then?" I asked, trying to blink away incipient tears that had welled up in an instant.

I had been about to ask which he preferred but stopped myself. They amounted to the same question.

"I haven't decided yet."

Later that day, Vivian's words came back to me: about his "almost" missing the anxious, self-conscious me. I wondered about that "almost". He had said once that I had brought a unique intensity to the studio. Was that gone, now? Was it that initial vulnerability, the feeling in me of being painfully exposed, that he was really looking for in a sitter or at least in this sitter? Was Susan right?

"...he'll probably say the same to an equally pretty young thing in a few months' time."

Might he be looking for a fresh model who would bring that sensibility again, a fresh muse, one who would tremble pleasingly under his searching gaze? Had he found it in that anonymous, lithe young woman, posing on the camp-bed?

The formless girl in the painting became an intermittent and unwelcome companion. I would find my thoughts returning unbidden to her anonymous shape, unable to stop myself from trying again and again to add some identifying detail to my memory of those slabs of colour as if I could, by some mental process, create from them an anticipation of the finished painting. I might put her out of my mind for hours or days but then, as I reclined on the couch, I would catch a glimpse of the back of her canvas amongst the others stacked against the wall, and she would be before me once more in my imagination.

It was not long before I noted that the order of those stacked canvases would change from day to day. When I had inspected them, the painting of her had been second from the front, but each time I entered the studio, unable to stop myself from checking, I would note where it was, at the front perhaps or maybe next to the wall or somewhere in between, as if its position in the pile gave some clue to its current ranking in an imagined pecking order of Vivian's interest. Where would the painting of me be placed, I would wonder, when I had left the studio for the day?

I do not think I dreamed of her, but sometimes, when I would wake from an unremembered dream in a state of momentary confusion, my mind's eye would see that canvas again and I would imagine the shapes taking form so that I was on the very edge of seeing a fully realised image, only for it to slip back again into flat anonymity or, on other occasions, the shapes, while remaining only slabs of colour might seem to move, as though that flatness could nevertheless sit up, step off the canvas and approach me.

On more than one occasion, I think I came close to betraying my mounting obsession with that other canvas. During one session in the days after first studying it, I realised that I had been staring over at those stacks of canvases for far too long. When I looked away, I thought that perhaps Vivian had noted my interest in them, might guess that I knew that he was painting another nude and had begun to obsess about it. In a moment of inspiration, I used the blank canvases, also stacked there, to cover my tracks.

"How do you feel when you approach an empty canvas," I asked, "when you are about to start? Do you get nervous, excited, does it challenge you, that blankness?"

"I like blank canvases," Vivian said. "At that moment in time, in the instant before I touch my charcoal to the canvas, there remains the possibility that the resulting painting will be perfection."

"And when you have made a mark that is no longer possible?"

"That's how it feels, yes."

"Can a painting be perfect?"

He did not answer. He seemed to be waiting for me to expand.

"As there is nothing to compare the finished piece against," I said, "it can't be assessed in quite that way, can it? I mean, two equally talented painters could paint the same person and, setting aside obvious error, they would paint completely different paintings. Not just their different styles but what they see in the person that is being painted too."

"Inevitably, but a painting can approach perfection if it realises in paint, in colour and texture, the exact effect that the painter is striving for. I am striving for coherence between what I want to show and what appears on the canvas."

"But the painting evolves as you paint. You told me that before."

"It does. If I'm painting well, the painting reveals itself over time."

"So, there's no perfection to strive for. There is an end and when it is reached you are hoping for coherence."

"It is a process, yes."

24

You don't know about me and Paul, do you?

Yes, Paul.

Christ, I wish I could see your face as you read this. I picture you going red, maybe having to re-read that sentence a couple of times to make sure it means what you think it means. And yes; it does.

Still reading? Or have you thrown these pages across the room? Even if you have, I know you will come back to them eventually.

It was at that barbecue at his and Peggy's. Do you remember? In June. I don't mean that's when we did it, that took time to arrange, but that was when I decided we would. I was wearing that green and white summer dress again, as it happens. I realise now that I took to wearing it quite often. I'm not sure why.

Anyway, I caught Paul looking at me, just a standard, everyday "Jane is looking pretty today" sort of look that any man might give to a female friend without it meaning anything special, but I returned his glance with just a flicker of a smile so that he would know that I had spotted it and he smiled sheepishly back. So far so normal but the next time our eyes met I made sure to hold his gaze just that fraction too long. That was all it took; every word we exchanged from that moment on, every glance, was laden with meaning.

It was just an idea at that point, sleeping with him, but then Peggy said something snide about what it must be like posing for "The Great Man". I don't recall exactly what she said, but I remember clearly how she emphasised those words, "The Great Man" and raised her eyebrows in a way that I just knew was meant to convey that she thought I must be having an affair with Vivian, not only that but that everyone else there would be thinking the same thing and, more, that she wanted me to know it. Did she say something about how it must be very tiring? I think she did. I smiled and said something anodyne in return but inside I was thinking how much I was going to enjoy seducing her husband.

Naturally, I let him think he was the one doing the seducing. I knew it would be much more exciting for both of us that way. Seducing your best friend's wife: it's the ultimate proof of superiority between men, isn't it? Did you not notice him standing a little taller when he was around you, being a touch firmer in his opinions? I did. I even thought it was so obvious that you might suspect something but I watched you closely and could tell that you remained completely in the dark.

It was easy, engineering his seduction of me. Do you remember the very loud Hawaiian shirt he had been wearing at the barbeque? I'm sure you do; it attracted a lot of comment on the day, which of course was his intention. When I sent Peggy a thank-you message, I made sure to mention it.

"Please tell Paul how much I admire his courage in wearing that shirt," I wrote.

I suppose there was a risk that she wouldn't pass the message on but evidently she did because on the Monday he sent a message from his work email defending his sartorial tastes in a suitably light-hearted manner; I forget precisely what he wrote; but the point was he had contacted me so he would feel that it was he who made the first move, no matter how subtle. From there it was child's play to keep a light-hearted email exchange going until he plucked up the courage to suggest we meet for lunch. He never stood a chance, really.

I won't bore you with the mechanics of how we arranged our liaison. I was spending so much time with Vivian by then it was very straightforward and Helen, who knew no more than you did whether I was really due to sit for Vivian, was on hand to babysit. I had also reached a point where I would hardly have cared if you had found out. Of course, I owed it to Paul to try and keep it a secret, which I have – until now.

I'm not sure you realise how much he admires you. He does you know, very much.

I know you sometimes felt, because he earns so much more than you in banking, that perhaps he looked down on you, when quite the opposite is true. He looks up to you for sticking to what you love, even though it left you in relative penury. Funny to think that, in so very many ways, he knows you better than I do.

I suppose I must have killed that friendship now. I should be sorry, I know. Perhaps I am.

He shook a little, which surprised me, when he started to undress me, it was just one little twitch of his hand as he reached for my top button and he quelled it instantly but I noticed it and it betrayed how excited he was, so excited that he couldn't quite contain that first rush of adrenaline.

When we were finally naked and in bed, I spent a moment licking and nibbling at one of his nipples, curious to see how he would react.

He sighed heavily and said, "Christ Jane, that's so good."

I really didn't want him spoiling things with an absurd porn-movie commentary so I placed my finger on his lips and whispered "Shhhh!" then slowly worked my way down his body, keeping my eyes locked on his all the time.

When my tongue first touched him, just the merest flick, he let out a little squeal. It wasn't very manly – I almost laughed, which would have been too cruel – but then I was suddenly aware of an immense feeling of power, of being completely in control. That little squeal had been enough to tell me how desperate he had been for me to lick him there, how much he wanted me to lick him there again. And it was completely up to me to give that pleasure or deny it. I licked him again, firmly with the flat of my tongue and he bucked involuntarily.

With that realisation of power over him came also the realisation that I wanted to do absolutely everything for him, with him.

I know you love to sixty-nine; but it doesn't really work for me, which is why we hardly ever did it.

I did it with him though, deliberately, precisely because it was something I generally denied you. I instigated it myself, turning my body round before he realised what I was doing and lifting my thigh over his face, straddling him with me on top, bending forward and doing everything my lips and fingers and mouth could think of to please him, making sure to respond to his tongue with my hips as well, so that he would know how turned on I was. It must have been the biggest thrill for him, don't you think, Michael, having his best friend's wife straddle him like that? I was impressed that he didn't orgasm, to be honest. I could tell that he was right on the edge on occasion. I suppose that he must have been desperate to hold on, not to let himself go, so that we could fuck properly.

Eventually we did. He was good, really quite skilled with excellent stamina. I had always thought that he might be; he has that look about him. I think he is a little bigger than you are too; although, to be honest, how big a man feels when he's inside me depends as much on how aroused I am as his actual dimensions.

Of course, I was so turned on by the whole thing that I was bound to come, but I actually came a couple of times before he did, which, as you know, is rare for me. We were in the doggy position, by the way, when he eventually came inside me that first time. And no, we didn't use a condom.

I kept him there for most of the day, fetching some wine and some snacks to drink and eat while we recovered. We chatted too, in between bouts of lovemaking, talked about all sorts of different things: private things that I'm not going to tell you.

We did it three times in the end and I orgasmed each time.

After we had done it that third time, when I had finished kissing him deeply the way I like to afterwards and I was hauling myself off him, exhausted and thoroughly sated, I saw that smug, self-satisfied look on his face that men get when they think they've been an absolute stud in bed. Even though I'd had a great time, probably the best sex I've ever had – sorry, Michael, but it's true – I decided right then that we weren't going to do it again.

I feel dirty, soiled, and sordid, after writing that. Not because of what I did but because of the relish I took in describing it to you, using those words to taunt you. You must realise I wrote it up that way to hurt you as much as I possibly could. You do realise that don't you?

And that was why I did it, too. To hurt you. I could never be sure that my affair with Vivian would pain you as much as it should. But I knew that this would. And what have I laid waste to in the process? A lifelong friendship, someone else's marriage.

I met up with Peggy a few weeks after my day with Paul: not to gloat; please don't think that; she suggested meeting up and I just couldn't think of an excuse not to.

I looked at this woman, as she burbled away happily about some domestic nonsense, half talking to me, half-playing with her son, and thought that I quite probably had already destroyed her marriage, her life really, that it was likely that sooner or later, maybe tomorrow, or maybe in a year, possibly several years, the secret already nestling in the dark recesses of her kitchen cupboard, the secret that was there every time she kissed her husband, when he fondled her breasts, lay sweating and panting on her after they had made love, would show itself in all its ugliness.

I had done it, without bearing even the slightest malice, to a woman who was in many ways a friend, who had never done me any harm, except perhaps the trifling matter of a couple of knowing looks, a snide comment or two, done it entirely for my own reasons, reasons that were nothing to do with her or even her husband, a husband who had been nothing more than a tool that came conveniently to hand, something that had proved oh so easy to turn to my purpose.

It will probably be him, I thought. There had been a curious expression in his eyes when I had seen him last. It might have been a yearning or a regret but it had seemed to me more akin to the look of one who is haunted, of a man who is visited by the same ghost whenever he is alone with his thoughts and will one day be unable to stop himself from doing the only thing that he thinks might possibly exorcise that ghost – introduce it to his wife.

As I was watching her, she bent down to kiss the top of her child's head. When she sat back up, she brushed her hair back where it had tumbled down over the right side of her face and tucked it behind her ear. She is still quite pretty, I thought to myself, although she has surely let herself get just a little heavier than either she or her husband would have wished. She is ten years older than me, remember. And then I was suddenly full of a loathsome smugness. I am superior to you, I thought; I summoned your husband to my bed and he came to me without a second's hesitation, without the smallest compunction or consideration of you and your happiness. I could do that because I'm younger, prettier, slimmer, more enticingly sexual than you are.

I could end your marriage here and now, I thought, turn casually to you and say, "Oh by the way, I slept with Paul the other day." watch your mouth loll stupidly open as you struggled to make sense of such an unexpected combination of words spoken in such an inapposite setting – Paul, slept, I, with – normal, commonplace words you might hear, do hear every day, tens of times a day, but which, grouped together in one particular combination, one order, and on my lips, would mean death to the life that you had thought you would lead forever.

"Yes, when you thought he was still in Birmingham," I might say. "He spent the day with me. He's very good, isn't he? He did it three times in one session. I bet it's been a while since he managed that with you."

Of course I wouldn't, but the very fact that I could felt like a huge weight or like a corset tied too tight, constricting me, squashing the life out of me, not just at my waist and ribs, but all over me: a straight-jacket.

You have that power too now, Michael, or will, if I go through with it and send this to you. Congratulations! I wish you much joy of it.

Vivian noticed. I should have realised that he would. I don't mean that he guessed that I had taken another lover, although, thinking about it, I suppose it is possible that he did; but he could sense that I was different in an important way, when next I sat for him.

"Something's changed," he said.

"In what way?" I asked, trying to seem only half interested.

"I can't quite tell. Has something happened?"

"Nothing new. Things aren't so good with Michael, but you knew that."

"It's not that, something else."

"I can't think of anything."

It was some time later when he said with a wry smile.

"It's another layer to add, I suppose. Bare faced liar."

I'm sorry, Michael: I lied earlier, in my description of my lovemaking with Paul. We did make love three times, but I only had two orgasms in total. I know that won't make things any better for you. That's not my reason for telling the truth now. It's just that I feel cheap for having embellished things just to maximise your pain. I could go back and change it but it's done now. I don't have the energy.

25

As the weeks passed, certainly from when he and I became lovers, my life, my real life, the life that mattered to me, was more and more my life with Vivian. The time spent away from him was empty for me, a matter of waiting for time to pass until I would be back with him and during that time, my mind would drift more and more to thoughts of him, even Alice's demands were seldom enough to keep me fully present.

When we went for Sunday lunch with your parents, at the Windmill, and sat outside – I'm sure you will recall: it was tremendously hot and your father sent his steak back because it was still blue inside – I remember looking across at your mother, so happily ignorant, playing with Alice on the grass, and wondering what she would think if she had known that you and I had not made love for weeks, that I was sleeping with another man, and that you almost certainly knew it.

And at that thought, my mind wandered back to Vivian's house. I wondered what he would be doing then, whether he would be painting: someone in the Day Studio, perhaps, at that time in the afternoon. Or, notwithstanding the time of day and the soaring temperature, might he be cocooned with someone in the timeless womb of the Night Studio: the worldly politician, perhaps: the unknown young woman.

Or there was another time when you had been talking about something to do with your career. I'm sorry. I can't remember what it was but that's the point. We were having supper at the kitchen table and you said, "What do you think?" summoning me back to the room, where I had not been for long minutes. I had been outside the door of the Night Studio, trying to catch something of the conversation going on behind it while the mystery young woman posed for Vivian.

"I'm sorry. I drifted off," I said.

You went so pale – pale with anger, I think – and stood up saying, "Christ Jane," before storming out, slamming the door behind you. I still don't know what it was you had been talking about. I suppose it must have been something important to you. It must have hurt to be ignored like that.

I knew then that it would soon be over for us, that you must have been close to breaking point. And I realise now, considering that moment, and others like it, how very selfish I had become. A woman who was not as self-centred as I had become, would not have stayed with you for as long as I did. Does that sound strange? I think you will understand, at least in part.

One morning, waiting for Vivian in the dining room, I forwent my custom of reading and instead stood by one of the tall sash windows that looked out onto the street. Below me, London came and went, like a hyperactive child, unable to sit quietly even for a moment, whilst inside the house remained constant, silently contemplative, remorselessly introspective. Vivian claimed to eschew introspection. I wondered whether that was really true. Could someone so artistic be truly artless, the painter as noble savage, always seeing the world afresh, as it is, untainted by artfulness?

I sensed a shadow move behind me and turned to catch a fleeting glimpse of someone entering the pantry. I made my way around the dining table and out onto the landing to check who it might be.

It was Susan, wearing only a dressing gown of black silk and a pair of socks. The dressing gown was not short but did not reach quite down to her feet either and was fastened very loosely so that a large expanse of wrinkled, sagging cleavage was visible between its folds. Her largely grey hair, which up until then I had only ever seen her wear up, was down and noticeably unkempt. It was all I could do to stop myself from deliberately scenting the air around her. Even so, I was aware of a melange of aromas, a woman's perfume, expensive, with an element of sweet spices, mixed with her own scents, unfamiliar to me, and, like a base note grounding it all, Vivian's familiar, distinctive odour.

"I needed a drink," she said.

She reached up for a glass where it stood on a high shelf and as she did so, the dressing grown rose slightly, revealing the backs of her knees beneath its hem.

"I may be well into my fifties," she said with a thin

225

smile as she turned on the tap and filled the glass, "but I can still entice him to join me between the sheets every now and then."

She turned to face me and leant back against the sink as she took a sip of her water, eyeing me with a look of restrained but nevertheless evident animosity, tinged with a touch of triumph.

"How old are your two children again, Susan?" I asked.

She laughed.

"They're not his you know," she said. "If that's what you're trying to insinuate. They really are my husband's. I was extremely careful on that score, I assure you."

I could feel the strength of my ill-feeling towards this woman dissipating, not in the sense of warming to her or of a developing empathy, more in the manner of not having the energy to maintain my animosity.

I brushed my hair back from my face.

"God, I'm tired," I said.

"You might be surprised to hear it, Jane, but I really do love my husband. I think I always have. This…" – she gestured to the building around us with a small circle of the hand in which she held her glass of water – "…well, it's complicated."

She contemplated her glass for a moment.

"Anyway, my husband has his own pleasures too."

What had happened to me? How had I come to a state of mind where I could have a calm, polite – outwardly polite, at least – conversation with a woman who had come fresh from making love to the man that I was sleeping with, knowing, as I did so, that this discovery would not make me hesitate to welcome him between my thighs the next time he sought to place himself there, even if that next occasion were that very same day.

Was I jealous? Yes. Not jealous of their recent congress, or, if so, only slightly, but jealous of the depth of their relationship, the long intimacy that she had shared with him over the many years of their affair. I was aware too, that she had come from his bedroom, a place where I had not been admitted. Colin had told me that by being welcomed into the rest of the house, I had reached an elevated status not granted to all Vivian's models and I felt that to be true but our lovemaking had been confined to the studio, the couch on which I posed. I had not been permitted entry into that inner sanctum.

But I was to be.

In the first weeks, before we became lovers, Vivian had asked me whether I had ever seen the Holbein portrait of Erasmus when, you will recall, the three of us had, in fact, studied it together. So, when he asked whether I knew it, although I hesitated, I said, "We saw it together at the National Gallery."

I won't pretend that I wasn't a little hurt that he had apparently forgotten that we had stood together in front of that painting for at least ten minutes, surrounded by a small clutch of respectfully eavesdropping tourists, while he expounded at length some of his theories of portraiture. I could have ignored the slight but, although I wasn't exactly angry, I was irritated enough to want to remind him.

He glanced at me, tacitly extending an apology.

"Well, do you think it's an accurate portrait? I mean as a representation of the physical object that was Erasmus, at the age of whatever."

"I don't know. I assume so."

"But is it important to you that it should? Surely, it is successful as a work of art, without our knowing, having any possibility of knowing, what the man himself actually looked like."

"I suppose."

He seemed disappointed with me.

"Actually, no," I said. "I can see how that might apply to an anonymous portrait. You know, *Portrait of a Young Man*. But Erasmus is such a significant historical figure that I think we do want to know what he really looked like. I think people are curious about that. I know I am."

"I'm not painting to satisfy people's curiosity; that's for sure."

"No. That I can see."

"Well, what about this then? This painting of you. You're not a significant historical figure, are you?"

I laughed.

"So, I've asked you before, what do you want out of it? What will you be looking for when it's done?"

"I think, above all, I'll be trying to see what you really think of me."

We were silent for a considerable length of time until eventually I said, "I suppose I should be careful what I wish for."

He did not respond, but everything about the way he silently considered the canvas made me think that I was almost certainly right about that.

As I say, that had been before we were lovers but I thought about it again after we were.

"We talked about it – when? – weeks ago," I said to the ceiling. "I think I tried to make light of it, but I really was worried what you're going to make me look like and I still am, even more so, now that we are lovers."

Vivian laughed.

"Is that what you think we are?"

He said it so lightly, so glibly, as if our lovemaking were merely an incidental detail of our lives. I took an involuntary, sharp intake of breath. It was as if he had slapped me hard across the face.

I sat up quickly.

"Fuck, Vivian!" I shouted. "I mean – Fuck!"

I had a sense of the building around me vibrating in response.

He was suddenly very still.

"How can you be so heartless?"

He remained motionless. My eyes started to well up, but then I sensed my anger growing, beating down my feelings of self-pity and I blinked the tears away.

"I'm not being paid for this you know?"

"Aren't you?" he said. "Not even in kind?"

I stood up and hurriedly pulled my knickers on.

"That's it. Fuck you and fuck the painting."

I didn't bother with my bra, just pulled my dress on hurriedly, grabbed the bra and my shoes, and headed for the door. Vivian was instantly at my side and had hold of my forearm, stopping me, still holding his pallet and brushes in the other hand.

"Let go of me!"

I shook his restraining hand away.

He stepped ahead of me and put his hand on the door.

"If you try and stop me," I said in a quiet fury, "I swear to God…"

"Please, Jane. I'm sorry. I really am."

He let go of the door and held his hand up slightly in a gesture of pacification.

"I'm unused to…"

He tailed off, as though he genuinely did not know what there was between us.

I stepped forward and took hold of the doorknob slowly, deliberately, waiting to see whether he would make a move to stop me again. He did not.

I opened the door, paused for a moment, then turned to him and held out my hand.

"Take me up to your bedroom," I said.

He hesitated just for a second, then took hold of my hand.

"No more fucking on the couch," I said. "Take me upstairs and go with me into your bedroom, where we can make love."

We made love fiercely, as though we were still fighting. I straddled him, sitting upright so that I was on full display, revelling in his lust for me as I rode him without restraint. At the end, I used my fingers on myself so that we came together. It was the first time that we had.

26

I realise that I haven't mentioned Clare very much. Looking over what I've written, I can see that you would easily form the impression that I saw more of Susan than of Clare, when the truth is quite the other way around. Clare would drift in and out of the house frequently. Often it was evident that she had stayed the night; I might cross her on the stairs on her way out or find her sitting at the dining table with her hair still damp from a morning shower or bath. She would even more frequently be there when I left, waiting to go out with Vivian to supper with friends or some event or other.

I find it difficult to believe that I could be so relaxed, knowing that I was sharing my lover with another woman – two, of course, since I would have to include Susan – and yet I was; relaxed I mean. I suppose it had never at any time been a possibility that Vivian and I would be exclusive. Whatever it was I was looking for in Vivian's arms, it was not monogamy. Nor had he asked me to give you up, although the truth is I think he knew that you and I no longer made love.

I liked Clare. In other circumstances we might have been friends. I don't mean to imply that we were enemies, far from it, but we were never going to be truly close.

Before one of my evening sittings with Vivian, she joined me in the dining room.

"Do you want a drink?" she asked.

I hesitated.

"I'm having one."

She opened a door of the sideboard to reveal a collection of spirits and took out a bottle of whisky. I felt rather uncomfortable at the idea of helping ourselves to Vivian's drink without him there, even though he was a generous host and I was sure that he would have told her on some other occasion that she should help herself.

"I won't, thanks."

She shrugged and poured herself a full measure.

"He wants me to move in with him," she said, after taking a sip. "He likes having a steady girlfriend; I think you know that already – even though she has to be…," she looked straight at me for a moment, holding my gaze. "… understanding."

"Are you going to?"

She shook her head.

"I don't think I would last ten minutes," she said, "I can put up with things as they are." She sighed and took another sip of her drink. "Just about. But the thought of me being up here, I don't know, reading a book, while he shags some journalist in the broom cupboard. I couldn't do it."

She turned to study me.

"He does that, you know," she said, "does it in the

broom cupboard."

From the way she studied my reaction, I think she was looking to see whether I had had sex in there with him.

"Wouldn't that be terribly uncomfortable?" I asked.

"Oh yes," she said and smiled mischievously. "It is."

I think that disarming frankness of hers was one of her characteristics that made it so easy to like her, to not resent her part in Vivian's life.

"Can you guess how we met?"

I shook my head.

"In a pub. I was there with a group of friends. He was drinking at the next table, just him and Colin, and he leant over to me and said, 'My name's Vivian Young and I want to paint you.' Simple as that."

"Had you heard of him?"

"Yes, but only vaguely if I'm honest. I didn't know any of his works or anything. But he had that thing about him, the whole famous thing. It's just sexy, isn't it? So I said yes. And the next morning we were doing it in the broom cupboard."

"How old are you?" I asked.

She smiled.

"Twenty-three."

I find it difficult to believe that I could feel old in the context of a relationship with a man some of whose children are significantly older than me and yet I did. I suppose I've always felt fundamentally young. I don't mean always youthful, just younger than most people in my life: my brother, you, most of our friends, all your colleagues.

Being an August baby might have something to do with it too. But at that moment, sharing a smile with Clare, I felt a fully mature woman, teetering on the edge of middle age. How ridiculous of me, I was only twenty-six and she is only three years the younger.

On my way out that evening, after sitting for Vivian, I paused in the hallway. There was a door opposite the Day Studio. I opened it carefully, revealing a broom-cupboard, with an upright vacuum cleaner, some mops and brushes, shelves of cleaning things. Would a couple really have room to make love in there? It would be a very tight fit, assuming they closed the door, which presumably would be partly the point. I was aware of a feeling of disapproval linked to one of superiority. I would never have sex in a broom cupboard. I was sure of that.

But was it so far removed from making love on a couch in an artist's studio?

I had said, "No more fucking on the couch." But it didn't work out that way. I had been admitted to Vivian's room, returned there with him from time to time for leisurely lovemaking, but we would still mostly do it hurriedly on the couch before I sat for him. That was what needed to be done so that he could paint me as he felt he had to.

Was it a trick, do you think, that protestation of need? As artfully contrived as my seemingly playful email exchange with Paul. Does it matter if it was? Might it even have been tending towards the mechanical, a matter of routine, like a middle-aged couple who make love once a week, always on a Friday night?

"You haven't slept with every woman you've painted, have you?" I asked him once. "I mean not counting your daughters, obviously."

Our eyes met for an instant. His rebuked mine.

"I'm sorry," I said.

We lapsed into a silence that was more awkward than most we had experienced in that room.

"I don't have to sleep with a woman to get to know her," he said, eventually, after I don't know how many uncomfortable minutes, "but I'll admit I feel that it helps."

He selected a tube of paint from the pile, a pile that seemed to have grown over the weeks.

"Not everything in my life is an aspect of my art. I sleep with women because I want to, because I enjoy it."

"I suppose I should be relieved," I said, glad that we were talking, after the strained silence. "Isn't it, though? An aspect of your art; I rather think it is."

The paint in the corner of the ceiling had peeled a little more over the weeks.

"The answer to your original question is no, of course not," he said. "I have not slept with every woman I have painted, very far from it."

"Good. It wouldn't be very flattering to me if you had."

He smiled.

"Happy now?"

I did not answer.

"There is an artifice," he said, "that is unique to humankind: the tendency to present ourselves as though we are not animal. And yet we are. The act of sexual intercourse is the simplest, most direct way to do away with that pretence."

"You might find it simple, Vivian," I said. "I find it anything but."

He laughed.

"So, you sleep with women to dehumanise them?"

"Christ, no. I'm looking to humanise them, by which I mean reveal them to be the fully functional human animal that they are and not just accept the demure, surface shimmer that they project. It's one of the reasons we can never know our parents properly. We stubbornly deny them their sexuality."

"You could say the same thing about going to the toilet, couldn't you?" I said. "People do. No one looks elegant sitting on the loo. But surely you don't need to see someone excreting before you can paint them well."

He laughed again and said, "It wouldn't do any harm."

We were silent for some minutes after that but his thoughts, it would seem, had remained on the scatological.

"The Romans built their public lavatories with the holes so close together that at busy times it was inevitable that you would be rubbing thighs with your neighbour while you took a dump. Did you know that?"

"No, Vivian, I didn't."

We took a break, went up to the pantry and had a little left-over grouse and a glass each of a deep red burgundy.

"Do you struggle then," I asked, cradling my glass and savouring the blackberry and cherry bouquet, "to paint women who are not your lovers?"

"I don't feel it to be an issue when I'm painting, no. But then, when I do paint a woman who is my lover, I feel a certain, well closeness, that I can't help but think will show itself on the canvas."

A certain closeness?

"It must be a very different experience for you painting a naked man."

"In some ways, indubitably, but at heart it is the same process."

He considered for a moment.

"I would say, however, that, whilst everyone is more vulnerable, more truly themselves without clothes, with men the bravado that clothes give them is so much of how they present themselves that the difference is all the more stark."

"Then why, in so many of your portraits of men, are they fully clothed?"

He smiled.

"That's what they want, mostly."

"So you would say that women want to be painted naked, mostly."

"Yes. I would say that."

"Do you ever actually ask them?"

He did not answer.

"Why would they want to be naked, rather than clothed?" I asked. "It couldn't be vanity, surely. Not the

238

way your paintings tend to be."

"I've thought about that quite a lot and I'm still not sure. Curiosity, maybe. I think perhaps they want to know how I really see them. You said something like that yourself once and, in that context, I am just a proxy for the world at large. I think that, although it frightens women, the thought of what the world really thinks of them, it fascinates them too."

"You didn't ask me whether I wanted to be painted as a nude or not."

"No."

He drained his glass.

"But then I don't recall telling you to take your clothes off, either."

27

Another party: I remember the reason for this one because it was the first time that I saw Susan and Oliver in the same room; I was going to say together but I'm not sure I saw them exchange a single word. It was a press screening of Oliver's latest production. I had not been invited to the screening but Oliver told Vivian that I should drop by to the drinks if I wished.

I'm not sure why I got into the habit of going to those parties, receptions. I suppose I enjoyed them, mostly, on balance. I think perhaps it was more because I felt that it was expected of me. Of course, they were also an opportunity to spend some more time in Vivian's company outside of the studio. I do recall noticing, when I arrived that evening, that I had met several of the guests before, enough to make small-talk easy, so that I did not feel awkward or out of place, even though I did not, at first, see Vivian among them.

When I did pick him out among the guests, he was in a group chatting with Oliver. I set out across the room to say hello, when I saw that Clare was also there. Her presence stopped my progress and I hesitated. I sensed that it might be uncomfortable to insert myself into a group with both

Vivian and she in it. Another person might have relished the chance to stimulate some awkwardness but I am not that person.

As I stood there for a moment, considering, I heard a voice behind me, which I recognised as Susan's.

"Hello, Jane," it said.

I turned.

"Susan. How are you?"

"Well, thanks. What did you think of the film?"

I felt sure that she knew I hadn't seen it.

"I missed it, I'm afraid."

"Oh! That's a pity. I would have thought it would be useful to keep on top of contemporary cinema."

I wasn't quite sure what she was getting at.

"Oliver tells me that you're an English teacher."

It struck me how little I had told her of myself. All she knew of me seemed to have come from her husband.

"Yes, that's right."

"I wonder you can find the time to sit for Vivian."

"I'm on maternity leave," I said. "I have a young daughter."

She pounced on that.

"So, you take time off teaching to spend with your new-born but end up spending all your time with Vivian."

It hit home. For a moment I looked down into my glass, unable to think of a retort.

"I wouldn't worry," she said, "we all find it difficult to say no to Vivian."

I couldn't stop myself from nodding in agreement. She

smiled.

Across the room, Clare and Vivian were chatting animatedly in their group. Clare laughed happily at something.

"What about your husband?" said Susan. "Vivian told me you were married. An English lecturer, yes?"

"Yes."

"What does he think? I mean, he must realise you're fucking Vivian, mustn't he?"

That word jarred, coming to me from another woman's lips. I hesitated for a moment, but I didn't have the energy to lie.

"Yes."

It was the first time I had expressed that truth so starkly, even to myself, that you must have known that I was sleeping with Vivian. Hitherto, in my thoughts, I had always hedged around that probability with doubt, uncertainty, but in the face of Susan's maliciously artful probing it felt less than useless to cavil.

"You know how restrained Vivian's titles for his works tend to be?"

I did not answer.

"*Blonde Woman, Figure on Bed*. That sort of thing."

There was a distinctly mischievous glint in her eye, I might almost say malevolent.

"He told me he was thinking of calling yours *Mrs. Michael Smith*."

Later, I wondered how Susan had been so sure that I was sleeping with Vivian. Had she just assumed it, as everyone seemed to? Was her question about you, perhaps aimed at verifying her suspicion? Or had Vivian told her?

Vivian had described Clare as his Pompadour, meaning his official mistress; but I wondered. One of Madame de Pompadour's roles had been to vet the king's subsequent mistresses, suggest them even. It seemed to me that Susan would be more likely to serve that function and thus be more obviously suited to that sobriquet. Had she vetted Clare? Was I perhaps someone who had not obtained her approval, that she had not vetted? That might explain her evident animosity towards me.

I looked back over to where Vivian had been, but could no longer see him or, indeed, Oliver. The group they had been with seemed to have dispersed. Clare was momentarily alone and came over to join Susan and me.

"So," said Clare, brightly, but slightly hazily, "the full harem is here."

I had the impression that the nearly empty glass of champagne in her hand was not her first nor, indeed, her second.

"What fun," she said. "Although I don't suppose this is all of us, not really, what do you reckon?"

Susan showed no sign of wishing to engage with her.

"Still," Clare went on, "I guess we are the main ones for the time-being. Shall we exchange notes? Helpful hints and tips, perhaps, about Vivian's likes and dislikes. I hear you give really good head, Susan."

Susan's reaction was instantaneous; too quick to be the result of any inner verbalisation or decision, she slapped

Clare hard across the face. The smack reverberated around the room, everyone seemed to give a gasp and then fell silent. Clare put her hand to her rapidly reddening cheek and her eyes were instantly brimming with tears. I instinctively reached my hand forward to touch her arm, but she shrugged it off and hurried from the room, barely stifling her first sobs, in irrepressible floods of tears by the time she reached the door.

"Christ, Susan," I said. "She's only a girl."

Susan countered any remorse that might have been welling up inside by turning her anger on me.

"And that makes you the mature grown-up, does it?"

Everyone else in the room was still, silently watching us so that her words rang clear and crisp to every ear.

The first to break the spell was Colin, who headed for the door, saying, "I'll check she's alright."

It was enough to moderate the general tension slightly; there were a few nervous laughs, and then, cluster by cluster, the room renewed its general hubbub. The guests might have resumed talking and were less obviously staring at Susan and me but I remained acutely self-conscious, not doubting that they were mostly, if not exclusively, talking about us.

"Well, as Clare put it, what fun!" I said. "Does Vivian relish the chaos he creates in people's lives, do you think?"

I looked around the room searching for him once more but still could not pick him out.

"It's all the same to him," Susan said, her anger and irritation apparently waning but still showing no signs of remorse. "All more colour for his pallet."

She looked down at her hand. It was flushed red.

"That actually hurt," she said.

I have come to realise that I am not one of those people, who can entirely disassociate the act of sex from love itself; the two for me will always be intertwined. I do not mean to say that I am incapable of making love without already being in love, far from it. I don't think I was even a little bit in love with Vivian when I first welcomed him inside me. And as for Paul, well... What I mean is that there is always for me, even when I am looking to enjoy sex in the most animal, most purely physical way, a question of where the act, the giving and taking of pleasure in that way will lead.

You must have thought me cruel when I refused to sleep with you anymore. Perhaps I was. But I think instead that I was merely being honest. To continue to have sex with you when I was making love to Vivian, would have been, I think, a terrible deception, a cruel lie. Besides, I honestly don't think I could have done it, physically, I mean. I'm sure I would have been too painfully dry.

I didn't tell him about that night, by the way. I'm sure you know the one I mean, when you turned to me and touched my hip with that irritatingly tentative manner you have and I cracked, telling you straight that sex was off the cards for the foreseeable future and that I wasn't sure when it would be back on – that I would let you know.

When you didn't say anything, anything at all in response, I remember thinking, What's wrong with you?

Why don't you shout and scream, throw me out or say you want a divorce, anything but lie there mute.

How long was it before you got up and went to the bathroom? Ten minutes? Twenty? You tried to move so that I wouldn't see it but I clearly saw your erection.

Then, when you came back you were entirely flaccid and I couldn't stop myself from saying, "Nice wank?" as you climbed back into bed.

It was horrible of me and I wish to God I hadn't said it. But there it is. I did.

You tried to hide them but I could sense your tears through the darkness. I'm sure that you were still crying when I eventually drifted off to sleep.

"I don't think I can do this anymore," Clare said.

"What?"

"This. All of it."

She made a gesture at the walls of the dining room with her dangerously full glass of whisky. It was a clear, fresh summer morning, promising growing warmth. It was not yet eleven.

"I thought I could share him, turn a blind eye to quick fucks in the broom cupboard. But I can't."

She took a swig, eyeing me over the rim of her tumbler.

"But then maybe it's not actually the quickies," she said. "The casual stuff, that I can handle. But I heard you two the other day, when you were in the studio. It was like being punched in the stomach. Serves me right for lurking around, I guess."

"I'm sorry."

"Are you?"

I honestly couldn't decide what a truthful answer would have been.

She went to one of the windows and looked out at the street below. After a few moments she placed a hand on one of the panes of glass.

"It's like a prison this place."

I remember thinking of the disjunct, how a place that was for me an escape, a sanctuary, had become a prison for her. We were both silent for a while as she continued to study the street outside, then she turned to face me.

"How long have you been involved with Vivian?" I asked.

"Involved! You do have a nice way with words, don't you? It must be being an English teacher. We met about two years ago. When was it? August, I think."

"So you were just twenty-one?"

She shrugged.

"He hasn't suggested painting me for months now. He painted me three times like that."

She clicked her fingers three times.

"But that was it. Now he spends hours every day with you. Not me."

"I'm not the only one sitting for him; you know that."

"Is that supposed to help?"

Her glass was empty. She held it up and contemplated it.

"I think that's enough," she said.

She went to the sideboard, hesitated a moment then placed the glass down with deliberation. She stood for a moment more at the sideboard, with both her hands resting on it, then went to the door and, as she reached it, half turned towards me.

"There's nothing here I need. Just a few toiletries that he can throw away. Tell him bye for me. Say it's been fun. He's all yours."

She gave me a last glimpse of her lovely smile. It was sincere, I think.

"See you around," she said.

And that was it. She just went straight downstairs and left.

He was all mine, she had said. We both knew that was not and never would be true.

28

It was far from being the first time I had cried in his studio, nor would it be the last, but it was the first time that I had brought my tears with me from outside. Vivian must have sensed that difference; at least I think he must, for it was the first time that he remarked on them.

"Do you think you could stop that?" he said.

That was enough to knock away whatever prop of self-control I had been resting on and I fell into unrestrained sobbing, so much that I had to break my pose and wipe my cheeks. He tossed a brush down, petulantly.

"This is hopeless."

I sat up and put my head in my hands. After a minute or so sobbing, I sensed Vivian close to me and looked up. He stood in front of me with a box of tissues, his expression had softened.

"I'm sorry," he said. "What's brought this on?"

I sighed and took a tissue, blew my nose.

"It's Michael. I've decided I'm going to leave him."

"Ah. And have you told him?"

"No."

I pictured you as you had said good-bye that morning with Alice in your arms.

"I think he must know though. He's been very quiet. For weeks now. Like a beaten man."

"Is that how you see this, like a competition between him and me?"

I studied the floor, the countless flecks of paint on the bare boards, the precise little chalk marks, like witches' conjuring symbols.

"How many marriages would you say you have wrecked, Vivian?"

"None," he said, "including yours."

We took a break but before long I insisted that we return to the studio and go on with the session. That afternoon, for the rest of the session, Vivian painted in silence. Scene after scene from our life together, yours and mine, rolled before my mind's eye: the look on your face when I told you I was pregnant, a walk in midsummer when we had been caught in a torrential downpour, the view from our hotel in Montmartre, which was almost all that we saw of Paris that weekend because we barely left our room.

We could have been happy, Michael. I'm sure of it.

"We'd better stop," Vivian said, "It's nearly six."

I dressed and, as always, the clothing, the re-covering was a moment of transformation, reconstitution, but that day it was not enough; I felt raw still, exhausted, unable to contemplate the journey home, your looks, whatever suppressed banality you would greet me with.

I slumped back down on the couch and buried my head in my hands.

"I can't do it, Vivian," I said. "I can't face going home. I just can't."

He did not hesitate; his reply was instantaneous.

"Stay then. Stay overnight if you wish."

Stay, stay in that house, sleep there, wake there. I took my hands from my face and looked around me at the blank, paint-flecked walls. It was as though I were seeing them for the first time.

"I don't..." I said but tailed off because I didn't know what it was that I wasn't sure that I was going to do.

"I have to go out, I'm afraid," he said. "It's Sophie's book launch so I can't miss it. Colin's coming too so you'll be on your own."

He was studying a brush closely as he cleaned it, almost as though he were talking to it, not me.

"But perhaps that will be for the best, for now, some time to yourself."

"Perhaps," I said.

Once he had finished clearing up his paints, brushes and pallet, he held out his hand.

"Come on. I'll fix you something to eat."

I took his hand and he led me out of the studio and along the corridor to the main kitchen, which is on the ground floor at the back. What intuition told him that I needed my hand held at that precise moment? His firm, gentle grip was cradling, comforting; it felt as though his hand had taken on itself all burden of decision, that I could relax and let it lead me where it would. He might have taken me upstairs to his bed, or out onto the street and into a taxi; I would have followed wherever he led. Where there had been anguish, mere moments before, there was something akin to joy; it was there where our palms touched so that I felt almost bereft when he let go of me so that he could start to cook.

We had a quail each, seared off in a hot pan then quickly roasted while he fried up onions and mushrooms in French butter, pale-white and unsalted, drizzling the juices from the pan, deglazed with a glug of red wine, over it all. The scents, the sounds roused an appetite I had thought beyond resuscitation. It was delicious, and we shared half a bottle of claret as we ate.

"That was lovely, Vivian," I said. "I feel almost happy again."

"Almost? That's one of my least favourite words," he said, with a rueful smile.

"Give me time."

"Time is something I can give," he said, standing to clear the plates, "But sadly, not now. I need to change. What will you do, while I'm out? I don't have a television."

I was not surprised, my only surprise being perhaps that he had not told me this before.

"There's the radio in here," he said, nodding towards a venerable looking transistor radio on the windowsill. "But there's plenty to read, up in the sitting room. Pick out anything."

"Thanks, I will," I said, following him out and up the stairs.

When we reached the doorway to the sitting room

and he made to continue up to the floor above and to his bedroom, I stopped him for a moment.

"Vivian!"

He turned and raised his eyebrows by way of question.

"Will you hold my hand again, just for a moment?"

I proffered my hand, which he took, cupping it between both of his. Then, still holding my hand in his left, he moved his right hand to my cheek and touched it. I pressed my cheek against his palm and closed my eyes.

"I need to change," he said, after a moment more.

I studied the books on the shelves of his sitting room for a while, noting one or two that interested me. I felt as though I would probably take one down later to read but not just yet; I had little doubt that my eyes and thoughts would not yet permit me to stay focussed on a page for any length of time. I went to sit on the sofa.

I thought of you.

You would probably have returned from the Faculty and relieved Helen of her duties by that time, I calculated. I pictured you feeding Alice, making funny faces and silly sounds, trying to encourage her to eat, imagined her squidging the food between her fingers and then licking them with a cheeky twinkle in her eyes.

That was when I sent you the text

"Staying overnight. See you tomorrow pm."

I may as well have texted "Marriage over." You understood that, of course.

Poor Alice.

Vivian appeared at the door. I looked up at him from where I sat on the sofa.

"The reception itself will be over by nine," he said, "but there's every chance we'll go on somewhere, so there's no telling when I'll be back."

"I'll be fine," I said, smiling at him. "I'm so tired, I think I won't be able to stay up and wait for you."

"Of course."

"Where shall I sleep?"

Four simple words. I might as well have asked him to tell me what my life was going to be from that moment on.

"In whichever room you choose."

The burden of decision was mine once more.

With a quick good-bye he turned and went downstairs. When I heard his steps reach the bare boards of the hallway, I rose and hurried out onto the landing.

I called down to him, bending over the bannister to catch a glimpse of him as he approached the front door.

"Vivian!"

He stopped and retreated a pace or two, looking up at me.

"What if I fall asleep in your bed?"

"I told you. Sleep wherever you wish."

I smiled down at him and he raised his hand by way of farewell, disappearing from view as he went towards the door again. I heard it open, but not close, heard him stepping back along the corridor. When he was back where I could see him from my vantage point, he looked up at me a second time.

"My bed is yours now, Jane," he said, "if you want it to be."

We shared a smile and then he left.

For some minutes after he had gone, I stayed there on the landing and listened to the silence of the house around me, a silence that was not a silence. Somewhere a clock ticked and, although the walls were thick, there was the constant low hum of the city outside. My eyes followed the elegant curves of the Newell staircase up to the third floor then down to the hall below. I seemed to have chanced upon the midpoint of the house, a house that was mine alone for the next few hours, a house that encircled me enticingly, willing me to explore.

Not wishing to give up too soon the pleasure of savouring that possibility, I returned to the sitting room and scanned more purposefully than I had before the book-laden shelves, picking out a biography of Rodin. The introduction alone was enough to tell me that he had had his share of "muses" too, a young Gwen John, sister of Augustus John among them, at a time when Rodin would have been roughly the age that Vivian was then. Muse. Was I beginning to consider myself as such?

No; I was not conceited enough to think that. If I were to have walked out then, never seeing him again, there would have been no effect at all on his art, save for a single unfinished canvas that he would be forced to put aside, just one of many that he had not finished for one reason or another over the years. If I had left then, no biographer of his, even compiling a tome as thick and heavy as the book that lay open on my lap, would so much as mention my name. I doubted whether I would merit a mention even if I stayed, save perhaps being identified as the subject of one of his paintings.

And yet, there I was, in sole possession of his house, sitting at his sofa, reading his books.

Rodin. Young. They could be named in the same sentence without foolishness, could be compared; it might not be beyond thought to consider Vivian the greater artist of the two. Most would not agree, I suppose, but that comparison could be made in all seriousness. I contemplated the thick book on my lap for a moment, not the words, but the physical object. It was a dizzying thought: the man I was sleeping with, whose bed was mine if I wished it, would one day be considered, like Rodin, worthy of five hundred pages of good quality paper and a hardback cover.

There was an irony, I was conscious of it, of finally, on that day of all days, feeling something of the significance of the offer to become involved in his life that had so beguiled you, that had made you push me towards his studio, towards his bed.

There was a rattle, faint but perceptible somewhere on one of the floors above, the breeze from an open window pressing on a closed door, perhaps. It was the house reminding me that it was there. I put down my book and stepped out of the sitting room, out onto the landing, returning to my imagined mid-point of the house: at the other end of the landing stood the two rooms I knew best outside of the Night Studio: the dining room and pantry, below, the two studios, the main kitchen, the salacious broom cupboard and another door, which I had not seen opened; above were Vivian's bedroom, the main bathroom, and two other rooms I had not entered; they might be guest bedrooms; I did not know; on the floor above that, the top floor where I had never ventured, there would be Colin's bedroom; what else?

I went first to Vivian's room, to prove to myself that I could. I had been admitted several times by then, but always with Vivian and always with my senses intent on impending lovemaking. I could not be sure but thought that this was probably the first time that the door handle had turned under my hand, not his. Entering at my leisure, undistracted by lust, made the room seem both familiar and fresh at the same time: the vast bed with its heavy, burgundy, brocade bedspread, the walls, like all the others in the house a neutral, pale coffee-cream but crammed with art, the two, low bookcases – what special books made their way up here and not to the sitting room? – the high sash windows that looked out on the gardens and mews houses behind and, in the corner, a cheval-glass, with its improbably ornate frame, in which I had caught glimpses of a woman making love and wondered that she could be so unrestrained, so vigorous.

It was not yet time to take possession of that room, so I left, closing the door behind me.

I could go upstairs, not to Colin's room, I had no need to pry into his affairs, but to see what else might be up there. I started up the stairs, four creaking steps, but halted. Vivian had not forbidden entry into any nominated room, issued no fairy-tale injunctions, his ex-wife was alive and well, living with her second husband in the south of France, no one was going to be immured in this elegant Georgian townhouse in West London. And yet each step seamed transgressive, provoking each a tiny frisson of a feeling that I can only call fear. After the fifth step creaked more loudly yet, I turned and retreated, laughing a little at myself.

Wondering what to do next, I remembered that, in the main kitchen where we had eaten our quail, there was some wine left of the claret that Vivian and I had shared with our early supper and I made my way down, only just managing not to hurry. After pouring myself a very full tumbler, I drank it, guilty of doing so too quickly to savour its soft richness, the cherry and chocolate bouquet, as we had done earlier, but it served my need and I felt both steadied and newly energised.

Down there on the ground floor, I could, if I wished, inspect the Day Studio, where I had been only once before, when Vivian had shown me in and explained the difference in purpose between the two studios. But the Night Studio beckoned, with its stack of half-painted canvases, the as yet anonymous nude.

The single light that lit, when I flicked the first switch my hand alighted on, fumbling in the dark by the door, hung from the ceiling rose. Its light was harsh in comparison to the soft array I was used to lying under but I had no wish to try and recreate the carefully crafted template of light that Vivian used when painting; I only wanted to inspect the stack of half-painted canvases once more.

My own canvas was at the top, having been the last that Vivian had worked on. Briefly glancing at it, I set it carefully aside; I had decided, weeks ago, not to study it in any detail; that could wait for when it was finished. As I set it aside, the familiar rear view of a canvas in landscape orientation was revealed as the next in the stack. Did that mean that she had been there that day? Spent her hour or so on the camp-bed before my arrival? It must have been so.

I turned it around with care, anticipation, trepidation, but it was still far from being a recognisable image.

The face now contained two eyebrows, one complete, as far as I could tell, the other nearly so. Although they were the only features of her face that had been even partially realised, together with the overall shape of the head they were enough to begin to give a hint of her. Without being able to place her, I was left with a strong impression that she was someone I had seen before, possibly someone I knew or at least had met, although it could equally have been someone famous, maybe a young actress or model.

It was tantalising to stand in front of that canvas unable to identify the young woman stretched out before me, like having a word on the tip of the tongue. After some minutes studying it, I replaced it carefully, exactly as I had found it, or as best as I could achieve, did the same with my canvas and left.

As I stood at the foot of the stairs, composing myself – yes, I found that I needed composing after the tension of having trespassed once more on Vivian's art – I realised that there was another room calling me, one that might perhaps be more cherished by Vivian even than his bedroom: his bathroom, the room to which he retired at least two or three times each day in undisturbed ritual. Colin, I knew, was under instruction not to interrupt Vivian in his bath, not if the queen herself were at the door.

The bathroom's white door, which stood across the landing from Vivian's bedroom, was as broad as the broad, blue front-door of the house. Pushing it slowly open, I saw that the room beyond, while comfortably sized, seemed to be all bath, a bath that was long and deep, roll-topped, pure-white porcelain placed exactly in the centre of the room.

I was to learn later that there had been a lavatory, but that Vivian had had it removed. "I will not bathe where I shit," he told me.

One side of the far wall was all deep shelving, on which were piled countless thick, white towels. I noticed too, at the other end of that wall, a shelf of soaps and bath salts and shampoos. Knowing that Vivian did not use soap when he bathed, I took them for permission of use, an easement.

The hot water, a fraction too hot at first, when I had filled the bath nearly to the brim, dropped in a mix of salts, perfuming it with citrus and pomegranate and climbed carefully in, was peacefully soothing, the gentle lapping noises whenever I moved, playfully distracting, teasing the house in its silence. I lay back and contemplated the ceiling. It was papered with ancient wallpaper, peeling and stained with nicotine. It was such a contrast to the uniform blankness of the walls and ceilings of the rest of the house. It's patterns of staining, its folds and flecks were mesmerising in their intricacy, and I thought I understood why Vivian had left it unrepaired, unreplaced. Its tones would change constantly, in different lights, in the steam of a freshly drawn bath, developing new creases and crinkles, endlessly intriguing to his artist's eye.

When the water had sadly cooled beyond comfort, I stepped reluctantly out and wrapped myself in one of the room's vast towels. I did not want to put on again the clothes that I had worn that day and had nothing to change into, so stepped across the landing to Vivian's bedroom still wrapped in the towel. There, hanging on a hook on the back of the door, I found the dressing gown of black silk that I had first seen on Susan when I came upon her fresh from Vivian's bed, fetching a glass of water from the pantry. I held it for a moment to my face, testing its scent. I thought I detected some traces of Susan on it, which I took as a challenge. Unwrapping myself from the towel, I put the dressing gown on, smooth against my skin after the towel's cotton loops, and went back down to the sitting room to read some more.

By the time Rodin was twenty-three, my tiredness, temporarily alleviated by the wine and the refreshing waters of the bath, had returned, but it was not unwelcome. I set the book down and took myself up, at last, to Vivian's room.

Hanging the dressing gown where I had found it on the back of the door, I climbed into the vast bed. The cotton sheets, clean and crisp, cool at that first touch, were inviting. I stretched then nestled down. I could not prevent a fleeting glimpse in my mind's eye of you, alone on our sofa, a glass of whisky in hand, from coming to mind, but I dismissed it. That was over. This was where I was meant to be at that time.

I expected sleep to come but it did not. A clock, an old-fashioned alarm clock with a bell at the top, like something from an animated cartoon, ticked softly on the bedside table, its luminescent hands clearly visible in the half-light to which my eyes quickly became adjusted. I noted the time. It was a mistake or was if sleep was what I truly sought. The passing minutes gave a focus to my anticipation of Vivian's return. Perhaps he would be back within ten minutes; he was not; then perhaps ten minutes more; and so it went.

At last, faint, barely perceptible against the quiet hum of the outside world, I heard the noise of a key turning in a lock and a door opening, the front door. Propping myself up on my elbow to listen, I could hear someone moving about quietly below, then, after a few minutes, steps coming up the stairs; they reached the first landing, continued up towards the second floor, where I waited. I held my breath as the steps traversed the landing, anticipating a movement of the handle of the door, and then exhaled as the steps turned away and continued up to the floor above. They must have belonged to Colin, returning alone, and making his way quietly to his room.

That moment of thinking that Vivian had returned and was about to join me made me aware of a mounting unease. What had begun as a lazy luxuriance in the soft sheets of that vast bed had become an increasingly anxious vigil. Conviction that I belonged had given way to doubt. I had entered the room alone, climbed between those sheets alone, and I would be no more than an interloper in another's room until he was there to join me, to confirm by his presence my right to be there.

After many long, counted minutes more, the front door opened noisily, closed again with a clatter. I heard loud, careless footsteps and voices: Vivian's and someone else's, a woman. For a moment I let myself imagine that there might be more voices, a group, but no; there were only two. The voices and steps ascended the stairs from the hall but diverted off at the first floor, to the dining room or perhaps the pantry. Something more than curiosity or pique made me get up, pull on once more the silk dressing-gown and go down to them. I had waited too long. I needed a decision to be made for me, to be taken by the hand and led again.

As I started down the stairs, the unknown woman laughed. They were in the pantry.

She was young and thin and beautiful, with strong, Slavic features and she was tall – in her stilettoes taller than Vivian. I judged that she would perhaps have been his height in her bare feet. She wore skin-tight jeans, accentuating the slimness of her long legs, and a crop-top, showing her lean stomach and a glittering piercing at her bellybutton.

"Jane!" said Vivian as though he had forgotten I would be there, as though the day had been just another ordinary day, as though nothing of significance had occurred. "Join us. Have a drink."

The girl assessed me, gauging my figure with a critical eye.

"Who is this?" I asked.

He turned to the girl.

"Who are you again?"

I had seen him drink – many times – but this was the first time that I had seen him near to being drunk.

"Natalia. You remember, Vivian."

Her accent confirmed her eastern European origins. She did not seem discomfited that he had forgotten her name.

"As you see, Natalia. She's a…"

"Model," she said, saving him the bother of trying to remember.

"This is Jane," he said. "She's also a model too, but a different kind. She poses for me."

He looked at me, assessed my figure the way she had.

"I'm painting her."

"How exciting," said Natalia, her tone of voice belying any enthusiasm.

I didn't have the energy for meaningless exchanges.

"I was waiting for you in your bedroom," I said to

Vivian. "I couldn't sleep."

The girl cocked her head and smiled at me. Her smile, so broad and even, was oddly disconcerting. The improbable regularity of her features rendered her face somehow blank, devoid of personality. Also, something in her manner told of more than alcohol.

"Then, I tell you what," Vivian said, slipping his arm around her slim, bare waist and taking a sip of wine from his glass, "we're just finishing our drinks. Why don't you go back up?"

It was all too much. I had no capacity for struggle. All I could think to do was what he told me to. I turned and made my way slowly back up to his room, slipped off the dressing gown and clambered once more into his bed.

It wasn't long before I heard, through the door that I had left open behind me, footsteps coming up the stairs from the landing below.

The next morning was the bottom for me; I was in a deep, dark well, the walls damp, thick with slime, offering no hint of hand or foothold, no hope of ever clambering out into the light, which was no more than a tiny circle far above my head, unreachable. I rose from Vivian's bed when he was having his morning bath, cleansing himself. Natalia had left, but her perfume, cinnamon and cedarwood, lingered.

I felt grubby, having to wear the same dress and underwear that I had worn the day before. The toast that I made in the pantry, mechanically, unthinkingly, was ash in my mouth. After the first bite, I stopped pretending to myself that I was capable of eating it. Only the coffee reminded me that I was human. When I heard Vivian moving about on the landing, his familiar soft tread, I made no effort to move to greet him and he did not come to find me. Later, after the doorbell rang and he had gone down, after I heard voices entering the Day Studio, I ventured downstairs and left.

And, as I was leaving Vivian's house, you were leaving our home.

I sometimes let myself think that we would have split up anyway, that however much in love we had seemed, had thought we were, however much wrapped up in each other and conjoined by parenthood, that, despite all that, whatever incompatibility there is between us that these past months have revealed would eventually have manifested itself, not so soon perhaps but eventually and inevitably. It is difficult to think of oneself as so buffeted by happenstance that something as fundamental to us could have depended on the chance of Vivian coming to your talk, would not have occurred but for that. But perhaps that is exactly what happened. Perhaps the truth is, that without that random event, not only would we still be together now, reasonably happy and basically in love, but we would have stayed together for life, not always happy, I suppose, or so much in love – that would be unrealistic – but mostly happy, mostly content, a life of shared affection: another me, contentedly juggling teaching and a family life shared with you, instead of being whatever I am now.

What is that? I'm not sure. It's something, and it's me now, but I don't think I would say that I was happy or content, not quite, not yet.

Poor Helen: you shouldn't have involved her, called her to babysit until I returned, if I was going to return. Was that deliberate malice on your part – because she is Vivian's daughter? The poor girl had sent several plaintive texts that morning but I had kept my phone switched off. It's not right, Michael, asking an eighteen-year-old to break the news to your wife that you have left her. She was very upset.

"Oh, thank God you've come. Michael just walked out," she said. "I was saying hello to Alice when he said, 'Say bye to Jane for me; I'm leaving her,' and walked out. I didn't know what to do. I really didn't want to stay but I couldn't leave Alice. When you didn't answer your phone or respond to my texts, I thought of calling your mother but I haven't met or even spoken to her and well…"

Can you imagine her trying to explain what was going on to my mother?

"Hi, I'm Helen, you don't know me; I'm the babysitter; Jane gave me your number for emergencies. Your daughter's husband has just left her. Yes, that's right, because she's having an affair with my father."

Did you even consider taking Alice with you?

29

My mother asked about you the other day. She always liked you, you know.

Actually, that's not completely true. She was a little wary at first, because of the age difference and because you were one of my lecturers. I think she didn't approve of the idea that you had seduced one of your students, although she never said as much. It's funny to think of her first thought of you as being some sort of Lothario. But then, perhaps her thoughts were closer to the truth than I would have said at the time.

I remember now that I had been a little embarrassed too; not about you – don't think that – not about the type of person you were, your character, but by your status. I first mentioned you to her when she was cooking. I think I did that so that there was something going on to distract us. I wasn't in the mood for one of my mother's interrogations. I remember that she was chopping onions because I moved away when I felt my eyes start to sting.

When I said that I had met someone, she just assumed it would be a student and asked what he was studying. It might have been anyone, of course; there was no reason to assume he would be from the university at all, although I guess it was an understandable assumption.

"Actually, he's a lecturer."

She paused her chopping with an "Oh!" but then started again, hoping to hide her instinctive reaction, I suppose, but it was already too late.

"Yes. But he's only visiting for a year. Then he goes back to UCL, where he's based."

"Right."

She went ominously quiet.

I've just remembered now. I told you that she was okay with it, didn't I? That wasn't quite true. It was just that she didn't voice any of her evident disapproval.

"How old is he?"

I told her, and she said "Right," again.

"Anyway, it's not anything serious."

She raised her eyebrows. It was probably a tactical error trying to dilute the news that I was in a relationship with an older man by telling her that it was not serious. It was also a white lie, because I think I was already half in love with you by then. I was certainly infatuated. That's a lovely feeling, being infatuated, if it is a little crazy. I wonder whether I'll feel quite that way ever again. I sometimes think you can feel that way only once in your life and that that's all in the past for me. Christ! Writing that makes me feel old.

She started to work out that there was something wrong, started putting out her feelers quite soon – my mother. She's not stupid or naïve; of course she's not; but I was a little surprised, to be honest, how soon she seemed to discern that something was up between us. I suppose we each naturally have a blind spot about our parents as sexual beings, don't we? You know the sort of thing, not wanting to contemplate that one's parents ever actually did it, let alone regularly and that they might actually have enjoyed it, or ever made love other than in the missionary position. And who would even contemplate, outside of knowing of a specific instance, that one or other of their parents might have had an affair? The thought! So, I guess from that starting point, it's easy to think too that a parent won't be alive to these things, won't have the necessary type of empathy, imagination. But she did.

She started dropping hints that she thought you weren't looking well. Were you perhaps ill? she asked more than once. She thought you looked troubled. Was everything right between us? Had we quarrelled?

And then one day she just came out with it.

"You're having an affair with Vivian Young, aren't you?"

I didn't answer, but I couldn't meet her eye. She knew what my failure to deny it meant.

"Jesus, Jane!"

She so seldom swears.

"How could you? How could you do that to Michael?"

"It's complicated."

"No; it's not," she said angrily. "I did some research about him. Did you not know how infamous he is? How many lovers he's had?"

Again, my silence told her all she needed to know.

"How does it feel just being the latest of a long list? And not the last either, you can be sure of that. How could you agree to pose for him, knowing that? How could Michael let you?"

I finally snapped and stood up.

"Oh, shut up Mum. Shut up! How could Michael let me? It was his bloody idea. He talked me into it."

Her face blanched.

"I told you it was fucking complicated."

I strode out, slamming the door behind me. Alice started crying.

And so did I.

How long have I been writing now? Weeks on and off. You and I have met often during that period, when you come to visit Alice; just yesterday you took her to the park. How far in the past will that day be when you get to read this, if you ever do? She had great fun playing in the sand pit, you said, if that helps you place it. It's been so, so strange saying hello to you, when I might have come fresh from writing about an argument we had, or perhaps some of the good times we had together. Sometimes I feel very guilty, the worst kind of hypocrite, smiling and being polite and friendly, when I've just been setting down in writing a bout of lovemaking with Vivian or the time with Paul.

I wonder when you will be ready to try again, Michael. Start dating, I mean. Somehow, I have a notion that it will be with another student, repeating the pattern. That would be like you, I think, going with what worked before. If you did, she would be younger than me by five or six years, younger than you by fifteen or sixteen; which would be quite an age gap wouldn't it? Unless you went for a grad student of course. Would you go for another redhead, if you could, do that thing famous men do when they ditch their wives of twenty years for a younger model who looks just like the original? Perhaps that only happens when the cause of the split is a mid-life crisis, when the husband dumps the wife, not the other way round.

I wonder if you really do like redheads generally, whether I was really your type, or whether I was simply pretty enough, in a general sense.

When it gets serious, what will you say about your ex-wife, I wonder. I suggest you don't say that she had an affair with someone famous, let alone name him. It might be tempting to get it off your chest, or vent your anger, if that is how you feel, but that sort of thing doesn't reflect well on the innocent party, whatever you might be tempted to think.

If you do eventually settle down with another woman, wouldn't it be funny if she came across the painting some time? I'm sorry; funny isn't the right word. But I wonder whether you would tell her who it was displayed on the canvas: *Picture of the Former Mrs. Smith*.

I realise I've just said I thought you would repeat the pattern, but what about me? I've barely slept with anyone my own age, just a handful of very forgettable, drunken fumbles. Is that mere happenstance or is there something about me that pushes me towards older men?

And I love doing it doggy style. Why I'm telling you now and never told you before I don't know. I should have. I'm sorry. But I'm shy about these things I guess, verbalising them, I mean, not doing them. I wonder whether the taste for doing it that way comes from something deep within me or if it is a sort of imprint from those first few times with James.

I was on the Tube yesterday with Alice. She was being a nuisance because she wanted to walk around the carriage and wouldn't keep still; you know what she can be like. And I found myself doing that thing where you speak loudly to your child, ostensibly reasoning with it, when what you are really doing is making sure that everyone around you knows that you are at least trying to keep her under control. I caught the eye of a boy sitting opposite us; I say boy, but I mean a young man – too young for me really; he can't have been more than twenty-two – and he smiled a kind, understanding smile. He wasn't bad looking.

I'm tired, Michael. This process is much more draining than I thought it would be. I'm going to stop typing now and I'm not sure I will ever come back to it.

30

Well, here I am, unable to stay away from the keyboard.

Just as I was unable to stay away from Vivian's studio.

I had invested too much, lost too much, to walk away then. When he is hungry, he eats, I reasoned. He had told me so himself. I had nothing to rebuke him for. Was I even angry with him? Or was I angry at myself? For not insisting that I was special, for not demanding to be treated in a certain way that I thought I deserved, for letting myself be swept away by him, into the torrent.

It was when my mother came round, which she insisted on doing as soon as she heard that you had left, that I realised I would be going back to him, that I would not stay away. She tried to take my side, to see the split from my point of view, but it was transparently clear that she couldn't. Every glance, every unthinking sigh was a rebuke. Every meaningless phrase directed at Alice was a thinly disguised criticism of me for failing as a wife and, by extension, as a mother.

At one point, she could contain herself no longer and said, without any preliminaries, as though out of nowhere, when she was midway through changing Alice, "But he's sixty-six."

I can't blame her: she had gone all the way in her marriage, until death came to part them, just as promised – I had barely lasted three years – but her disapproval made me want to rush back to Vivian's uncritical arms. He had at first made me feel sometimes like a foolish schoolgirl and he could still make me feel ignorant and lacking in understanding but I realised that under his remorseless gaze, for all its merciless intensity, I had never felt judged for being me.

Was there an element of stubbornness too, in my determination to continue to sit for Vivian? I had broken my marriage doing this. Surely, I had to see it through to the end.

One night, alone in my bed, the bed that had been ours but was now only mine, unable to sleep, I said out loud to myself, "It had better be a bloody brilliant bloody painting."

My mother rebelled initially, when I first asked her to take Alice overnight so that I could spend the night with Vivian. She said some very harsh things, things that hurt, things that hurt because they were true. As Vivian had said, it is justified criticism that stings most. She relented when I told her, which was not true because I had not asked him, that Vivian had said that I could bring Alice to stay too if I wanted.

I do not remember any dream that might have prompted the feeling, although I suppose there must have been one, but I woke in the middle of the night, one night, in Vivian's bed, with a strong sense that when I turned to check, I would find that he was dead. Have you ever had such a feeling, a conviction that something is the case, despite knowing at the very same time that it would not be? It may have been only seconds that I lay there on the very edge of panic, unable to make myself move my head even the tiniest fraction, which was all it would have taken to glance at his sleeping form and watch for the rise and fall of his ribcage that would testify that he was still alive, still there in the bed next to me. It felt like minutes. I held my breath for a moment, listening for the sound of his, but all I could hear was the ticking of the bedside clock, which seemed to whisper, "Vivian's dead, Vivian's dead, Vivian's dead," in a mocking, taunting rhythm.

When at last I turned my head, the sheet, which was all the cover we had needed on that warm summer night, moved perceptibly where it lay draped over Vivian's dark shape in the half-light, up and down, up and down. He was still in the room with me, still there. A corpse is nothing more than an object, that I knew from my father's death; from the very moment of passing, the person that you knew, loved, is no longer there, all that is left is matter, indistinguishable in any way that is important from the furniture that surrounds it.

No. Vivian was very much still there.

The realisation that Vivian was alive, the relief, gave way to a tumult of anxious imaginings of what would have happened if he had indeed been dead: shallow, practical anxieties remote from any thoughts or emotions of shock or grief or sorrow. What does happen if there is a sudden death outside of hospital, I asked myself. I did not know, but there would have been an ambulance, I supposed. Would there be police? There would certainly have been publicity: Famous Artist Dies Naked in Bed next to Lover Half His Age.

Sleep, in my then state of mind, I knew to be impossible, so, without disturbing Vivian, I rose, put on the silk dressing gown that I had done my best to make my own, and went as quietly as I could down to the pantry for a drink of water. The light in the pantry, when I switched it on, was dazzling to my dark-accustomed eyes and I stepped back out as soon as I had poured myself a glass, instinctively returning to that part of the landing that I had designated the mid-point of the house. The house loomed darkly around me, the heights and depths of the stairwell deepened by the shadows thrown by light escaping from the half-closed pantry door.

Released from the dark bedroom, a place that, at that hour, seemed to hover at the confused point between wakefulness and sleep, my thoughts became more ordered, rational, but dwelt still on a life in the wake of Vivian's death. The notion of his absence made real to me how much he had become the focal point of my life. The painting of me would be unfinished, I thought; and, in a way, so would I. I had been groping towards the creation of a different me under his gaze and that process of reformation would stop without him there to provoke it as surely as the process of his painting me would come to its own, incomplete end.

And paintings of others too.

I thought of the anonymous young woman, so tantalizingly close to being recognisable when I had last inspected her canvas. That had been weeks ago. I looked down into the darkness of the ground floor. She was down there now, waiting for me.

I had descended those paint flecked stairs so many times before, yet each step seemed unfamiliar, precarious, as though the wood might give way beneath me at any moment; the creak of each board as it took my weight, which should have sounded familiar and comforting, was harsh, resonating up and down the stairwell like an alarm.

"Get a grip, Jane," I whispered to myself.

When I reached the door to the studio, I tried the handle, half expecting it to be locked, although I had never known it to be.

It was not.

Opening the door and switching on a light, I found that the studio looked markedly different from how I was used to it being, for the couch on which I posed, which I had only known in position for my sittings, was pushed to one side. In its place, but at a right angle to where the sofa would sit, was the camp-bed. I sensed, before I looked, that the large, landscape canvas of the young woman that I had been obsessing over would be at the top of the stack of canvases that leant against the wall.

I was right.

I went to it and took hold of it. I knew, just knew that

it would be complete enough to tell me who it was, if, indeed, I knew her at all. I took a breath, then turned the canvas.

I gasped.

It was Maggie.

Maggie, Susan and Oliver's daughter, brilliantly depicted in all her sweet, artless vivacity. I still cannot decide whether I gasped because of who the subject was or because of the exceptional quality of the piece.

I set it down resting against the wall and studied it.

Her pose was notably more modest than the one I had chosen to assume; her left arm lay across her chest just below her breasts as though she had been tempted to cover them; her legs lay close together so that all we could see of her sex was a neatly trimmed triangle of close-cropped, dark hair. She looked not at the viewer but slightly to the side and into the middle distance with the gaze of someone who is puzzled by something, perhaps by her own thoughts. Above all, she looked exquisitely vulnerable: sweet and young and vulnerable. I was put in mind of something Guy Johnstone told me once: how a certain type of youthful beauty in a woman can provoke a man to desire, at one and the same time, both to protect her and to ravish her.

There was something else. I can admit it here. The bravura of the painting, the uncanny reproduction of the essence of the girl, felt like a challenge to me, a threat. I could not help but wonder whether the portrait Vivian was painting of me could possibly match it. At that moment, studying it in the very room where we had both been painted, I doubted it.

And I was jealous: jealous and hurt and upset.

And I hated myself for feeling that way.

I don't know for how long I studied the painting: many, many minutes. At one point I heard a noise from somewhere above, a muffled creak of the type the old house would make on occasion, reminding me that Vivian might wake and come in search of me. I had no doubt of his fury at finding me disturbing his canvases. The question that intrigued me more was how I would respond. Would I meet fury with fury? She was not my daughter. Of what could I accuse him? Of being Vivian?

In the height of summer, dawn comes early. Even in that light-sealed room, I sensed its onset that morning, perhaps in a softening of the darkness of the hallway outside, where I had left the door open behind me. It was time to put Maggie back against the wall, re-place her portrait alongside that of the relaxed politician, alongside that of me.

As before, I did my best to ensure that I put it back exactly as I had found it, so that Vivian would not guess that I had discovered his secret, that he was painting a naked portrait of his oldest lover's daughter.

Was it even a secret? He did not seem to have taken any pains to hide the canvas. There it was leaning against the wall where anyone might turn it and see. And yet I had not seen a single person examine those canvases, not one, not even Vivian. Surely there was a rule, perhaps expressed to others, never mentioned to me but one I understood, that no one was to disturb them. He would be sure enough of that to take no special precautions, hide her in plain sight. I even supposed taking an unusual step would perhaps draw attention to that canvas, pique interest, make discovery more likely not less, like the locked door in Bluebeard's castle.

Perhaps I was overthinking things.

Perhaps it wasn't such a big deal.

It's funny, Michael. I've just realised that I wrote those previous pages, relating how I found out that Vivian was painting Maggie, without thinking of you at all, as though I were no longer writing this for you to read, but only for myself.

31

I've mentioned before how controlled the light was in the Night Studio. There was the constant, exposing light on me and a carefully arranged set of neutral lights trained on the canvas from several angles so as to flatten the light there as much as possible. A side effect of this lighting set-up was that Vivian, as he prowled the room, was often not directly lit. It would be wrong to imply that he was completely in shadow, but his features might at one moment be brightly lit then at another in shade. At one point that morning, during the first sitting with Vivian after I had discovered that the other nude was Maggie, he stopped in a position where his face was lit from above and his eyes lay deep in the shadow of his brow. "What else lies hidden behind those eyes?" I thought. "What other secrets?"

"I'm not sure who is studying whom more intently, I you or you me," said Vivian, with a smile. "It's quite obvious, you know. Do you have something on your mind?"

It seemed worse than useless to deny it and yet I was not going to tell him that I knew about Maggie. A half-truth seemed best.

"I was wondering whether you have any truly dark

secrets," I said, trying to sound gently playful, only half serious. "I would imagine you do."

"That depends how you define 'dark'. I have many, many secrets."

He had advanced to within a foot or so of my feet and was studying the left one.

"Actually, secrets isn't quite right. Let's say, instead, things about me that I will share only with care. I'm not sure there is any single thing that I wouldn't tell the right person."

He looked up at my face.

"Of course, there is also no one person with whom I would share everything."

"We all hold parts of ourselves back, don't we," I said, thinking of you, Michael, for the first time in weeks. "Even from the ones we love."

"We certainly do."

In the next days after discovering the identity of Vivian's' other sitter, I found myself looking out for the next possibility of seeing Susan. What I was expecting from any anticipated encounter with her, I could not say exactly. I suppose I might have been looking for an opportunity to confirm my instinct that she did not know that her daughter was posing for Vivian. I felt sure that she would not know, that Maggie and Vivian had kept it secret from her and from Oliver too, that no one would know other than the two of them, and Colin perhaps; but I think I felt that seeing her with Vivian again would tell me for sure.

What of Maggie? I knew by then the thrill and burden of holding tight to a secret knowledge, a knowledge that conferred a terrible destructive power. She must have been transformed by it. Had I seen a consciousness of that power in her gaze as depicted by Vivian, an element of confusion with herself, that it could please her so?

I had not yet seen Maggie and Susan together, could only guess at the nature of their relationship. Indeed, I had only met Maggie once and briefly. It was testament to Vivian's skill that I nevertheless felt that I knew enough of her to believe that he had captured the essence of her in his painting.

I did not picture Susan and Maggie sharing the same kind of easy, jocular affection that I had witnessed between father and daughter, sensing instead that their relationship would include moments of conflict and tension – Susan's character would provoke that, I thought – but I also imagined Maggie as freshly immune from such provocation. I do not mean to suggest that I pictured her being insolent or unkind to her mother, far from it – she had not seemed to me that type – but I felt sure that the dark secret she harboured would act as a charm of protection, shielding her from barbs, imparting to her a new imperturbability.

And that secret was mine too, just as I carried with me the power to reveal Paul's infidelity, if I chose, I now had power over Susan as surely as I had over Peggy.

It was some days – more than a week, I think – before I had my chance, but eventually we coincided once more,

Susan and I. As I watched her chatting to Vivian, I was very conscious of finally having an advantage over her. I had tried before to tell myself that I was younger and therefore more physically appealing, that he must prefer my arms to hers, and though I felt that to be true, the notion left me feeling hollow, not at all superior to her, she who had such a long history with Vivian, had shared so much with him. She was, in a way, the woman to whom he had been... I was about to say been faithful but that wouldn't be right, obviously: I suppose I mean with whom he had been most constant.

But I knew something she didn't, something important and personal to her: that Vivian was painting her daughter. You see, watching them chat, I was completely, absolutely certain that she didn't know and I know now that I had been right, right about that at least.

32

It was a Thursday, a Thursday like countless other Thursdays in Vivian's studio. He had been painting for less than an hour, perhaps forty-five minutes, prowling around the room in his usual way, periodically scrutinising some part of me at close quarters, returning to the canvas from time to time to make what must have been miniscule adjustments. Then, after pausing, frozen in the act of applying another brush stroke, he stepped back, sighed audibly then put down his brushes, put down the pallet, unhitched the rag he had tucked into his belt, wiped his hands on a clean one, and said, "Right. You can get dressed now."

I was momentarily puzzled. Aside from those occasions that I have already described, when we had argued or been interrupted, I could not recall him stopping a session after such a short length of time and it was clear that he did not mean that we were to take a break, as we habitually did after an hour or so.

I sat up.

"Is something wrong?" I asked, not marking at the time that I had asked that same question on another notable occasion.

"No, nothing's wrong," he said with a smile, a wistful, almost sad smile. "It's finished."

I could write for days and days, but I do not think that I could manage a complete description of the overwhelming confusion of emotions that those words unleashed in me.

It's finished. Posing for Vivian is finished: coming here almost every day, the sustaining meditative ritual of silence and exploration and discussion, my purpose over the last four months; it's finished: making love each morning, settling back, mottled and sweaty and sated: it's finished.

I felt something akin to bewilderment, or of being adrift at sea with no bearing or anchoring point, also a hint of fear, of having to face the unknown, face it at that exact moment and for the foreseeable future. Above all, I would say that I felt puzzled.

I got dressed.

I had considered going over to look at the painting naked as I was, but somehow it felt more fitting, more respectful to clothe myself first: to mark the occasion. I paused for a moment when I had zipped the zip at the side of my skirt and smoothed its cloth. This is going to be the last time I get dressed in Vivian's studio, I thought. Then, taking a breath, I stepped the five steps over to the canvas and turned to face it, standing silently next to Vivian.

What did I think of it? It's hard to say; I was still reeling inside with the realisation that it was all over, the process of sitting for Vivian, a process that had come to be my entire life over those last few months. I think perhaps that my first response was simple relief; it was recognisably me and, although my body had a more sculptural look to it than I considered myself having, I was certainly not repelled by it, did not find it ugly. I was struck most by how physically present I looked. We largely think of ourselves as mental entities, don't we? But in it, when I first looked on the finished work, I seemed an exclusively physical being. I don't mean without spirit or animus, don't misunderstand me; my expression certainly spoke to me of an inner life. I mean, I suppose, that the fact of my body dominated the canvas.

I am speaking of my initial reaction to it, you will understand, my response when I first looked on it, standing there next to Vivian in his studio. I have seen other things in it, fresh things, each time I've seen it since.

"Are you happy with it?" I asked.

He shook his head, and I was momentarily afraid that he was unhappy enough that he would discard it, even now, but my fears were groundless.

"I've never been completely happy with even one of my paintings, at least not since I was very young and very ignorant," he said.

He continued to study it with an air of contained sadness.

"But I can say with near certainty that anything I did to it now would make it more imperfect than it already is, worse not better."

We continued to study it together for minutes more.

And then I said, "What do we do now?"

What do we do now?

I remember those words from another time.

It was when we first brought Alice home from the hospital. You looked so proud carrying her up the stairs to our front door. I remember thinking how handsome you looked and how lucky I was.

Do you remember the way we put her down, still asleep in her car seat in the middle of the living room and just looked at her?

"What do we do now?" you said and I laughed because that was exactly what I had been thinking.

When I woke in the flat on the morning after Vivian had finished painting me, the day ahead seemed empty and purposeless. I am ashamed to confess that the mundanity of caring for Alice did not seem to me to count as a purpose.

It was the day I had feared. Almost from the first time Vivian and I made love. A nameless, inarticulate fear at the beginning but one that solidified, took form over the weeks, the reason why I did not leave you earlier, waited until you yourself broke, realised that you couldn't go on and left. The fear of being alone.

I had lost sight of that fear at times, distracted in Vivian's arms or by the exhilaration I felt in his studio as we talked, by the feeling of being nearly famous when I was out and about with him, even sometimes at home, when my scorn for you gave my moments purpose. But Vivian had other people to paint, and when my painting was done, what then? If you and I had split, if I had burned my boats with you...

When I took Alice for a walk in her pushchair that morning, a mile or so to the supermarket and back, I cried all the way. I dreaded returning to the flat, being alone in there with Alice all day: all day that day and all day the next with no one but her, no you, no Helen to smile and say hello to, to share a joke with or a conversation about her father, no one but me and Alice. But there was nothing else to do but go home and so I did.

The day dragged, as empty and tedious as I feared it would be. I'm so ashamed, but when Alice knocked a cup of coffee over, I shouted at her so loudly, in a way I had always thought I never would. I frightened myself, Michael; I really did.

He didn't call. He had said he would, in a general, unfocussed way when we had said good-bye on the morning that the painting was finished. But I just knew that he wouldn't and he didn't. I could have called him, I suppose, and asked when we would see each other again but I would have felt so desperate and needy, which was ironic, because I was desperate and needy.

And he didn't call the next day either.

I could feel that I was close to cracking, to doing something dreadful, and felt that the only way to get through the next few weeks, at least until I returned to work in the new academic year, was to move back in with my mother. I was just about to pick up my phone to call her when it rang, which made me jump.

It was Vivian.

"Oh, so you've called," I said, unable to stop myself from sounding bitter.

He ignored that.

"My dealer has identified a buyer for the painting."

"Oh!" I said, blankly. I had somehow imagined a public sale of some sort. I'm not sure exactly what: an auction, a showing at a gallery. "Who?"

"His name is Milo van der Hauser. Despite the name, he's Swiss, a commodity trader; at least that's how he describes himself. My understanding is that there are holes the size and shape of his fingers in pies all over the world. I rather like him; there's something disreputable under the smooth, globo-rich polish that appeals. He already has two pieces of mine."

"So, he has the advantage of having been pre-vetted," I said.

"He's coming to see it tomorrow morning. Would you like to meet him?"

I considered for a moment.

"Yes, I think I would."

It would be the first time that I would see a stranger viewing the painting.

"If he buys it, will that be it, then?" I asked Vivian as we sat and waited for the buyer to arrive. "The painting just vanishing into some black hole forever?"

"Not exactly, no," he said. "If he does buy it, he's going to let it be displayed at a forthcoming exhibition at the Tate, as part of the deal."

A woman from the dealers', Annabelle, Australian and very straight-talking, was waiting with us. I had met her a couple of times before.

"He also loans his pieces to public galleries from time to time," she said. "So, it's likely to emerge somewhere every now and then."

"Have you decided what you will call it?" I asked.

Vivian smiled.

"I toyed with calling it *Onion*," he said. "but, in the end, I've decided to call it *Young Mother with Red Hair*."

When the doorbell rang, we all got up, but Annabelle turned to me.

"Would you mind staying up here to start with, Jane?" she said. "It's probably best if Mr van der Hauser views it first without you being there. So that he can judge it as a stand-alone piece if you get my drift."

"Sure."

Her words made me understand, in a way that I had not until that point, that the painting had already taken on an existence of its own, just as Vivian had once warned me that it would, that it was something entirely separate from me; it had become a work of art, the sitter as anonymous as any Renaissance youth in a *Portrait of a Young Man*.

It was half an hour before they returned, Vivian and Annabelle, a strange half-hour; I felt a little as though I were waiting for a job interview or perhaps for some test results – the doctor will see you now. When they did come back, the two of them, they told me that the buyer was waiting down in the studio and I could go and meet him if

I still wanted to.

The door was open and even before entering I saw a tall, trim, handsome man of forty or so, with a deep tan, dressed very casually but expensively, who was examining the painting with marked focus. He was standing a little closer to it than I would myself and leaning in even closer from time to time – to observe the brush strokes and pallet-knife markings, I suppose.

"Mr van der Hauser?" I asked as I entered.

I think I startled him slightly, such was his concentration on the canvas but, as he turned to me, it was obvious that he recognised me as the subject of the painting.

"Quite so; but you must call me Milo."

As I approached him, offering my hand, I said "Hi, I'm..." then hesitated because it seemed almost unnecessary to introduce myself when it was so obvious who I was; but then, of course there was no reason to suppose that he would know my name.

"A young mother with red hair," he said, smiling broadly. "Annabelle tells me that your name is Jane. It is a great pleasure to meet you."

We shook hands. His grip was not so firm as some I have known but still a little too tight for my taste. After relinquishing his hold, he studied me intently in a manner I found unnerving. We talk about women being objectified, but in that moment, I felt that literally to be true of me, that I had been rendered temporarily inanimate under his gaze, a physical thing only. He turned back to the painting, studied it with the same intensity then turned back to me, granting me a suave, revivifying smile.

"How many children do you have?"

"Just the one: a daughter, Alice. She's about to be one."

He nodded as though he had anticipated the age and sex of my only child.

"I can tell that I shall grow to love this painting," he said. "Please do not take it personally when I say that I think it is amongst Vivian's finest."

"I won't."

"I considered, at one point," he said. "That I would wish Vivian to paint me: with my clothes on, I must admit." – that smile again – "but, when I learnt how long the process takes, I knew that I would not have the patience, or frankly, the time, to sit for him."

I could almost admire the deftness with which he established, within the first few moments of our acquaintance, his superiority over me, his manifest busyness and hence importance. I suspect it is a habit of his.

"It is certainly a process," I said.

"And a very intense experience: I am given to understand."

For a moment I was back on the couch under Vivian's pitiless gaze. How inadequate that single word "intense" was, to convey all that I had been through, all that I had undergone in those past months. I shook my head.

"Until you've done it…"

Milo gave a nod, as though he understood more than I did myself, then turned back to face the painting.

We stood side by side and studied it together. Already, it seemed to me, that a separation, a gap had appeared between the woman in the painting and myself. We were already differentiated by time, only a matter of a week at that point, but that differential was growing, rather in the way a photograph of oneself is undoubtedly of a different person, the person you were when the photograph was taken not the one inspecting it, a difference that is marked and obvious in a picture from one's past but already there even on a first viewing, no matter how immediate. But that sense of separateness was more than a matter of time. I felt rather as one might in the presence of an identical twin who had grown up unknown, kept apart and thus, despite the similarity of appearance, had experiences completely other from one's own.

But more than that, she was, this woman stretched out before me, an image, one mediated by Vivian's great, unique, exceptional skill, of a woman that was not and never had been me, but Vivian's idea of me, an idea that could never match my own, were he and I to spend our entire lives together from cradle to grave. At that moment, the time that he had spent observing me, the hours spent in the studio, the time together elsewhere, which had always until then appeared to me to be inordinately, selfishly long, seemed paltry, obviously inadequate for the task that Vivian had set himself.

"This is only the second time I've seen, it," I said. "Since Vivian finished it, I mean."

"And it looks different to you this time, yes?"

"Yes, yes, it does."

"I have two Vivian Youngs hanging on my walls in my house outside Geneva. I do not think I will ever tire of them or fail to find something new in them each time I observe them closely, even though, like this, they each consist solely of a single person as the subject. But then, we are endlessly fascinated by the human, are we not? I think that is what makes Vivian so great as an artist: he enables us to indulge that fascination, feeds it."

"You are going to buy it then?"

"Oh, yes. Although Vivian is relatively prolific despite the length of time he takes, an opportunity to buy one of his works is a rare thing, especially by private sale."

"If you don't mind me asking, how much are you going to pay?"

I felt a little rude and wondered whether he might refuse to tell me but I had learnt by then, from being so often in Vivian's company, that the rich like to talk about their money. It is the single topic that most interests them.

He smiled and told me. It was an enormous sum.

"You can buy a person for less," Milo said.

He glanced at me with his smile of teeth that were too white to be true.

"Do not misunderstand me; I do not refer to modern slavery," he said. "Alas, in such trades a person would be much, much cheaper."

His smile broadened.

"I want to say that, for that quantity of money, there are few people who will not be persuaded to do something they otherwise would not."

"So you mean buying more than the person. You mean purchasing their soul."

"Precisely."

Our eyes met. I had the clear impression that he had indeed bought many people; in business mostly, I would have said, but not solely in business. I may have been mistaken but I also felt that an offer of purchase had just been made.

In the half shadows thrown by the lights positioned around Vivian's studio, Milos's handsome, tanned features and broad, glistering smile took on a Mephistophelean quality and I thought I caught a whiff, in his expensive aftershave, already too heady and sweet for my taste, of a sulphurous afternote.

"Naturally, unlike people," he said, "Vivian's paintings tend to increase in value."

"I'm sure they do."

He raised his expensively furnished wrist to check the time.

"I would so much prefer to look at the painting than at my watch, but..."

He gave a continentally exaggerated shrug.

"I must soon be elsewhere. Please, if you are ever in Geneva, or if you would like to visit, do not hesitate to get in touch. My house is your house. Stay for as long as you wish."

"That's very kind but I don't have any plans to travel to Switzerland."

"But you can make them. You would enjoy it greatly; I can assure you of that. Besides, it would be something to be able to show my friends both the model and the painting side by side."

I gave a non-committal smile.

"Please do not think that this is just politeness," he said, "with no intention of following through, as is so common here in England. I am quite serious in my offer."

He gave the ghost of a bow.

"Oh, I'm sure you are," I said. "But, unlike the painting, I'm not something to be exhibited and I'm very much not for sale."

"Of course not."

He smiled again, all gracious charm.

"Nevertheless, Annabelle can put you in touch with me if you ever change your mind."

He turned back to the picture saying, "You will find that people often do."

33

I expect you are familiar with Guy Johnstone's review of the exhibition where the painting was first displayed. I assume you have a copy. It wouldn't surprise me in the slightest if you knew it off by heart. I remember every word – not the result of committing his words to memory, I can assure you, but of being unable to forget them.

It's a masterpiece of insinuation; isn't it?

-

In *Young Mother with Red Hair*, perhaps the most successful work in a room full of successes, we are again presented with one of Young's characteristic depictions of uninhibited nakedness: in this case a conventionally attractive young woman with striking auburn hair, lying sprawled before us in a manner that suggests that she has only just come to rest. Of the fact that she is a mother, as stated in the title, we are given no clue, unless there is just a hint of slackness to her breasts that might suggest that they have, in the not distant past, served an end other than sexual pleasure.

The patterns of freckles on the model's face, her upper chest and most notably about her shoulders and arms have been reproduced with an obsession that recalls Young's earliest works, when reproduction of detail bordering on the oppressive was his most characteristic trait. It is an illusion, but it seems almost as though he has depicted every single freckle with extreme exactitude, an illusion, certainly, but an illusion created by a master at the very peak of his talents.

Although he has not shied away from the redness of the model's hair, has embraced it enthusiastically, Young has resisted the temptation to depict the sitter as in any way flame-haired, when to do so might provoke comparison with some notable works of the Pre-Raphaelite Brotherhood. Her hair tones are altogether more earthy, corporeal. In any event, it is not the hair on her head to which the eye is first and repeatedly drawn but an uninhibited clump of equally orange-brown hair (Would it be unkind to say ginger? It seems the word most apt and no slight is intended.) situated elsewhere, the colour of which, if anything, is even more obsessively accentuated. Indeed, every angle of the composition works to draw the eye, both on first viewing and repeatedly, to her sex so that, without having quite the same ferociously explicit, gynaecological exactitude, it nevertheless invites comparison with Courbet's *L'Origine du Monde*, although, again in contradistinction to that piece, the fact that we see all of the model and not an anonymous torso, lifts the painting away from being only sexual in theme.

She gazes directly at us, an attitude that is rare in

Young's nudes, but she is neither confrontational nor inviting. Her expression seems solemnly questioning, as though she is waiting for something from us: perhaps an answer to the question her body asks of us.

Whilst the painting may not be, clearly is not, only sexual in theme, to my mind it remains primarily so, with the most sensitive parts of her body, fingertips, toes, nipples, and genitalia, accentuated with slight yet powerful touches of vermilion. One has a sense, not quite of arousal, more of recent stimulation slowly dissipating, and an encroaching lethargy. Perhaps I might venture *tristesse*.

Am I supposed to be grateful that Guy at least considers me "conventionally attractive," do you think?

I had met Guy several times by then. I've already mentioned that. How many people reading his article would guess that he knew the woman in the painting, do you think? That she was someone whom he would see again not long after it had been published.

One day – When will that be? Too soon, I know it. – Alice will stand in front of that painting. Perhaps, on that first occasion, she will see it and suffer only a child's embarrassment at the strange, unfathomable behaviour of a parent, a deep, painful embarrassment, I have no doubt, but an emotion of a type that most, maybe all children suffer at one time or another, an acute but nevertheless ordinary aspect of any childhood. But then later, when she has become a woman – might she be fifteen, as I was? – she will look upon it and know what sort of a woman her mother is.

Did you go to the exhibition? I half expected to bump into you there. Naturally, Vivian invited me to the opening, but I just couldn't. I went on a Tuesday, early in the morning, in the hope, partially realised, that there would be almost nobody there. I spent a good hour looking at the other paintings: so many fabulous pieces. I thought again that I may have been too hard on you, in the face of such talent.

When I finally went to look at the painting of me, it wasn't long before I was joined by a gauche looking youth. He can't have been more than sixteen or seventeen. After a while, I noticed him darting furtive glances at me. When I smiled at him, confirming his suspicions, he went bright red, the poor boy.

I realise that I don't know whether you have even seen it – the painting – but I can't believe you haven't. What I would have given to watch you, unseen, when you first saw it, to see your face. Did you cry? I imagine you probably did. I know I would have in your position but then, as you know, tears come easily to me, more so these days than ever.

34

When Milo had left, Vivian took Annabelle and me to lunch. He had someone sitting for him that afternoon but he invited me to stay, if I wished, so that we could have supper together. And so, after a seemingly unending hiatus of no more than a week, I was a regular part of Vivian's life once more.

"I seem to see more of you now that you are no longer sitting for Vivian than I did when you were," said Susan, finding me alone in the house when Vivian and Colin were out together on some errand or other.

"I suppose you're right," I said. "But there's a logic to that."

She threw a questioning look at me.

"Well, when I was sitting, I spent most of my time locked away with him. Whereas now..."

I looked around at the sitting room, where I seemed to spend a lot of my time then, in contrast to the previous months, when the dining room that was a waiting room had been my natural resting point.

"I suppose there is a situation vacant, after Clare moved on."

Susan had not lost any of her taste for goading me.

"On the day she left," I said. "She told me that she couldn't reconcile herself to sharing him."

"Unlike the pair of us," I did not say.

"People seem to like to confide in you, Jane," said Susan. "It must be that innocent, artless look you have about you."

I refused to rise to this, was determined to keep my cool.

"It upset her that he hadn't asked to paint her for a while."

"It's how we feel we can get close to him isn't it?" Susan said, thoughtfully.

As I had once before, I sensed her animosity being tempered by introspection. I considered her for a moment. She had posed five times for Vivian over the years, which might add up to nearly three years of that special intimacy that posing for him brought, three years of being, for hours each day, the sole focus of his attention.

"Helen – his daughter, Helen – said more or less the same thing," I said.

"Did she? Another confidante."

She appeared to have recalled her innate animosity towards me.

"I've seen it before with other girls."

On her lips, the word 'girls' sounded pejorative. It was obvious that she wanted me to know that she counted me as such. I was immune. The painting of Maggie, my knowledge of it, was a magic penny in my pocket that I could take out at any time.

"They start by doing everything they can to get out of his studio, to work their way into the rest of the house," she said, smiling her mirthless smile, "but then they realise that it is only in there that they can be really close to him. Don't you find?"

"I'm not sure I could go through the whole process again."

"Yes," she said. "I would imagine it is very tiring, always bringing a special intensity to the studio."

It was too much. Throwing Vivian's words in my face was a taunt too many. The composure I thought the secret had conferred on me vanished.

"Perhaps you should ask Maggie."

The blood drained instantly from her face. I don't think I have seen such pallor outside of a hospital.

"What... what do you mean?" she stammered, clutching her shirt at the topmost fastened button.

"You know exactly what I mean," I said. "Did you think you would always be the only one of your family Vivian has painted? Why don't you go down and see for yourself?"

She stared at me for a moment with wide eyes, then turned and rushed from the room. I heard the clatter of her shoes banging hurriedly down the stairs. There was silence for a second or two and then I heard a half-strangled shout.

I followed her down. Just as I reached the door to the studio, a wail of anguish greeted me. I feared to go in but I couldn't not.

There, on the bare boards in front of the painting of her naked daughter, Susan, in her smart tweed skirt, sensible cotton blouse and cashmere cardigan, had collapsed onto her knees and was hugging herself, rocking back and forth, emitting a low moan that was animal in its wordless despair. From the little I knew of her, and it was so little, I had expected anger, indignation, vitriol but instead I was confronted by a woman who seemed to have been hollowed out in an instant, leaving a space filled only with desolation. When she looked up at me with reddening eyes that overflowed with tears, I thought I saw there a feeling of being utterly ancient and unattractive, sexless. I think now that there was also a deep self-loathing, that she hated herself for feeling that way, when her only thought should have been concern for her daughter, that, where there should have been determination to prevent her daughter from coming to harm, to protect her from any risk of being damaged, there was instead only envy of her young body and fresh beauty.

Eventually, after covering her face with her hands, she fell silent.

When at last she lowered her hands and looked up at me again it was to whisper, "He promised me. He promised me he wouldn't paint her."

We both knew, how surely we both knew, that the implication, the probability, inevitability even, was that Vivian had also slept with her, but I honestly think it was the fact of his having painted her that hurt Susan most.

She did not act as I would have anticipated, with

confrontation, waiting to pounce on Vivian upon his return to accuse him; instead, she fled, although not before letting go in front of me a damburst of hurt and recrimination, barely intelligible accusations against him, telling of slights nurtured over years, of chances of happiness foregone, of previous betrayals with others close to her. It was difficult to stay with her, not to flee myself in the face of her emotions, her strength of feeling that threatened to overwhelm me, but the guilt at my own part in her distress, my remorse for so thoughtlessly destroying her idea of the life she thought she was leading restrained me. I tried to comfort her, held her in my arms for long minutes as she sobbed into my shoulder.

"It has been a lie," she said, "all of it: every touch, every loving caress, every unspoken promise, every meaningful glance thrown my way, all of it a lie – for nineteen years."

She had composed herself and stood for a moment with her hand on the front door before she left.

"It's done," she said. "I'm going now and never coming back. He knew he was risking this moment and he went ahead anyway. That's what hurts the most: the insouciance of it all."

She smiled at me: the smile that I had thought mirthless but seemed to me then to be pained.

"Do you think it will be any different for you?" she said. "Take my advice and run too, Jane. Run as fast as you can."

Run as fast as you can.

But I didn't.

I went back upstairs.

I considered returning the canvas to its place against the wall but it seemed pointless to try and pretend that nothing had happened so, leaving it on display where Susan had left it, I trudged wearily upstairs to the dining room and helped myself to a glass of whisky. I was conscious of an echo of Clare but I needed fortifying and nursed a measure until Vivian and Colin returned nearly forty minutes later.

"Jane!" Vivian shouted as soon as they returned.

"In here," I called down to him, "the dining room."

I heard him come hurriedly up the stairs. He strode into the room, studying his smartphone.

"Susan has sent me an email: an email, Jane. She and I have been…" he hesitated. "She and I have been lovers for more than twenty-five years, and she sends me an email."

He brandished the phone at me for a moment.

"It's barely intelligible, but I'm sure you can guess the gist of it."

He looked down at the screen and then back up at me.

"Happy now?" he asked.

"No."

I noticed a tremor in his left eyelid.

"Come with me."

There was no handholding now as I followed him down to the studio. He gripped me by the upper arm and led me over to stand in front of the painting of Maggie.

"So, what do you think of it?"

At that moment it seemed to me one of his finest works.

It told of a life not yet lived, full of hope and possibility, almost limitless potential, of a life that would inevitably contain sadness, perhaps tragedy, but also great joy.

"Come on," he said, "I want to know."

"I think it's magnificent," I said, in barely more than a whisper.

"Then what do you want of me, Jane?"

He let go of my arm, stepped forward and picked up the canvas from where Susan and I had left it leaning against the wall.

"Do you want me to burn my books?"

"No."

"I will. I'll do it right now if you tell me too. I'll put a foot through the canvas here and now, cut what's left into shreds."

There was a wildness in his face that I had not seen before. I did not doubt that he would go through with it.

I hesitated for just a moment and then said, "No. No. Please don't do that."

His anger subsided and he took a deep breath.

"Right," he said.

He carefully fixed the canvas on the easel, then stepped back and studied it for a moment more.

"That's all I've got to say about this, Jane," he said, and left.

I stayed studying the painting for a few minutes more then followed him back up the stairs.

After moments such as these, lovers either part forever or make love.

In his bed afterwards, when we had both recovered our breath, I leant over to kiss his shoulder.

"I've just realised something," I said.

"What?"

"The painting of Maggie, it's not finished yet, is it?"

"No," he said to the ceiling. "Not yet."

I only saw her once, Maggie, in the next weeks during which Vivian finished the painting, even though I was often at his house. I didn't even realise that she was there, just happened to glance down when I was passing across the first-floor landing, and there she was at the door to the studio. Whether she heard me or sensed my presence, I don't know but she looked up at me and our eyes met.

It seemed to me that her look was one of hate, hate and animosity, perhaps envy too. It filled me with sadness that I should provoke such feelings in her. But why should I deny her the right to feel that way, just because my image of her had until then been of a sweet and vulnerable young woman, all smiles and pleasantness? And what had it cost her, to continue to sit for Vivian, after I had betrayed her secret? What sort of home did she return to each day, if she still had a home to go to?

Perhaps you think I should have known all those details, where Maggie was living, what had happened between her and Susan; I was spending so much time with Vivian, why not just ask him? He was sure to know. But living with Vivian wasn't like that. I've told you before how he would move focus from one person to another. When the spotlight of his attention was turned on you, you didn't want to shift it away by talking of others, least of all his other lovers. Besides, I think he deliberately compartmentalised his life, as a way of keeping some control over it. I said before he was an intensely private person.

I just wrote "living with Vivian", didn't I?

In that period after Susan broke with him, it sometimes felt as if I were living with him but technically it wasn't true. I might spend two, maybe three nights a week with him, much of my days, but I was living at my mother's, just as I told you I was.

35

My mother's voice on the line was clipped, tense and disapproving, when I called to say that I would be staying at Vivian's again that night, but she said nothing to voice that disapproval. It was the first time that I would have spent two nights running with him. By then, Vivian had finished the painting of Maggie and I had passed a last ruminative half-hour alone with it and my thoughts. I didn't ask where it would go, whether someone had bought it and if so who, although I did say, only half joking, that I hoped it wouldn't end up on Milo van der Hauser's wall next to me. Vivian smiled and said that it would not.

She bit her tongue, mostly, my mother, during that period. She knew that I was fully aware how much she disapproved of my behaviour and I think she must have realised that no good would come of provoking a confrontation with me. I suppose she reasoned that, if she kept her head down, cared for Alice whenever I asked, kept on top of her own emotions, we could come through it still a family. She must have feared losing me if she and I ever had a head-to-head, screaming argument. I think she feared too that I might lose custody of Alice if she weren't always willing to take charge of her. Would you have done that, Michael, if the chance had offered itself?

The occasion that prompted the call to my mother was a reception at Sotheby's, a private viewing of the pieces for an upcoming auction, including two Youngs.

Before getting ready to go out, I spent a happy half an hour in Vivian's bath, the inner sanctum, the holy of holies. As I gazed up at the crazy, hypnotic patterns on the peeling wallpaper of the bathroom ceiling, I felt relaxed and at ease, completely at home. I will be able to note how the patterning changes over the coming months, I thought, just as I imagined Vivian doing.

After reluctantly leaving the bathroom's steamy, floral scents, I put on a new red cocktail dress. They say redheads should never wear red, but I was in a convention-defying mood. I had a feeling it wasn't the way that Vivian would have chosen that I dress; I don't mean that he would not appreciate the look but that he would have considered that it drew just a little too much attention to me but that was one reason for wanting to wear it, a small gesture of independence, even if it was perhaps only perceptible to me, a statement that I would be staying with Vivian on my terms.

Vivian would be going to the viewing from another meeting of some kind – I didn't know what – so I made my own way there. How familiar I had become with such events: the smiling, deferential welcome of the attractive girl checking the guest list, the pleasant, beckoning murmur of conversation, swelling as I approached, that drew me along the corridor towards it, the happily proffered glass of champagne that had become nothing special, a matter of routine.

When I reached the main reception area, I realised that I knew, certainly not all, not even half, but perhaps a third of the people there and as I circulated, stopping to exchange small talk with groups of half-acquaintances, smiles were aimed at me from all aspects of the room, smiles of familiarity and acceptance. More than anything, I was aware that people had been expecting to see me there.

I went to inspect the two Youngs that would be sold. They had both been painted more than fifteen years ago. They might have been painted the day before, such was Vivian's consistency of style.

I studied one. Who was the blonde woman? A lover, one of his daughters, just a friend? I did not recognise her and there was no way of telling from the typically prosaic title, *Woman with Hair Up*. She looked to have been in her early thirties so she would be well on her way to fifty now; yet, here she was, preserved forever as she had been, or seemed to Vivian to have been, at the age of thirty-three.

I had seen in the catalogue, that there was a sketch by Rodin waiting to be sold and I sought it out. It was only a sketch but the contrast with Vivian's pieces was marked. The Rodin, a man and woman dancing naked, was all movement. Vivian's pieces seldom have that kind of dynamism. That is not an effect he strives for. Of the pieces of his that I knew well, only the one of Susan smoking seemed to hint at movement; although her pose is static, one has a definite sense that she is just about to move the hand that holds the cigarette and take another drag.

Then I saw Oliver. It did not feel like only the third time that I had seen him. He and his relationship with his wife, their relationship with Vivian, whatever that had been, his daughter Maggie had figured so largely in my thoughts over recent weeks that I felt almost as though I knew him well when the reality was that I had been introduced at a reception, said hello, listened to some of his theories of cinema, been told gossip about him as he walked away, and, on another occasion, witnessed him have a conversation about a vintage car: not much of an acquaintance.

I was not surprised that he had come and when he spotted me and smiled as if he were an old friend, it did not feel odd to smile back.

He does not know, I thought. He does not know about his daughter, may not even know that his wife had ended her affair with Vivian.

Whatever Oliver's and Susan's tacit understanding of each other's behaviour had been, I could not see her announcing the end of the affair at breakfast – "Oh by the way, I'm no longer sleeping with Vivian."

I turned away from the Rodin, looking for Vivian, but was intercepted by Annabelle and stopped to chat to her and the little group that she was standing with. One of them, a thick-set balding man with a distinct Edinburgh accent whose name I can't recall launched into a story about a famous British artist of the twentieth century, something about his trying to paint a cat.

And then I saw them in a mirror, a large, ornately framed mirror set between two huge vases of flowers. That image of them will stay with me forever; I am sure of it, the four of them in a discrete, intimate group all of their own: Oliver and Maggie and Vivian and Susan.

I remember that my first thought was that the image of them in the mirror made for a very satisfactory, almost symmetrical composition, the type that Vivian strove so hard to avoid on canvas. The irony.

And my next thought was that Susan's face was awry. We all have an asymmetry of facial features – I'm sure you know that – even those with the regular features of what Guy Johnstone would call the conventionally attractive, and I've noticed that this often appears more clearly when one sees someone in a mirror, as though the reversal of the image in the glass in some way doubles those asymmetries. How stark they seemed in Susan's face at that moment, how askew she looked.

I turned to see what she would look like unmediated by reflection. She was retransformed instantly into the elegant, fine-featured woman I was familiar with, just as I had first observed her sitting at Vivian's expansive dining table on a bright morning a few months and a whole lifetime ago.

When she saw that I was watching her, I think her chin lifted just a fraction, almost imperceptibly in response to my gaze. I summoned up the vision of her on her knees in Vivian's studio with her head in her hands, her body wracked by sobs. I found it difficult to believe that it could be the same woman.

The Scot was still speaking, but I had zoned out completely at the sight of them. I looked at Maggie; she seemed very much the sweet, vulnerable girl whose image, so perceptively, so brilliantly realised, I had, in a series of furtive, obsessive glimpses, seen emerge on canvas.

And Oliver: I studied his amiably patrician features, his charming demeanour, redolent of ease and comfortable, unthreatening charisma, searching for any signs of a beaten man, a man sick at heart. I could detect no trace of what I was looking for. He could not possibly know, could he? How could he know and still look like that in the presence of the others? If he did know, what did he see in the mirror when he shaved in the morning?

Without me noticing his approach, Guy was at my elbow.

"I understand Susan has started sitting for Vivian again," he said, adding with relish, "I expect you knew that, of course. That will make six paintings of her: more than any other person."

Vivian said something, and the three Brown's laughed as one, Susan reaching forward and touching his forearm for a moment.

"I don't know whether it's a nude or not," Guy said. "I suppose we'll just have to wait and see. I wonder what he might call it, *Old Mother with Greying Hair* perhaps."

It was the end. I felt faint and was aware of a mounting queasiness, a pooling of saliva in my mouth. I knew that I could not stay in that world a day, an hour longer. The feelings of belonging that I had imagined that I had felt earlier when luxuriating in the scented steam of Vivian's enchanted bathroom were illusory. I did not belong there. I had no conception of how Susan could pay the price of membership of whatever club it was that she and Oliver and Vivian between them had established.

I had to go.

I felt suddenly self-conscious, foolish, and jejune in my red dress, like a fourteen-year-old at a party for the grown-ups who has unwisely tried to ape their dress, embarrassed at how much I stood out, as though eyebrows were being raised at me behind my back. I was instantly ill at ease, as though I might at any moment be propositioned by a sweatily sinister family friend who insisted that I call him uncle. The thought of Vivian coming over and putting his hand possessively on the small of my back or calling me over to come and join him with Susan and her family filled me with revulsion. I think I may have shivered.

I looked around for somewhere to put my glass of champagne, still three-quarters full. Stepping towards the mirror, I had just placed my glass on a side-table, when I saw Vivian's reflection looking at me. I held its gaze for a moment, then turned and left.

36

I would like to say that I did not waiver after that moment of revelation, that I did not nurse a bottle of chardonnay deep into the night in my mother's sitting room, wondering whether I had the strength to break with Vivian. But that wouldn't be true.

It was not just a matter of the investment that I felt I had made by then in our relationship, the many things that I had given up to be with him. I can also admit to myself, now, a line of thought that was fundamentally mercenary, although perhaps it would be fairer to me to talk in terms of a series of vague, half-formed fantasies, rather than a line of thought. The truth is I had begun to contemplate letting myself get pregnant by him, have his daughter. For some reason I was sure that, if I did bear him a child, I would have another daughter. He does seem to have produced many more daughters than sons. Is that a thing, biologically? Do some men produce more X chromosome sperm than Y?

It is a strange world, the world of Vivian and those whom he has drawn into his orbit, but it is undeniably a gilded one, one redolent of achievement and success, of talent and beauty and wealth. If I allowed myself to remain there for a time, arranged for me to become pregnant by him, bear him a daughter, that child, and by connexion I also would remain attached to that world forever, whether closely bound or loosely associated I could not know, but a part of it. And I suppose I should also admit that I had met enough of his children to know that a daughter by him would in all likelihood be both attractive and talented.

Doors open, opportunities beckon for such children; it is undeniable, not solely by the cachet of his name, though surely that has a power that is potent indeed, but also by introduction to the circles in which he and his move, all those talented and well-connected people. Even Alice, I sometimes imagined, might have doors opened to her by reason of her half-sister and all that that association could bring.

Ah, but there we have it: Alice.

Sometimes, in the dark hours of a sleepless night, I cannot avoid an image coming to mind, an image of myself, wearing a sensible tweed skirt and tailored cotton shirt, collapsed in tears onto my knees in front of a half-completed canvas.

He offered to let me have a cut of the proceeds, you know. To tide me over after the divorce, he said. It would have been an awful lot of money, Michael: close to a million. But I couldn't.

Are you cross with me? Perhaps for Alice's sake. Don't be. I'm sure it was for the better. I don't mean to imply that I would have felt in any way beholden to him if I had taken the money. I'm certain that was not his intention and I'm sure it would not have been the effect. But it would have been a connection with him that was more than a memory and I was quite convinced that I had to avoid leaving in place even that faint link to Vivian and his world.

I sometimes find myself missing Helen. We were hardly close and she's so much younger than I am but it's a shame that I feel that we shouldn't keep in touch, when I would otherwise so like to. I wonder whether she ever thinks about Alice.

I do have one last link with him, though. A week or so after I left for the final time, when it must have been clear to Vivian that I would not be going back, I received a parcel from him containing a sweater, scratchy to the touch against bare flesh, heavy and old-fashioned, cable-knit in Aran wool.

Term starts soon. I'm not the first to point out that Autumn is a more natural start to the year than the first of January but it's true isn't it? I suppose as academics it is particularly so for us. A good case can be made for spring too, I suppose: Lady Day, as in mediaeval times. Why it has been set for midwinter, I don't know.

Mrs Cooper was noticeably put-out when I told her that I wasn't going back to St. Bede's and would be starting at Manorfield instead. I'm not sure that I believe in fresh starts any more, clean breaks as catharsis, but I just knew that those familiar corridors would speak too much to me of our life together, of us before Alice and all that has happened since she was born. Everyone there would know me as the Jane who left Michael, the one who had an affair with Vivian Young. I imagine I would interpret every sideways glance at me, rightly or wrongly, as a rebuke. Presumably, the staff at Manorfield will find out sooner or later, if they don't know already, but even that will be better. To them, I won't be the woman that has changed from a respectable wife and mother to an adulteress, the one that they had misjudged entirely. To them, I will be someone who has always been like this, a single mother with a colourful past. I think I will be able to cope with that preconception of me, look them in the eye at staff meetings. The pupils on the other hand...

You'll never guess who got in touch the other day; or perhaps you will.

James. Yes, my James, the hero of my youth, the man to whom I first gave my heart and, in time, my body.

He sent an email saying that he'd heard about you and I splitting up and that if I wanted to unburden myself on an old friend I knew where to turn. I think we both know what he meant by unburden myself; don't we?

God! He even wrote, "I hear you've been a naughty girl."

Ughh!

I mentioned my father's funeral earlier. As we made our way out of the crematorium, James came over to me and gave me a special hug. Just recalling that moment now makes me want to go and take a shower.

I wrote near the start that I was sure that I came out of Vivian's studio a different woman from the one who went in. I'm no longer sure that that's true. Of course, it is true in a trite sense; we all change ineluctably over time, don't we? The multifarious incidents of life each leave their mark on our characters and on our bodies but I think there is a limit to how much the essential self changes. It would undeniably be true to say that I felt different. Nevertheless, the most I would say, now, after all I have written is that I emerged from my time spent with Vivian with a clearer notion of who, what I am.

I've been thinking about the start of term; yours I mean. I wonder how it will be for you. I have a horrible feeling that your natural enthusiasm will have been dulled. If it is, I'm so very sorry. I thought I hated you when I started writing this, but now I'm not sure. But even if I did, I wouldn't want to take that away from you. And yet I think I have. When I saw you last, there was a beaten look about you, the sort of expression I was searching for on Oliver's face but couldn't find. I prefer your vulnerability to his apparent imperviousness. That won't be any comfort to you, I know, but it's true.

I still haven't made up my mind whether I will deliver this to you. I'm glad I've written it, for my own sake, but I'm not sure what it would do to you to read it. I think I had in mind, when I started, that this would be my final act of revenge, a plunge of the knife by the hand of Nyssia herself, but I'm not sure anymore that I want to do that to you.

I worry also, what it might do to your relationship with Alice. I'm sure she'll want to have her father in her life and I don't want to do anything that might endanger that.

In truth, it hasn't come out quite the way I thought it would and I see things revealed in it about myself that I was only vaguely aware of before.

I'm tired Michael. I think I'll stop now. Alice is asleep and I think I'll turn in too.

Printed in Great Britain
by Amazon

78403770R00189